I Don't Know What I'm Doing

a novel by Michael Suarez

To my family –
I am who I am because of you all

ISBN 978-1-7356294-0-7

"Okay," she says, clearly not buying it. I'm so screwed. I put the cap back on, wanting desperately to taste whatever "Peach Madness" is supposed to taste like. I carefully step down onto the cold bathroom tile and quietly put the step-stool away. I unlock the door and step out. Mom's not there, and I let out the breath I didn't realize I was holding.

I walk to my room, hand tapping the pocket holding the secret lip gloss, glad to have escaped possible punishment, and find my mom sitting on the edge of my bed. *Aw, crap. What's going on?* I think

"Hey," I say. *Why did I say that? Katie, you idiot!*

"Katie, can you sit down?" she asks me, her head motioning me to sit next to her. I carefully do so. Mom shifts and faces me. "Sweetie, something happened. With your Aunt Jess."

"What?" I ask, confused. What does Aunt Jess have to do with anything?

"I, uh…well, actually it's about both Aunt Jess and Uncle Thomas." She ˈs a deep breath, the kind she does when she doesn't want to cry. This ˈs makes me want to cry, but I try my best to hold the tears back.

Thomas is gone."

ˈead?" I ask, barely above a whisper.

ˈs.

And, like that the tears fall on their own.

"Your aunt Jess isn't doing too well, either. She's in the hospital."

"What happened?" I ask, crying but not crying.

Mom's own tears begin to fall. She looks like she wants to say something, but she also looks like she's holding something back. "Accidents," she says, nodding.

"Like?"

"Like…accidents. Freak accidents." More nodding.

I decide I don't want to know whatever it is she doesn't want to tell me. I hug her, and she hugs me back. Mom is always so soft and warm. I love her. And, I feel bad that at this moment I wish Aunt Jess were here, so I could hug her, too. Uncle Thomas died, and Aunt Jess has to be sad about it. I want to make her feel better, but all I can do is sit on my bed with my mom and hug her and cry until we can stand up, leave the room, and try to do things as if the world hasn't changed.

That night, when Dad comes home and after we've had dinner, they go to their room, close the door, and talk. I try to hear a little, but not too much. Sometimes, it's clear that things are going on that I shouldn't be listening to, but this night is just talking. Mom sounds really upset, and Dad sounds like he's comforting her. After a few minutes, she starts sobbing loudly. It sounds like he's hugging her, her sobs muffled in his chest. I decide then to just leave them alone and take a shower.

Afterward, when I'm dry but have the bathroom all to myself still, I try the lip gloss. It looks okay and tastes very little like peaches. I hold on to it, though, because I stole the stupid thing. It was a pain in the ass, too. Luckily, the teenager behind the counter couldn't have cared less. I think back on that girl and wonder if that'll be me in a few years. Why did I have to steal it? So stupid.

Eventually, my mom and dad say goodnight and go back to their room. I fall asleep with a clear memory at the forefront of my mind. Last year, for my birthday, Uncle Thomas and Aunt Jess threw me a birthday party at their house. It was pretty awesome. My mom said she was worried that they were spoiling me, but I didn't feel spoiled. Most of the family was there, along with eight of my classmates, all of whom I considered friends. Two moved away, and five are still nice, even if they don't talk much to me anymore. CeCe, though, is probably my best friend. Jess baked me a gigantic strawberry cake with real strawberries in it. There was even a DJ who played whatever requests I had, even stuff Mom doesn't care for. It went on until it was dark and all of my friends had gone home. A few of the adults in my family drank, but not too much. My mom always makes sure no one gets drunk around me. I appreciate that. I hate drunk people in movies or on TV. Then, Thomas and Jess let me stay in their bedroom, and I got to sleep in their massive bed. It was nice. They were nice. Always. I love them.

Even though Uncle Thomas isn't with us anymore, I still love him.

As I drift off, I wonder how Aunt Jess is doing.

A few days later, I'm finally allowed to see her. We go over to her house before the funeral, and she smiles through her tears whenever she talks to me. For some reason, she avoids my parents, but not in a mean way.

At the wake, she gives a funny speech about Thomas, wiping away tears occasionally. She tells a story I've never heard before about their second date. She and Thomas had gone to the movies on their first date, which had resulted in an awkward kiss outside the men's bathroom. It was supposedly a funny story, but I've never really understood why. For this date, though, they decided to just go somewhere and talk. And talk. And talk. And talk. Uncle Thomas was apparently quite the talker, eager to say things to Aunt Jess. She actually considered bailing on the date, until he confessed that most of what he was saying was, as Jess says, "bullshit."

This makes everyone laugh, including the preacher off to the side, who shakes her head at the same time. I smile to myself.

Thomas was so intimidated by Jess, which she says surprised her. He didn't think he was good enough for her. She was in medical school at the time, and he was working odd jobs after graduating with an English degree. This made her take his hand and tell him, "'I'm nobody special.' 'You are,' he said. I shook my head. 'No. I'm not. And, guess what? Neither are you. We're nobodies. But maybe we're nobodies who found each other.'" She takes a deep breath. "Maybe," she says, her voice cracking the way it does when she gets emotional. "Maybe that's corny. But it was true. Me and Thomas were nobodies. Most of us are. But we try. Again. And again. And again – to be somebody. That's what makes most of all this worth anything. Otherwise, we just sit on the couch and never do anything.

"Afterward, we finally got around to talking – really talking. About ourselves. About what we wanted and didn't want. Turns out, he hated the idea of having children. At the time, I hadn't really thought of it. Now, I think, 'Man, that would've been nice.' But, maybe not. And, I guess that's the problem. Being stuck with all these maybes. One thing I *am* happy about it how often we said I love you to one another." She nodded and smiled. "We should do that, shouldn't we? I mean, if we *really, truly* love someone…shouldn't we say it?"

About an hour or so later, the casket lowers. Everyone is quiet. A few people are crying. I look over to Aunt Jess, and she doesn't have any more tears. She just looks at the rectangular hole her husband is in now, her eyes sadder than I can remember seeing them. I feel nauseous, but I don't move. I'm confused. Maybe one day I'll know more, because it feels like so much is being kept from me at this moment.

Then, Aunt Jess turns to me. She gives me a smile. Then, the tears return.

I don't see her again for two months, the day of my tenth-birthday party.

That night, however, Aunt Maddie comes to stay over at our house. She hangs out with me most of the night in my room, saying she wants to give my mom some space, whatever that means. "Let's watch something," she says.

"Yeah. Let's watch *Beetlejuice*."

"*Beetlejuice*?"

"Yeah. Lydia is the *coolest*."

"I thought *I* was the coolest."

"You're cool, but Lydia has really awesome hair."

"Yeah, yeah. Lydia's pretty awesome."

"I want to ask Mom if I can go as her for Halloween this year."

"Really?"

"Yeah."

Maddie smiles. "You go, girl," she says.

I'm seated crisscross, applesauce, while she's lounging her left arm propping her up on my bed. Like me, she's changed from the black dress she had on earlier. As I'm noticing how similar the two of us actually look, from our hair to the way we speak, she seems to drift off, her mind elsewhere. After about a minute, I ask, "Maddie?"

She turns to me. "Hmm?"

"You okay?"

She considers this and then answers. "I'm just worried about Jessie." Aunt Maddie is the only person in the family "allowed" to call Aunt Jess "Jessie." Apparently, Aunt Jess isn't a fan of this nickname, so Aunt Maddie says it to her on purpose. As time's gone on, she's grown to like it. But even *I'm* not allowed to call her that. Not that anything will happen if I do. I mean, I get it. I don't like being called Kate. I like Katie. Even though my real name is Katherine. "She loved Thomas so much," she adds.

I nod. Aunt Jess always seemed happy with Uncle Thomas around. "They've been together since before I was born. It's weird that he's not going to be around anymore."

"Yeah. It's not cool."

"No, it's not."

She sits up and opens her arms, calling for a big bear-hug. I get on my knees, and we hug. It feels good.

"Aunt Maddie?"

"Mmm-hmm."

"Why do some hugs feel really good?"

"Because sometimes, we *really* need it."

"But why?"

"I don't know."

She stays in my room, and we end up watching the movie, followed by *Edward Scissorhands*. I fall asleep halfway through, Maddie on the floor at the foot on my bed.

I hate that I had to stay to take my stupid midterms instead of going home for Thomas' funeral. A part of me believes Jess will never forgive me, regardless of the circumstances. I sent her several texts throughout that week, but eventually life went on, and here I am studying for finals, my mind constantly thinking about what it's going to be like when I go home in a few days and see her for the first time.

My roommate Nicole stops by after her morning run to change, wash up, and head to her first exam. Luckily for me, my first one is tomorrow, but I do kinda wish I didn't have to wait. There's the good of having more time to study, but the bad of having periodic stress cramps and – so help me! – gas. I'm sure Nicole's noticed. She's applying some makeup, playing it cool as to why I have so many Febreze plug-ins set on high. All year has been like this. Nicole has never once made me feel like the gross person I am, especially given that she's so perfect and clean. Ugh. If I didn't love her so much as my best friend, I'd hate her.

"Good luck," I tell her when she finally heads out.

She pumps her fist in the air John Bender-style, and we both laugh. Alone again, I let out some more stress-gas. Thankfully, this particular gas has never smelled bad. But it does tend to be noisy.

I check the clock by my bed and see I have well over twenty-four hours until my English exam. We've already been given the prompt. All we have to do is show up and write. It sounds simple enough, but that basically means I'm setting myself up for failure. I tend to blow easy assignments. Not sure why that is.

Now, of course, I'm thinking of Thomas. Jess was the first to be married. We were so happy for her. According to Maddie, most of the family thought she was a bachelorette for life. She seemed to love being alone too much. But I guess she always talked about how her life flipped when she met him. A part of me worries that maybe she'll reject all that she was over the past fifteen years. I hope not. Jess is the best oldest sister ever. I wouldn't want her to change. Then again, it's her life, isn't it? It'd be selfish of me to demand otherwise.

Guilt returns as I'm reminded that I not only didn't go home but Mel probably isn't doing much. I know she and Jess got into it pretty bad this past Christmas, but family is family. Then again, Mel can be stubborn from time to time. Still, for what it's worth, she's always been supportive of me, even giving me a few grand before I left to UT. I love her. Of course, I do.

There's always Maddie, but chances are she's more focused on her own shit than to worry about Jess. Then again, maybe I'm being too judge-y. After all, Maddie's been crazy-busy since starting as an editor a few years ago. I mean, reading's fine and all, but I couldn't imagine having to not only read the amount she does but do so in a way that involves finding errors and making suggestions, and ugh! My contacts hurt just thinking about this. I take them out and put on my glasses. Thankfully, no one's here to see me in them.

I begin to think about my English professor and how she's able to read so much every semester. God bless her. Thomas was a professor for a few years, but he was so over the politics of it fairly quickly. He told me that professors have to publish multiple works every year. "No, thanks," he said. He then began work on a novel, but I never read anything from it. I felt it wasn't my business to ask. The thing is, now I'm wondering if it's sitting somewhere, completed, waiting for a pair of eyes. I make a note to see if Jess has found it anywhere. I'd actually love to read it.

I receive an email from Penelope about her junior prom, so I use this as an excuse to put off studying for just a little bit. Judging by the photos, it seemed fun. She looks cute in her bodycon short prom dress, something I could never pull off. I didn't go to my junior prom, but I did attend senior prom.

Thinking of that inspires me to go back to studying.

As I finish packing what little I have, I realize I'll have to wait a week to get my grades, which sucks. More time and more gas. I'm confident, though.

"I'm sure you kicked ass," Nicole tells me. She's staying a few more days, so she's lying on her bed, legs crossed, looking pretty comfortable playing with her phone.

"Yeah?"

"Yeah. You studied your ass off."

"I did, didn't I?"

"Yep. Now it's time to hit the gym and get it back."

"We're not all born with a bubble butt."

"Yes, but maintaining a healthy bubble butt is the hard part."

I smile. "I just wish I wasn't so short."

"Nothing wrong with being five-two."

"I know. It's just sometimes I look at my sister Maddie, and – yeah – you know what? I'm jealous. I'm jealous of my older sister."

"Is she the one who looks like Jennifer Lawrence?"

"Yeah."

"You're so much prettier than her."

"I wasn't fishing for that, but I'll accept. Also, don't say that about my sister."

"Yes, ma'am," she says, saluting me. We laugh.

When I zip up the last bag, I take a look around and find nothing else to pack. I sit at the edge of my bed, facing Nicole.

"So what happens now?" I ask.

"What do you mean?"

"I mean, are we gonna be roommates this fall?"

She rests her phone on her chest and considers the question. Then, she turns her head to face me and smiles. "Duh."

I smile.

"Did you really think otherwise?"

I shrug. "I don't know. We never talked about it."

"Look, as far as I'm concerned, you're my best friend. When we go home this summer, we'll reconnect with friends and all that shit, but by the end, we're coming back here. In fact, *this* is home now. Going to school here. Living here. Being with you. *You're* home."

"Well, aren't you cheesy?"

She shrugs. "Hey. Why not? We're not gonna see each other for months."

"Text me, 'kay?"

"You got it."

I gather up my backpack and a carry-on sized luggage bag. "Love you," I say.

Nicole gets up, hops to me, and gives me a big, tight hug. "Love you too, Hales," she says, opening the door. I can feel her eyes on me as I make my way to the elevator. I turn back once I hit the down button. She waves bye and then goes back inside. I will miss her. Of course, I will.

I drive my over-stuffed car to my childhood home, and I think about my mom and little Katie, who's turning ten in a few days. I pat the bag sitting on the passenger seat, her gift nestled carefully inside. I hope she loves it.

Just the thought of seeing Mom for the first time in months creates a lump in my throat, and I have that stupid thought I've been having for the past year – ever since I realized her age affects her bladder and that's why she always has to use the bathroom. Mom's getting old, and one day, she's going to die. I dread how grey her hair is most likely going to be when I see her. I shake off these ridiculous feelings and focus on the happiness of being able to come home to a mother I actually get along with. Nicole and her mom don't see eye to eye on most things, apparently, so she was very much dreading going home.

I get to the house and unlock the door. "Hello?" I call out. No answer. I close the door, kick off my shoes, and walk upstairs to my bedroom. Inside, I'm already comforted. I drop the bags I brought in by the door frame and just throw myself face first onto my bed. I take a deep breath. I'm truly home. After rubbing my face on the comforter, I decide to bring in the rest of my stuff and clean up before getting too relaxed. I eventually take a shower and get some clean clothes on. Thankfully, Mom keeps my room clean and dust-free, so there's that.

Hungry, I go to the kitchen, fix myself a sandwich, and text Mom, wondering where she's at. "mom, where r u?"

The bubbles appear and disappear. She replies four minutes later. "getting groceries for tonight. Be home soon. Kisses"

I get excited at the prospect of cooking dinner with Mom. We used to do it so often. It was our thing. Being so much younger than everyone else in my immediate family was lonely, but Mom was always there for me. Jess is two decades older than me and Mel is seventeen years my senior, a fact that consistently blows my mind every time I think about it. Maddie's ten years older, and even though she was closer to my age, by the time I was starting school, she was a full-blown teenager and wanted to spend more time with her friends than with me, a fact that changed once she started college, and I guess, matured. Still, she's had her own life for as long as I've known her. So, that means it was mostly me and Mom.

Dad left when I was one. He moved to California and met a woman named Clara, and in less than a year, I had a younger sister named Penelope. We've met in-person only once – when I visited a few years ago – but we email and text one another often. I smile to myself, my mouth full of the plain turkey sandwich I made myself, finish chewing, and then down some Cherry Coke before deciding to text Maddie where she is.

She answers immediately: "hey I know u. I'll be there tonight. Luv u"

"Luv u too"

I wonder if everyone's coming over. Then, I suddenly remember Jess. Feeling like shit that I forgot to swing by her place before I got here, I decide to call. There's no answer. Rather than leave a voicemail, I call again. No answer. I text: "hey, big sis. I'm home. Hope to see you tonight maybe? Luv u always"

No bubbles. No answer.

I text her best friend, Samantha. "hey. Sorry to bother you. I tried calling and texting Jess but she's not answering. She okay?"

About a minute later, Samantha replies: "she's fine. She's a bit down still, but I go over every day. Don't worry, baby girl, I got this. See you tonight."

So many thoughts cross my mind at once. First of all, Sam's coming tonight, which is awesome. She's always been nice to me. I figure it's because she's an only child and she sees herself as a part of this family, which she totally is. It also seems like just about everyone's coming over tonight, presumably as a welcome home kind of thing? Sounds great. But, what about Jess? She's still down, which is expected, given what happened. Still, she's not answering calls or texts, and Samantha has to see her at her place every day? That doesn't sound good. I make a note to ask about this tonight and to see her in person tomorrow.

I finish up and decide to watch *Rushmore* and maybe take a nap. Finals nearly destroyed me.

Mom wakes me up.

I open my eyes and see her, upside down, looking at me. I get up and hug her. She *does* look older, and my heart *does* break a little bit, but I tell myself that she has a few good decades left and push those thoughts aside.

"Oh, honey. You look so such older."

I want to say, "You, too," but decide on, "Thanks."

She kisses me on the cheek, and we sit down. She wants to know everything, and I'm happy to let her in on just about everything.

"Meet any cute girls?"

"Mom."

"What? It's not like I asked about sex or anything."

"Mom," I say again, getting up and moving to the loveseat. I kick myself for thinking she wouldn't ask.

"Oh, come on. You're almost twenty. I assume you're having sex."

I adjust myself, wanting this to end ASAP.

"But, I'm not asking about that. I'm asking if you've met anybody special."

I sigh dramatically. "One girl. But it wasn't that serious."

"What was her name?"

"Suzy."

"Suzy," she repeats, considering the name. "What happened?"

"Nothing. It just…it didn't work out."

"Did something happen?"

"No. It…I found out she had a girlfriend. And, I didn't want to be the other woman, so I broke it off. We only went out a month, so I wasn't that big a deal."

Mom nods. I add, "Plus, she was a Trump supporter."

"That's not nice, sweetie."

"It was a joke."

"I hope so."

"Mom."

"Okay," she says, throwing her hands up. "Fair enough."

I'm glad to be done with this part of catching up but it feels good that Mom cares enough to ask.

"So, you're here all summer?"

"Yeah. I'm happy to have the break."

"That's good. Well, just about everyone's coming tonight to celebrate your return."

"Yeah, I tried getting in touch with Jess, but –."

Mom's already nodding, so I stop. "Yeah. She's…she's not doing good, sweetie."

"How bad is it?"

She takes a deep breath. "She doesn't come out of bed much."

"Mom, it's been almost two months."

"I know."

"There's something seriously wrong."

"Haley, we know."

"Well, what's being done?"

"What we *can* do. Every day, Samantha goes by to check on her. I go a few times a week. Maddie's been there."

"Mel?"

Mom gives me a look, like I should know better. That isn't good enough for me. "Seriously? Mel hasn't gone to see her?"

"She thinks she'd upset her more."

"Maybe. Maybe not. They're sisters. Jesus."

"Haley. We know. Your sister's going to be fine."

"Maybe I should go over."

"We'll go over tomorrow. The two of us. For tonight, we have dinner. Now, I bought a bunch of stuff to make, so let's get to it." She stands up and pats me on the back.

My mind's still reeling from the possibility that Jess will never be the same.

"Honey," she tells me.

I look up at her. She doesn't say anything. She doesn't have to. I nod, get up, and follow her to the kitchen. Because life goes on, ten minutes later, I'm laughing it up with her.

It's after eight by the time everyone arrives. Seated at the large dining room table is Mom, Maddie, Mel and Katie, Samantha and Kris (Jess' other, crazy-funny friend), and Aunt Greta. There's plenty of food and conversation, and I'm loving the opportunity to catch up with so many people I love.

"So, Katie – excited about Friday?"

"Oh, yeah," she tells me.

"Katie's been toying with the idea of dressing up," Mel adds.

"Is that right?"

"It's between Cinderella and Belle. Right?" Maddie says.

Katie nods, excited.

"Well, my vote's for Belle," I say.

"Here, here," Kris adds, lifting her cup to toast no one.

"I like Belle," Katie begins, "but Cinderella has a blue dress, which I like better than the yellow one."

"Well, you could go as Belle at the beginning of the movie," I say.

"Yeah, but I wanted a princess dress."

"Here, here," Kris adds again, even lifting her glass for good measure. Laughs this time.

"Fair enough," I say.

"So, Haley," Maddie begins. "You'll never believe who I ran into yesterday."

"I'm sure you're about to tell me."

"Well, if you're gonna be like that."

"Maddie, come on."

"Nope."

"Who?" I demand. She's clearly loving this. After finishing her glass of wine and saying, "Ahh," she says, "Dani."

Shit, I think. I swallow without chewing much. "Oh," I say, trying and most likely failing to play it off.

"Oh?" Maddie says, barely able to contain the smile forming on her face.

"Oh, Dani," Mom says. "How is she?"

"Doing good. Her and Sasha are scraping together cash to make a horror movie."

A few at the table offer a few impressed words, but I unconsciously scoff. They all look my way. I take a gulp from my soda, hoping everyone will move past that. They do.

"You know, Dani was really great," Mom says.

"She really was," adds Maddie.

"Who's Dani?" Katie asks.

"She's your aunt Haley's ex."

"Really?"

I decide to just face this head-on. I wipe my mouth and say, "Yeah. For a little bit."

"Right. All through junior and senior year of high school. Including summers."

"Oh, yeah," Aunt Greta joins in. "Whatever happened with her?"

Maddie, who can't seem to keep quiet, answers for me again: "She dumped her."

"Wait. You dumped *her*, or she dumped *you*?" Katie asks.

"Poor Haley was dumped."

"I wasn't dumped."

"You were. But it wasn't super horrible or anything. Haley was going away to college, and Dani wanted to stay here."

"That's not why."

"Then what was it?"

"Will you just drop it?" I ask, my voice rising.

"Geez, Louise. Calm down, crazy."

I'm fuming all of a sudden. This was not how tonight was supposed to go. I love everyone at this table but being reminded of Dani and how she broke my heart – well, it's shitty that Maddie would bring it up so cavalierly.

"Okay. Okay," Mom says, trying to calm me down without singling me out. "Let's everyone calm down."

"*Everyone*? I'm not the one getting upset."

"Maddie," Mel says, *finally* saying something, which suddenly blows my mind, since she always seems to have to say something. What took her so long? "Drop it."

"Drop what? What did I do?" She turns to me. "Hales. What did I do?"

I'm trying to control my breathing, and I want so desperately to give it to Maddie, but my eyes catch Katie's, and I think better of it. I take a deep breath, and without looking at her, I tell Maddie, "Nothing. It's on me."

"See? No big deal."

It's awkward now. *I've* made it awkward. Maddie may have started it, but I escalated it, and now it looks like I ruined the evening.

About a minute passes without anyone saying a word. Katie is the first to speak up. She tells me, "Sorry she hurt you."

I want to break down and cry, but I don't. I smile at her, and thankfully, the dinner continues with no more talk of exes. And, by the time it's over, I'm on solid terms with Maddie again. Family, am I right?

Tomorrow, it's all about Jess.

<u>Maddie</u>

I hear about Mom and Haley's plan to visit Jess, so I decide to make it a family outing and go along. I stay the night, and we all pack into Mom's compact car and head over to see my red-headed older sis. Haley and I are on good terms, which makes me feel better for bringing up Dani dumping her last night. I was being an ass. I blame it on the wine. I thought I was being playful, but I clearly wasn't. That's on me. Neither of us bring it up, though, so I figure it's ancient history.

When we get Jess' place, Sam's making breakfast.

"Hey, guys," she says, as we walk into the kitchen. "So, Haley – feel weird sleeping in your old bed?"

"You know, it *was* a bit weird. I prefer it, but I couldn't sleep that well."

"Man, I remember coming home from school ready for my old bed, but it always took like a week to get back into it."

"Where's Jessica?" Mom asks.

"She's showering. Should be about done."

"I'm gonna see if she needs help." She walks to Jess' bedroom.

I turned to Sam and lean over the counter conspiratorially. "How she doin' today?"

"Not bad. She didn't even have to use the f-word to get me to leave her alone once we were in the bathroom."

"Well, that's progress."

"So," Haley asks, "what happened exactly?"

"Your mom didn't say? Maddie, you didn't tell her?"

"She knows. Right? You know?"

"Yeah. Mel told me. Mostly. But, I'm still not too clear."

"It was *bad*, sweetie. And, ugly. But, she's okay now. She's not gonna do that again."

"How do we know?"

29

"We just do. We gotta give her the space and freedom to live. We can't hound her."

"Says the best friend who literally checks in on her every day," I tell her.

"Hey, it's on my way to work, and if you'd seen the damage she did that night, you'd want to hover ever-so-slightly, too."

"Fair enough," I say to that. After all, who the hell am I to judge anyone taking care of my sister? I suddenly feel the urge to hug Sam, but for some reason decide to save it for later.

Mom comes back. "She's just getting dressed. She's happy *you're* here," she tells Haley.

"Really?"

She nods. I'm not completely convinced. Regardless, Jess comes in, and the first thing she does is smile at Haley and give her a hug. Her eyes look like they're tired of producing tears and her voice cracks occasionally. Jess, the one who always seemed the strongest, looks like she's ready to fall apart at any second. I'm on edge and sense everyone else is, too. I see her every other day, but I have yet to get used to seeing her this way.

"How you doin', kid?" she asks Haley, her hands cupping my little sis's cheeks.

"Good."

"Yeah? Awesome." After another hug, she thanks everyone for the visit but assures us that she's fine.

We sit and have Samantha's tasty eggs and toast, while she leaves for work.

"So, Jess," I say. "How's *Lost*?"

"Just ended season three. Holy shit."

"Right?!"

We laugh, and it feels good. "Yeah, man. I mean, the season was a bit rocky, but those final episodes, and that last scene? So good."

"Well, keep me up to date. We'll watch the last episode together."

"It's a date."

Mom starts talking to her, and I think to myself that Jess *is* doing fine. I don't doubt that living here alone, amidst the former life she had with the man she loved, must be horrible. I consider just why she's subjecting herself to this form of self-torture, and then I'm asked by Mom, "Right?"

I snap out of my reverie and say, "Yeah. Totally."

Everyone seems to buy it, and so I decide to keep that trust and stay focused on the conversation, which isn't about anything particularly special, but it's fine. It's the kind people have around those who've just gone through something life changing. It's, like, everyone knows what's going on and what's wrong, but no one's talking about it. I can't really say that it necessarily bugs me, but it also feels dishonest.

"I wanted to ask," Haley says to Jess, "if it was cool that I hang out here today."

"You want to hang out *here*?" she responds. "Don't you have some old friends to see?"

"I got the whole summer. I want to spend time with you. My favorite sister."

"Ha-ha," I dryly say.

Jess smirks, gives me a quick look, and then tells Haley, "Sure. Why not?"

I drop Mom off at home and go to meet Angie at her bookstore. I enter and find no one around – not even behind the counter. The score to *Blade Runner*'s playing, I believe, but I do my best to shout above it, "Hello?"

There's some noise, and then Angie comes out from the back room, carrying a box. "Hey," she says.

"Hey. Where is everybody?"

"It's 10:45 on a Tuesday," she says walking behind the counter.

"And…?"

“And, it’s quiet, because people are working.”

“Oh, please. So, if we go to Target right now we’d find no one?”

“It’s also a bookstore, not a Target. Smartass.” She says that last part under her breath as she sits the box down on the counter and then slices it open with a letter opener.

I walk to a table with new releases. “So, Haley’s home.”

“Oh, I love little Haley. How she doing?”

“Good. She’s actually spending the day with Jessie.”

“Really?”

“Yeah.”

“Well, that’s good, right? Doesn’t that mean Jess is getting better?”

“I hope so. She *sounded* better, but she still looks bad.” I add, “I had breakfast with them.”

Angie nods as a customer enters. She coolly turns the music down a little. “Hello,” she says.

“Hi,” the middle-aged man replies. He starts at the shelves near the front right windows and begins browsing. I move closer to the counter.

“This is a nice place, by the way.”

“Right?”

“Music, too.”

"I love being able to choose my own playlist for the store. That way, I don't go crazy hearing the same shit over and over."

I lean on the counter and ask, "Can I ask you something?"

"You know I hate that question."

"Is it stupid that I'm a little freaked out about turning thirty in two months?"

"Hmm. Not really."

"I never asked how you handled it a few months ago."

She shrugs. "It wasn't a big deal. You were there. We even counted down to the minute."

"I know. I just thought maybe you were hiding something."

"I don't know, Mads. I was pretty excited about turning thirty. I mean, why wouldn't I be?"

"Because you're no longer in your twenties."

"So, what? Just because I'm in my thirties I can't do certain things anymore? I mean, think about it. What exactly changes aside from the number?"

"I mean, fair enough, but I'm still freaked."

"Why?"

"I don't know why. I really don't."

"Well, best friend, alls I can tell you is that you need to find a way to get over it. One second, you're twenty-nine and the next, you're thirty."

I let it go, knowing she's right. Angie's been my best friend for well-over a decade now. As cliched as it sounds, I'm damn sure she knows me better than I know myself.

I stay for about an hour. At one point, the guy buys himself a copy of David Foster Wallace's *Infinite Jest*, and we roll our eyes at one another as he walks out. I go and pick up lunch at this sandwich place about a block away, and when I return, there's a half-dozen people inside.

"Damn," I tell Angie as I make myself comfortable behind the counter.

"Five potential customers. Not sure I know how to handle this."

"I can call riot control."

"Please?" Angie takes a bite of her sandwich and tells me, "You know, I've actually been thinking about what you said, about being freaked out, and I have a little bit of an idea, but mentioning it means I'll have to break the Bechdel Test."

"Well, shit, Angie."

"I know, I know, but how the hell are we supposed to get through *every* conversation and never once talk about a guy?"

"You disappoint me."

"Whatever. Here's my hot take: you're freaked out about turning thirty because you haven't had a relationship in years, and for some insane reason, you're linking leaving your twenties with leaving behind the possibility of meeting 'the one' and starting a family."

I admit to myself that she's close, but as I mull it over and she takes a huge bite from her meatball sub, I realize that's not it. "Nope. Sorry."

"Really?"

"Yeah. You betrayed women everywhere for no reason."

"Well, Ms. Ass, I tried."

"*You're* Ms. Ass."

"Thank you. I work hard on it." With plenty of food still in her mouth, she gives me a toothy grin.

When I get home that night, I decide to wrap Katie's birthday present. As a big fan of reading and writing, I got her three of my favorite things: a copy of George Eliot's *Middlemarch*, a Moleskin with a fancy pen to write with, and a porcelain teapot with some Earl Grey to go with it. I put it all in a box and carefully wrap it, as *Spirited Away* plays in the background.

I shower, get dressed for bed, and find myself unable to sleep. I turn my bedroom TV on and flip through the channels, finally landing on a rerun of *Friends* I've seen at least two dozen times. It's the one where Ross is giving a speech and everyone – except Phoebe – is taking forever to get dressed, as the clock is counting down the entire time. I remember seeing this episode for the first time with Jess and Mel, back when they hung out.

Mel can most definitely be a handful, but I've never understood what led to their falling out. I mean, I know what the fight this past Christmas was all about, but that was more of the straw that broke the monkey's back (or whatever). But, before that? Beats me.

I've often thought that maybe Mel had a thing for Thomas, or maybe even that Jess had a thing for Stephen, but I tend to shake all that away, because that just doesn't click for me. Honestly, it's probably some bullshit that always seems to destroy relationships. Hence, why I'm not a fan of them – romantic-wise anyway.

I begin thinking about what Angie told me, and I consider it again. Cliched or not, plenty of women think about this kind of thing when they turn thirty, but that's just not me. I consider that maybe I'm lying to myself, but there's nothing really to support that.

I think about Dad and if that's affecting how I'm feeling. Again, nothing.

My thoughts turn to Katie, and I begin reflecting on how it was for me when *I* turned ten. I had two older sisters, one loving parent, a dad who was starting a new family in another state, and a cool aunt. Am *I* that cool aunt for Katie? I'd like that. I remember how it felt to have someone who supported you and kept your secrets. Aunt Greta wasn't necessarily *that* for me. Mel was, though. Jess was off doing her own things, mostly, by the time I was ten, but Mel was there for major support for things I couldn't bear to share with Mom. Yes, even as a ten-year-old, I had my secrets. Does Katie? Would she feel comfortable telling me? I hope so.

Jess. I'm happy she has Samantha and Kris.

Haley. I'm happy she has Mom and Nicole.

Me. I'm happy I have Angie and Marie.

Mom. I'm happy she has Greta and all of us.

Mel. I'm happy she has Stephen and Katie.

Yeah. I'm not freaked out about turning thirty. I'm happy about it.

Camel. Not monkey. It's the straw that broke the *camel's* back. *That's* what it was.

Once Haley finally leaves, I go to my bedroom, unscrew the top to the vodka bottle by my bed and don't even spend the time to pour it into a glass. I down several fingers worth, taking heavy breaths after the final swallow. Damn, it burns. But, it's a good burn.

A few minutes later, and I can barely keep my eyes open. Which is just as well. I'm in bed and don't feel the urge to pee just yet. I take a look at the broken picture frame at the far corner of the room. Sam knows not to touch it. It stays there. I keep an eye on it as best I can, until everything goes black.

Someone shakes me awake. I don't open my eyes, but I let whomever it is know I'm up.

"Jess?"

It's Sam, of course. Who else would it be?

I tell her I'm up.

"Jess." She sounds funny – like far away. "Jess?"

I hear her walk away. She's in my bathroom. The water from the tub rushes out, and moments later she's walking back to me and then –

SPLASH!

I get a bucket of water tossed on me.

This definitely gets me up. "What the hell?"

"Oh, you're up. Breakfast is ready." Sam sounds eerily calm. With that, she leaves the room, carrying the bucket with her. I'm soaked and need to change, but there's a part of me who thinks I should just go to the kitchen to show her what she did.

"I'm gonna dry off first!" I call out, making sure she knows I'm angry.

"Sounds good," Sam says back. She doesn't sound upset, which freaks me out a little.

I get out of bed, dry off, and put on some new clothes, scoffing at the bras I haven't worn in months. Who needs 'em?

In the kitchen, Sam is drinking coffee and checking her phone. She's always super-busy and always has been. "New haircut?" I ask.

"Yeah. Thanks for noticing," she says, not looking at me. She's angry.

I sit at the table where a stack of pancakes sits waiting for me. "Thanks," I say.

"No problem." She puts her phone in her purse and begins to gather her things. "I'll see you tonight."

"Tonight?"

"Yeah. You said you were finally coming out of your shell and were gonna spend the night with me and Kris. I got stuff planned."

"Yeah. Yeah – sure. No problem."

"You promised."

"Yeah. Yeah – absolutely. I remember."

"You don't remember. God, of course, you don't remember."

"I remember."

"Really?"

"Yeah."

"Wow."

"Wow, what?"

"I made that up."

"What?"

"Those plans you say you remember promising? I made them up." She shakes her head. "I'm so sick of this shit." She heads to the front door, exiting the kitchen.

"Then don't come over anymore. No one's forcing you to."

She comes back. "Oh, yeah – sure. Who gonna make sure this place doesn't devolve into a junkyard?"

"I can take care of myself, okay?"

"You could've fooled me."

I get up, take the plate of pancakes, and drop them and the plate into the garbage can by the island. Sam's face says it all. With one gesture, I break her heart. I want in that instant to take it back. I'm about to say I'm sorry when she looks at my empty hands and then back at my face, this time with her eyes glistening.

"Sam…," I start to say, not knowing what I can possible say or do to fix this.

It doesn't matter. She looks like she either wants to hit me or let me have it – or both. Instead, she walks out of the kitchen and then the house. The thing that breaks *my* heart is that she doesn't even slam the door. She closes it softly and then locks it.

It started like this:

I woke up about ten hours after returning from the hospital, in my bed, to find Sam in a chair beside me that she must've quietly – a feat on its own – brought in from the living room. She was snoring. I remember not feeling much at that point. I went to the bathroom and returned to find her still out. I got beneath my covers again and fell back asleep. I don't think I dreamed.

Sam woke me up a few hours later by softly touching my arm. We didn't say much to one another, but we managed to get me showered, dressed, and fed. Then, we spent the rest of the day watching episodes of *Supernatural* in mostly silence, a reaction every now and then resulting in a noise or a comment, like, "That's so gross." There was even a little light laughter.

The day after, I woke up at a better time, and Sam was still here. Her clothes were the same, but her hygiene was still up to par. Kris joined us after work, and we spent the night eating take-out and watching some John Hughes movies, commenting on how oddly sexist and racist parts of *Sixteen Candles* and *The Breakfast Club* were.

The next day, Sam was there again, but this time she left after breakfast, promising my mom would be by and that we'd all meet at the funeral parlor for the wake. Sam needed to take care of a few things at her office. I told her she should take care of her own life first and stop worrying about me, but she ignored that, told me she loved me, and left. And, that's how it's been for the past two months or so.

That's also when the drinking began. Well, I guess I mean that that's when the drinking *returned*. Back in college, I was quite the drinker. It started with a few beers and then to the heavy stuff. By the time I met

Thomas, I was drinking half a bottle of scotch or vodka daily. How I managed to do anything I chuck up to being young. Now, I wouldn't say that Thomas got me to or inspired me to quit drinking, but he was a piece of it. His presence even helped in the days following what I did to Melanie. Something she, rightfully, has never forgiven me for. I vowed to quit, and he made sure I did it. He wasn't much of a drinker, and even though he didn't have to, he stayed sober, too. We were clean for about fifteen years.

But I went out and bought a bottle before Mom came over for lunch. And then I drank a quarter of it throughout the day. I did wonder if anyone could tell. Maybe they did. Maybe they were letting me process it all. Mel *did* give me a look when I hugged Katie. She could probably smell it, so I did my best to stay away from her. That probably didn't help any chance for a possible reconciliation.

Katie. She's everything to me. Because of my...*condition*, I made a conscious decision to be a close part of Katie's life. She isn't my kid, but I pretty much see her that way. As her godmother, I'm there for her always.

Which is why, after Sam leaves, I wrap Katie's gift for her birthday tomorrow and finish the latest bottle.

Sam isn't there when I wake up.

                    *   *   *

Katie's party isn't until four, so I figure it's fine to have a drink. By

3:45, I decide it's probably best to take an Uber, in case I get into an

accident on the way. I mean, I'm fine, but because I have a *little* alcohol in

my system – well, you know how these things go. The woman driving me

is nice enough. Her name's Karen, I think. I tip her well when she pulls up

and then I'm out of the car, present in hand, and walking to the front door.

It opens before I'm even close enough to knock.

"Jess!" Stephen says, excitedly.

"Hel-lo!" I respond. He makes a weird face, but then plays it off like he

didn't.

"Come in."

"Was just going to. Duh." I laugh to make sure he knows it's a joke.

Maddie comes in from the dining room, beaming. "Jess!"

"That's my name."

"I'll take that," Stephen says about the gift. I hand it to him, and Maddie

hugs me. "We're all outside."

"We'll meet you," Maddie says, and he's off.

I shake my head. "What a lame-o."

"A 'lame-o'?" Maddie's smile fades away, and suddenly, she makes the same face Stephen did less than a minute ago, but she doesn't try to hide it. "Jess, are you drunk right now?" She says that last part quietly.

"No." Stupid question.

"Yeah, you are. Mel's gonna *kill* you. Or, worse, beat the hell out of you."

"I could take her."

"Maybe a few years ago, but Mel works out now. Like a lot."

I roll my eyes. "Please. One on one, I'm the victor."

"Okay. Regardless, you need to realize that you're at your niece's birthday party, and you're drunk."

"I'm not drunk! Did I have a few drinks? Yeah. So, what? *You* drink. You drink all the time."

"At night, with friends. Not during the day, and not during a time like this. Come on, Jess – you're supposed to be the older, responsible one."

"Well, maybe I'm not the older, responsible one. Maybe it's Mel. Maybe it's always been Mel."

She shakes her head. "You know what? Let's go."

"No."

She takes a hold of my arm. "Come on."

I shake her arm off and say, "Get off!" I walk right through the dining room and the kitchen, and out through the patio doors to the back yard. The party's already going on. Looks nice. Maddie ends up beside me and turns me her way. "Hey. What's the matter with you? You're gonna make a scene."

"Get off. I'm fine."

I walk through everyone, trying to find Katie. Where *is* she? I see a bunch of people I don't know with familiar faces scattered around like chocolate chips. I see Mom, who looks at me concerned for some reason. I offer her a courteous smile and continue on. Finally, I see Katie at the far end of the pool, talking with two other girls. She looks happy. I come to a stop and just look at her.

"Hey," I hear a voice say curtly.

"Hey," I respond, not really caring who it is.

"Jess."

I turn around and see Mel. She's dressed up and holding a glass of water with a slice of orange in it. I want to throw up right on her that second, but I don't. "Mel," I say, doing my best to match her tone.

"What are you doing here?"

"I was invited." I hold back on saying, "duh," but she knows I want to say it, so it's enough.

"By who?"

"Whom?"

"What?"

"Whom. Not who."

"Whatever. That's not the point."

"Well, whatever. If you want to speak incorrectly, that's on you," I say over her response.

"Excuse me?"

"I'm here because it's Katie's day. Can't we just celebrate Katie's day?"

"I know it's Katie's day. I've been planning this party for a while now."

"And, what? You want an award or something?"

"I want to know *why* you would show up here drunk?"

Again, with that accusation. This time, though, I decide to take a quick glance around. People are looking and clearly talking about what's happening between us. I try a trick from my college days, and I look inside myself and try to count to thirty. I can make it to ten, no problem, but then my mind gets tired or bored or both before I can make it to twenty-five. I lick my hand and smell it. I can smell liquor. Of course. I'm drunk, and I'm about to ruin Katie's birthday.

Mel seems to suddenly soften. She steps toward me, and I think she's actually going to hug me for the first time in years. Perhaps it's the alcohol, I don't know, but I step toward her, arms beginning to stretch out when she moves past me and meets up with Katie, who looks so happy to see me.

"Aunt Jess!"

"Hey, little dude." I get lower and we hug. It feels so good I don't want to let go.

"Okay, Jess," Mel tells me after a few moments. I don't let go. "Jess." Fine. I let go. Katie doesn't seem to have minded. I look at Mel. She wants me to leave, that much is clear. I decide she's probably right.

"Listen, Katie. I gotta go."

"What?" she says, sounding unbelievably disappointed.

"But I tell you what. How about we hang out this weekend, huh? We can go somewhere. Get something to eat. Have fun."

"That sounds good, right?" Mel says. I wonder if she'll even agree to that or if she just wants me to go.

"I want Aunt Jess to stay."

"Katie, I would. I'm just…a little sick right now."

Katie looks like she's about to cry. Mel gets lower. "Katie. Don't cry. Aunt Jessie's just being honest with you." This seems to stop Katie's tears, but it also seems to silence her, which doesn't sit well with me. I'm the last person to tell Mel she's not being a good mother at this moment but seeing that makes me want to. Katie's just a kid. So what if she wants to cry?

I want to tell Mel that it's okay. I'm leaving. Instead, I say, "Don't call me Jessie."

"Excuse me?" Mel says, her voice rising.

Mom comes over. "Would you two keep it down?"

"No, I want her to say what she said."

I scoff and smile. Screw her.

"This is my house, Jessie," she says, putting emphasis on my name. "Don't tell me how to act or what to say."

I get in her face. She meets me.

"Okay, now *stop* it."

"Mom?" Katie asks. She's scared now, and I'm the reason for that. Still, I'm not backing down from this.

"What?" Mel asks. "What are you gonna do? You're gonna fight me here in front of everybody?"

"Maybe I should."

Maddie gets in between us. I stumble back a little. "Okay. That's enough. Mel, walk away right now."

"Are you serious?" she asks, sounding like she can't believe what she's being told.

Maddie turns to me. "Come on. Let's go get something to eat. I'm starving anyway."

"Fine," I say.

We begin to walk away when I hear, "And, don't come back, *Jessie*!"

Without thinking, I turn around and take a swing at Mel, but I don't connect. Instead, I hear my mom yell, "Oh my God!" Katie yells, "Mom!" Maddie seemingly tries to hold me back, but it's unnecessary. I trip on myself and fall nearly face-first on the pavement. "Ah," I say. There's small commotion with a lot of mumbling. My mind gets fuzzy. I hear a lot of yelling from Mel and Katie. Stephen tells Haley to get the car. My mom's saying something, and Maddie's helping me up. I'm dragged back into the house and back out of it again. I'm put into the backseat of a car, buckled up, and driven away. I look out the window and don't see anyone.

I look to the passenger seat up front and see Maddie shaking her head, talking with whoever's driving. I can't see who it is.

I wake up and find no one beside my bed. I want to kill myself. It's simple, really. I have plenty of medication. I'll just take it all. I'll make sure this time.

I'll write a note first; maybe a few. One addressed to everyone and a few for specific people. Katie, of course. Maddie and Haley. Mom. And -.

Sam comes in from the bathroom wearing my robe, which looks freshly dried. She looks at me funny. "You okay?"

I'm at a loss for words, so I nod.

She nods back and leaves the room.

After everything, Samantha is still here. My best friend in the whole world. That's that, then. Today, I'm getting myself out of bed. I'm going to clean up, eat breakfast with Sam before she's off to work, and then I'm leaving the house. Not for booze or anything like that. I'm back on the wagon. I'm pretty sure I can do this.

<u>Greta</u>

I have no idea how hard Sarah's taking what happened yesterday. After Jessica made her debut and fell down, knocking over the table with Katie's presents, she went inside Melanie's house and just watched TV the rest of the day. I spent some time with her, but she didn't say much. Melanie tried to get her to see that she wasn't in the wrong and that it was all Jess' fault, but Sarah wasn't having it. She did smile at Katie and tell her everything was fine. She even accepted Haley, who fell asleep with her head on her lap.

Maddie sat on a chair beside the couch, sipping wine and not saying much, once she returned from taking Jess to her place with Samantha, who is the sweetest person ever. Having had to take care of an ill husband during the final years of his life, I recognize the healing spirit in her. Jess is hurt. Maybe not physically, but certainly mentally and spiritually. I'm so happy she has a good friend to be there for her.

I took Sarah home once things were really over. She did her best to say her goodbyes to everyone, while keeping a neutral tone. On the way back, Haley sat in the passenger seat and Sarah in the back.

"You okay, Mom?" she asked.

"I'm fine," Sarah said, tired.

"Are you sure you don't want me to drive, Aunt Greta?"

"Oh, I got it, sweetie. Thank you."

Haley turned on the radio and found a station playing some '80s hit. She kept it at a low-ish volume, and we continued on without saying much to each other.

I wake up a little after eight and go check on Sarah. She's still in bed – something of an anomaly, given that she's always the first person up in the morning. I want to get under the covers with her and talk, but I also knows she needs her space and that she'll open up when she wants to.

When I go to the kitchen, Haley is still in her pajama bottoms and t-shirt, eating a banana and looking out the window into the backyard.

"Good morning," I say.

"Morning."

"Anything for today?"

She shrugs. "I was thinking of going to the movies. Want to come?"

"I think, maybe, I should stay close to your mom today."

She nods, understandingly. "What do *you* think about yesterday?" she asks as I turn on the coffee maker.

"Well," I say with a heavy sigh. "I don't think Jess should've shown up to Katie's tenth birthday party drunk, that's for sure."

"Right."

"And, I also think Melanie pushes things too far with her. I understand that things aren't great for them right now -."

"Like when they were younger?"

I nod. "Yeah. Like before you were born, they were almost inseparable."

"Really? What happened?"

"You know what happened."

"I saw them fight last Christmas, like always, except it got really bad, but it also seemed like the fight was about something else."

"I'm sure it was. But I don't know anything about it."

"Me neither."

"Anyway, Jess was wrong. Melanie was wrong. It was Katie's day for crying out loud. Am *I* wrong?"

"No," she says, mouth full. She swallows. "Jess is sad right now, though."

"We know. But, two months, Haley."

"I don't know how I'd feel losing Mom. If I had someone I'd chosen to be married to and that person…well, I don't *know* how I'd feel." She throws the peel away. "But *I* give her the benefit of the doubt."

"You think Melanie was wrong."

"Of course. She was egging her on. I mean, yes, Jess shouldn't have shown up wasted, but there's a reason for that. She was also there because she loves Katie to death. Mel went right up to her and wanted to fight. I could tell."

"Right. Well. Let's hope my fiftieth birthday next month isn't as controversial."

"Oh, I'm sure you and Mom will duke it out in front of everyone."

I chuckle. "Is that right?"

"Oh, yeah. Even odds, too."

"Even odds. Well, I take those."

She laughs. I laugh. Fine way to start the day, I suppose.

I'm reminded that I'm turning the big 5-0 when Sarah and I go shopping for Maddie's own big birthday. We find ourselves in Macy's, trying to find a top she'd love, and seemingly failing every time we think we've found something.

"I can't believe she's turning thirty already."

"I can't believe you'll officially have daughters in their twenties, thirties, and forties by the time the year ends."

"Don't remind me, please."

"I know, I know. But, just so I know, what can I look forward to in my fifties?"

"Nothing. More body aches, maybe."

"Well, I do work out regularly still."

"Good for you." She holds out a blue top meant to show quite a bit of cleavage. "How about this one?"

"Well. Maddie *does* have a big chest."

Before I can go on, Sarah looks at it, gets what I'm saying, and says, "Never mind."

"Maybe she'll like it."

"Moving on."

I smirk. "Your daughter wears sexy clothes, I'm sure."

"Oh, I'm pretty positive. I still remember the stuff she wore in high school."

"Oh my God," say, remembering the skin tight and/or revealing stuff she tried to get by her mom. "Jesus, Sarah, how did you do it?"

"Do what?"

"Raise four girls."

"It wasn't that hard. Especially when Roger was still around."

"How is he? Haven't heard from him in a while."

"Me neither."

"Not surprising."

"No, it's not. But I *am* happy Haley talks to him regularly. And Madelyn, too, sometimes."

"That's good."

"It is. They *should* have a good relationship with their father. Things didn't work out." She shrugs, slightly deep in thought but also still in the moment. "But we tried. We really did. *I* don't blame him."

"For the record, I side with your older girls on this one."

She nods. Then – "New subject, please."

I hold up a black, elegant top that I think would work with jeans or whatever nice pants girls wear these days. Sarah looks it up and down.

"That's the one," she says.

"I know. I've got great taste."

I have a bucket list. So help me, I do. I brought this up to Haley once, and she admitted to having one, as well.

"What's on it?"

"Travel, of course."

"Ooh, where?"

"A few places."

"Like…?"

She took a deep breath, and said, "Well, I'd like to go to the Telluride Film Festival. It's in Colorado. I've seen pictures and videos for years. It's so beautiful. Plus, I mean – come on. A film festival. Like, a real one. I don't know. Stupid, I guess."

"Haley, that's not stupid. I think that sounds lovely. And, even if I didn't think so, so what? It's your dream."

"I guess."

"Where else?"

"Um…well, there's this Viking Cruise that goes through France. Sounds cool."

"We should do that."

"What? The cruise?"

"Yeah. Why not?"

"Just you and me?"

"Sure. Or anyone else. But, if that's something you're interested in, I'm willing to pay for it. Besides, it's on my bucket list, too."

"Really?" She brightened up at the very real possibility of this happening.

"Yeah."

"That'd be so cool."

"Then, okay. I'll look into it."

I did. And so, for Haley's twentieth birthday, I'm giving her the cruise. I figure we can go during her winter break. Her birthday isn't until October, but she'll be away at school then. The plan is to surprise her sometime before the big day.

Haley is such a sweet girl. I'm not naïve to think she's little miss perfect, but she's got a good head on her shoulders. Her mother and father divorced when she was one. By this time, Jess was in college, with Melanie right behind her, and Maddie was a tween. It was decided one day. They couldn't do it any longer, so Sarah and Roger called it quits.

It was a long time coming. In the early days, there was certainly love. Frankly, in my opinion, the love never went away. But it wasn't enough to sustain the changes both went through. It's an interesting thing how some people are able to meet when they are young and grow together. It doesn't happen all that often. I saw that with Jess and her man. They were lucky. Sarah and Roger had to work for it, and sometimes, there was a lot of shouting, even in my presence. Things never got *that* bad, though. Roger never crossed a line. From what I know for sure, there was shouting and crying and horrible things said, mostly, though not exclusively, from Roger, followed by stretches of not talking to one another. Sometimes, Roger would leave for weeks at a time. This was during Melanie and Jess' childhoods and teenage years. They would grow to not like their father very much. By the time Maddie was born, the fighting began to occur less and less, but the love that was so clearly there in the beginning was hard to see. Less laughter in the home. A lot of quiet. Jess sometimes starting fights with Roger for no good reason. Melanie staying out all night, sometimes for days. It wasn't pretty.

I'm unsure as to how any of this truly affected the girls. Melanie's in a good marriage. Jess was in a great one. Maddie seems okay being on her own. Haley – well, I'm not too sure. She seemed to be fine in that department, until Dani broke her heart. I hope her parents' divorce and that heartbreak didn't do any lasting damage, but who's to say?

I love that girl with all my heart. I would never dare say Haley's my favorite, but I'll admit this: we're closer than the others. That's okay, I think. Haley's never had too many close friends. I'm happy to say I've been one of them.

Sarah and Haley come with me to the cemetery a few weeks later. It's been about a month since I've gone by to see Phillip. I notice that the grass has been cut and the ornamental flags for Memorial Day are gone. My knees find the soft turf before his stone, and Sarah puts a hand on my shoulder. I haven't cried in years, and though seeing his name reminds me of how much I miss the man, no lump in my throat appears, let alone tears.

Haley echoes my thoughts and says, "I miss him. He was funny."

I stifle a laugh. "Yeah." I put a hand over Sarah's. She turns hers over and holds mine. I feel safe.

Back in the car, Haley drives us to lunch. Sarah looks at me through the rearview mirror and asks, "Are you ready to turn fifty, grandma?"

"Oh, sure. Why not?"

She smiles. "I've invited everybody. It's going to be quite the evening."

"Should be good."

"Jess *and* Mel are gonna be there?" Haley asks.

Sarah takes a second before answering, "No. Jess is going to come by in the morning and have lunch, but…no. She won't be there."

"Understandable," I say.

"Is it?"

"I'm not taking sides, Sarah. But it's obvious that they don't like being around one another anymore."

"I hate it."

"I know you do." It's my turn to put my hand on my sister's shoulder. She rubs it.

"Can I ask you guys something?" Haley asks.

"Sure," Sarah answers.

"Did you guys ever get into it the way Jess and Mel are right now?"

"No," we both say in unison. Everyone sort of laughs, things oddly relaxed now.

"We used to fight," Sarah says, "but never anything like this."

"Well, there was that one Valentine's Day during my senior year of high school," I say. "Remember that?"

"When I talked to that guy you liked?"

"You told him I had a crush on him."

"It was an accident."

"Mom," Haley says, as I shake my head, even though I'm smiling.

"I was so embarrassed. God – I hated you so much. I think I said that to you, too."

"Oh, you said a lot worse."

"Really?" Haley asks, sounding a bit amused.

"Oh, your aunt said some pretty blue things to me."

"And, you to me."

"Only as a reaction."

"Fair enough."

"So, you guys fought. But how long until you made up?"

"I'd say," Sarah begins and then looks to me for confirmation. "A week? Maybe?"

I nod. "About five days."

"Who apologized to whom?"

"Neither, right?"

I shake my head. "Neither of us."

Haley seems disappointed by this.

"I'm sorry, by the way," Sarah says.

"I'm sorry, too." I turn to Haley and put a hand on her shoulder, which she rubs, just like her mother. "It'll be okay, Haley."

"Will it?"

"Sure. They're sisters. Even if it takes forty years."

"Even if it takes forty years," she replies softly, maybe even to herself.

I turn to Sarah who looks solemn. "Sarah."

She turns slightly, looking at me through her peripheral.

"It'll be okay."

She nods curtly and turns back, facing the road before us. I am not looking forward to turning fifty, but perhaps there's a way to get two of my nieces talking before that happens.

Part Two: "It's more for you than anybody else."

<u>Greta</u>

On the morning of my fiftieth, I call Jess. She sounds better than she has in a long time, which makes me feel good about what I want to do. I let her know I'm glad she's coming over for brunch at my place and that Haley and Maddie will be joining us. She says she's happy, too, and that's that.

I call Melanie immediately after and invite her to brunch at my place. She says she doesn't want to be wherever Jess is, but I tell her she can't make it and that she's welcome to come over and join me, Haley, and Maddie. Though she's a little upset with Maddie still, presumably over her seemingly sticking up for Jess at Katie's birthday party, she agrees.

It's a bit sitcom-y, but so what? Sometimes, a lie like this works in getting two people to meet who would rather not. The only thing that can hurt this is either of them recognizing the other's car and figuring out this whole charade. Also, how angry will they be with me over the fact that I've tricked them to come over? Hell, Haley and Maddie won't be here, either! I'm such a liar. But I don't care. Jess and Melanie *will* talk.

*   *   *

Jess arrives first, and it's like I haven't seen her in years. She looks so much healthier than she did at Katie's birthday.

"Look at you," I say.

"Yeah, well – thank Sam."

"I will."

We sit at the kitchen table, and Jess looks the clock behind her and then back at me. "So. You're turning fifty tonight."

"I know," I say, playfully scrunching up my face.

She almost smiles. "What?"

"Turning fifty. I suppose it's a big deal."

"Isn't it?"

I shrug. "I've lived a life already. To think I'm just now turning fifty." I shake my head, trying to contemplate how that's possible. "It's strange."

"Yeah. I turn forty this year."

I nod.

"Didn't think I'd be a widow when I turned the big 4-O."

"None of us think that."

"How'd you do it?" she asks me. I'm caught off guard. I wasn't expecting her to be so open so quickly. "I'm sorry. I didn't mean anything by -."

I wave it off. "Oh, no. No. It's not that." I sigh. "Let's just say it wasn't easy. But, a very obvious and cliched thing is always happening, and it happens even when it seems *your* world has ended."

She nods, already understanding. "Life goes on."

"Yeah." Jess has always been so quick. "Yeah."

She pours herself some tea, because I'm a terrible host. I get up and finalize some small sandwiches behind the counter. Melanie will be here soon.

"So, where is everybody?"

"Huh?"

"Haley and Maddie." She turns around to face me. "They running late?"

I lick some mustard off my finger and respond without looking at her. "Mm-hmm."

I hear her turn back around. After a few seconds, I hear a chuckle and then a full-blown laugh. She ends it with a long sigh. "Melanie's coming." She turns back around. "Right?"

I don't answer. Instead, I begin slicing.

A shake of the head, and then she's standing up and walking out of the room. I put the knife down, grab a towel, and head after her. "Jess." I catch her at the front door. "Jess. Please."

"What is this? What do you think's going to happen? We'll talk, smooth things out, maybe even share a hug?"

"That'd be nice, but no."

"Then what?"

"I just want you guys to talk."

"About what? Seriously, what do we have to talk about? The fact that she hates me and doesn't want anything to do with me? Is that what we could talk about?"

"It's a start," I joke, but Jess isn't having it. She crosses her arms.

"I'm leaving," she says quietly. "Please open the door and let me leave."

"What happened with you two?"

"Oh, come on."

"No, what?"

"You know what happened. Everyone does."

"I know things were said. But that can*not* be it. I mean, did one of you do something to the other?"

"Oh, yeah. Absolutely. I had an affair with Stephen, and in return Mel had an affair with Thomas." Her voice breaks when she says his name.

I let this hang there for a few moments because I ask, "Really?"

"No!" she says, almost comedically frustrated. "Jesus." She takes a few steps away and puts her hand on her forehead.

"I'm sorry."

She nods, rubbing her eyes with her palms.

"I just want things to go back the way they were."

"That's never going to happen."

"Not if neither of you try."

"I've tried. I've tried for a long time. You guys just don't know because I don't broadcast it." She takes a deep breath. "Every month for the past three years I've called to talk to her. She's always busy, apparently. The last few months, Stephen began telling me how he had been trying to get her on the phone and that she didn't want anything to do with me. And then Thomas killed himself." Her voice cracks again and I can see her eyes begin to glisten. "And I tried to call her from the hospital, because I wanted to hear her voice, and guess what happened. She was busy."

She sits on the third step of the set of stairs nearby, taking deep breaths, not wanting to cry. I walk over, devasted by what I've heard, worried about what's possibly coming next in this tale. "And then." She holds in the sobs. "And then I went home." The sobs break through, and she begins to cry, breathing heavily and shaking.

"Shh…shh…," I tell her, as I sit next to her and hold her. Part of me wants to cry with her, but I also recognize I need to do the important thing: I'm here for her.

"Why does she hate me?" she manages to ask.

I shake my head. "She doesn't hate you."

"Yes, she does."

"Shh…shh…."

Melanie never shows up. Or, perhaps, she arrived, saw Jess' car, and decided not to come in. She calls about an hour after she was supposed to show up, explaining how busy she was with work. I tell her it's fine.

I spend the rest of the day with Jess.

My party is held at Sarah's, who hasn't gone overboard on anything except the food, which I get excited about. She's hired a chef to prepare eight courses consisting of takes on my favorite foods. "Oh, sis, you're the best."

"I really am," she says.

It's a little after 7:00 pm when I arrive, a little over two hours until I'm officially fifty. I feel good about it. Jess and I spoke about a great many things for a few hours, watched my favorite movie, *Casablanca*, which

71

Jess had not seen in ages, and got takeout from McDonald's, because why not? When she left, it was like seeing Jess from months ago. I wondered if she was capable to staying herself anymore. Maybe Jess from months ago is gone, replaced by a new Jess who struggles with being the old her and the new her. Maybe. As she drove away, she waved, and I waved back. An hour later, she texted: "Today was great. Let's do it again soon. Love u"

Haley comes over wearing her old prom dress, which seems loose on her.

"I knew I should've gotten a new dress."

"Jesus, Haley. How much weight have you lost?" her mother says.

"A few pounds."

"I thought freshman put *on* weight," I add.

"People deal with stress differently. My roommate runs. A lot. I don't eat."

"Haley."

"Mom. I'm fine. I eat. I'm not *starving* myself. I just don't have snacks around when I'm studying. Which is most of the time."

Maddie comes over wearing a simple black dress and owning it. Haley gives her a once over and then looks at herself, clearly hating the decision she made to dress up for this party. "Hey, gang. What's going on over here?"

"We were just discussing your little sister's weight."

"Mom."

"What?" Maddie asks and turns to her sister. "What's wrong? She looks healthy to me. Maybe a little skinny."

"Bye."

Haley walks away. We call for her to come back, but she disappears into the house, probably to change.

"Oh," I say. "She's so cute."

"She *is*," Maddie agrees. "So, Aunt Greta. What's on your wish list for tonight?"

"What do you mean?"

"Presents. Looking forward to any."

"I mean, I wouldn't say no to new sneakers." I lift my foot, sporting old All Stars beneath my dress.

"Damn. How *old* are those?"

"A few years."

She nods and takes out her phone. "I'm getting you a new pair."

"Maddie...."

"What's your size?"

"Seven."

"Seven," she repeats, actually ordering them.

"Are you really ordering me shoes?"

"Of course." She lifts the phone up. "Stupid wi-fi."

"Just forget it."

"No. You need new shoes."

"I really don't."

"Ooh. Finally." She sits down with us and continues on her phone. I shake my head and turn to Sarah.

"Your daughter is something else."

"Tell me about it."

Loud laughter has all three of us turn to the entrance to the backyard. Melanie's just arrived with Stephen and Katie, who is holding a wrapped box with a fancy bow wrapped around it. She sees us and waves.

When they meet up with us, Katie holds out the present to me. "Here you go, Aunt Greta." I reach for it, but then Melanie intervenes.

"No – Katie. Presents go over there." She points at the table holding all the presents, and there are quite a few, I must admit. "Aunt Greta will open it later."

"It's all right. I'll just take it now."

"Oh. Okay." She sounds…embarrassed almost.

I focus my attention on Katie and hold out my hands. Her smile returns, and I receive the gift from her. "Thank you, honey."

"It's from all of us."

"Well, isn't that nice." I look up at them and say, "Thanks, guys."

"You got it," Stephen.

Melanie smiles. It seems genuine.

I open it and find a very lovely purse. "Oh. Oh my." I take it out of the box, and Maddie actually gasps.

"Oh, my God, that's beautiful," she says.

"Oh, guys. Thank you *so* much."

"Why don't *I* get gifts like that?" Maddie asks Melanie.

"Talk to me when you've turned fifty," she answers.

"I'm turning thirty in a few. Maybe I can get a fancy coin purse?"

"Ha-ha."

"Seriously, guys. Thank you." I hug it. "Especially you," I say to Katie.

Katie smiles wide. I open my arms, asking for a hug. She gives me a big one.

The rest of the evening goes smoothly. Sarah gets everyone to countdown until my actual birth time. It's cheesy and sweet, and everyone is game. Then, the cake is brought out by Maddie and Haley, who of course *did* change her dress. As everyone sings "Happy Birthday," I take a look around at family and friends and realize something. I don't actually have a best friend or my own family. That went away with Phillip. I suddenly miss him, so when it comes time to blow out the candles, I make this wish: I want to see him again.

<u>Jess</u>

For some reason, Sam and Kris take me lingerie shopping. I finally ask why as we walk into Victoria's Secret.

"We're here to find you something sexy," Sam says.

"Why?" I ask, dumbfounded.

"Because I've seen your underwear. There's no lingerie."

"I have lingerie."

"Yeah, but it's all ancient. You need a new bra and a new pair of panties."

I turn to Kris. "Is she serious?"

"We're here, aren't we?" She holds up a thong. "How's this?"

76

"No."

"Jess doesn't do thongs."

"Why? 'Cause of the weggie?"

"Um, yeah."

"Huh. To each her own, I guess."

"Well, pardon me if I don't want floss up my ass crack."

"Very classy, by the way," Sam tells me.

"Sorry. I forget I'm in the land of people."

"What's wrong with saying ass crack?"

"Kris."

"What?"

I see an employee walking our way, an awkward smile on her face. "Hello. Anything I can help you with today?"

"No, thanks," Sam says. "We're just taking a look."

"My best friends want to buy me some sexy underwear for some reason."

"Oh. Well. I can recommend Sexy Illusions, -."

"You know what?" Kris interjects and reads her nametag. "Thank you, Taylor. But we got this."

"Okay. No problem. Just holler if you need anything." She walks away, and I note just how fit she is. I suddenly feel fat.

"Can we go, please?"

"No. You need this."

"Why?"

"Because buying and wearing sexy lingerie makes a woman feel, well, sexy. And feeling sexy makes you feel wanted. And feeling wanted makes you feel…good."

I smirk. "Well said."

"I tried. Whatever. The point is, it's a gift from me."

"Wait – what? Why don't *I* get a gift?" Kris says.

"Why should I buy *you* lingerie?"

"Um. So, I can feel sexy and wanted, too."

Sam rolls her eyes and turns to me. "Jess. Trust me." She gestures to the store. "All of this…it isn't for significant others. It's more for you than anybody else."

I gently hug myself, hating how much I've put on since Thomas's death. Sam's tried to get me to go on walks with her, but now I suddenly want to hit the gym more to get back into shape. I walk further into the store, past all the lingerie and into the workout attire. "Jess?"

I see a cute outfit and point to it. "There."

"What?"

"Buy me *that*."

"Come on, Jess. I'd said I'd buy you -."

"I want *that*. Or, we can leave."

Minutes later, we leave the store, and I'm holding a bag with a new outfit for the gym. Yeah, this is getting better. Healthy life. Healthy body. I just need a healthy mind, and I'm working on that.

I wake up the morning, wash-up, eat, and then I head to the gym. I don't have a job anymore. The hospital was told about what happened and suggested I take an "indefinite sabbatical," which is the nicest way they could've fired me. I still haven't been by to collect my things, but I assume that everything's packed and in storage. And, well, isn't that nice of them. Of course, I can hardly hate, or disagree with, their decision. I doubt it was easy, but the least they could've done is simply fire me. Technically, I can return at any time, but I probably wouldn't have an office or even a locker to return to, so…yeah.

I find I have a lot of time on my hands. I'm grateful Thomas and I were responsible and paid off the house and both cars. I still have Thomas's

Chevy. It hasn't been turned on in months – it's probably done for and pretty gross inside. One day, I'll get up the guts to do something about it, but his stuff is still all around the house, and I have yet to do anything about all of that either. Ugh. I need to get out of the house.

So, I do. I go the gym. I work out. Hard. No trainer. No friends. Just me, music, and sweat. When I go the first time, I feel incredibly self-conscious, especially wearing the ridiculous outfit I made Sam buy me. I look cute enough in it, but I'm definitely not fit. Months without much cardio, or anything really, didn't do me any favors. Terrible eating habits, too. But that can change. After a few weeks, I feel great.

I visit Aunt Greta at her place for her birthday, only to be sort of ambushed in to talking to Mel, who ultimately doesn't show up. I get a good cry out of it, though, and I spend some quality time with Greta. I realize just how full my life was before. There was work, Thomas, and Sam and Kris. Everybody else was secondary. Now, I have the time for someone like Aunt Greta, and I admit to myself that hanging out with another widow makes me feel comforted. No one else will ever come close to really getting it. She does, though.

About a week later, I get call from Katie. She wants to video chat. I answer straight away. She's in her bedroom, talking quietly. I guess she's not supposed to be calling me, but I don't mention anything.

"Hi, Aunt Jess."

"Hey, Good Looking."

"You look happy."

"I'm always happy when I'm talking to you."

"I miss you."

"I know."

"Mom doesn't want me talking to you."

"Yeah. About that, Katie. I'm so sorry I ruined your birthday."

"Are you okay?" My heart nearly breaks with that question.

"Yeah. Yeah, I'm fine."

"I liked your present." She shows off the shirt I gave her that says,

"~~GIRL~~ SCIENTIST."

"That's awesome," I say through an involuntary smile so wide it almost hurts. "That's my girl."

"I think I want to do research, but also maybe a doctor like you."

"Well, you can start in medical school and then -."

I hear a door open on her side, which startles her. She looks to her left.

"Who are you talking to?" Mel asks. She takes the tablet from Katie.

"Oh my God. Katie, I *told* you…"

"I know," Katie says quietly.

"Look at me."

"Hey," I say, not liking her tone.

Mel brings the tablet up and looks at me.

"She just wanted to talk."

"Excuse me, but who are *you* to say anything?"

"I'm her aunt, that's what."

She looks down at Katie. "Sweetie, it's fine, but you've lost your iPad privileges for today." She leaves Katie's room and begins to walk down a hall into her bedroom. On the way, she starts on me. "Don't you ever get involved when I'm talking to Katie about something she shouldn't be doing."

"Well, she's my niece, so…."

Mel laughs. "Oh, yeah. You're such a great aunt. Tell me, are you drunk right *now*?"

"Actually, I've been sober since her birthday."

"Well, good for you, but until I say so, stay away from Katie."

"That's fine."

"And you stay away from the house, too. I *will* call the police."

"Fuck you," I say, so help me, wanting to suddenly cry.

"Nice. Such a great role model, aren't you?"

"Yeah. Better than someone who's mean to their own child."

"At least I have one."

My mouth opens, agape.

Mel seems to snap out of it, her angry gone in an instant. She looks like she wants to say something. Instead, she hangs up.

I sit at my kitchen table, phone still in my hand, a bit shaken at what she said. It's a low blow, for sure, but it seems right. In a weird way, I feel a little better. Given what I told her all those years ago, it feels like we're finally even in a way. I set the phone down carefully, aware now at just how quiet my house is.

"Damn," Maddie says taking another fork full of lasagna. "I forgot how good of a cook you are."

I invite Maddie and Haley to dinner, which I cook, because I want to spend more time with them. Mel may want me out of the picture, but she's not the only family I have.

"Thank you," I say.

"The place looks good," Haley says.

"I've been trying."

"Can we have wine?"

"Jess isn't drinking anymore, dumb-dumb," Maddie tells her.

"And, more importantly, you're not even twenty yet."

"For the record, I do drink."

"Well, aren't you an inspiration to us all," Maddie says. Haley gives a her a face. It's nice to see that we can bust each other's chops and still have fun. Not everything has to turn into a fight.

Maddie gives me a little rub on the leg and asks, "So. Really, Jessie. How you doing?"

"Good. I think. It's still weird being here."

"You thinking of selling?"

"Not really."

"I can stay here instead of Mom's," Haley offers. "In case you want company."

"You know what? I'll take you up on that offer."

"Sweet."

"You do realize you now have to babysit this kid," Maddie says.

"I'm not a kid."

"In this family, you're practically Katie."

"I am not."

I smile at the playfulness between these two. It warms my heart. Sure, it'd be nice to still be close to Mel, but it's also nice to know that some sisters stay close. I hope that never changes for them.

"What are you smiling about, weirdo?" Maddie asks.

I shrug. "Why not?"

"Yeah, get off her ass."

Maddie throws I small piece of bread at Haley, who throws her hands up, terribly defending herself. I shake my head.

"So, I, uh, went to see Mel today," Maddie says, the rest of the bread being chewed in her mouth.

"Yeah?"

She nods. "Katie says hi."

"Well. Tell her I said hi the next time you see her."

She nods again.

Haley says, "God, it sucks that Mel is doing this."

"Well...," Maddie says, drawing out the word into nothingness.

"What do you mean?"

"I mean, it's not like Mel is completely out of line here." I shift in my seat, and Maddie seems to note this, immediately adding, "But, at the same time, doing it in a bad way."

"I don't get it."

"What I'm saying is, I get why Melanie is mad right now. But she's taking it too far. If Katie wants to see and talk to her aunt, she should be allowed to."

"Mel's a bitch."

Maddie shakes her head, and I say, "Hey!"

Haley seems to freeze at my tone more than the word.

"Don't you ever call her that. Understand me?"

She nods, her eyes avoiding me.

For a minute or so, Maddie eats for the three of us, no one saying anything. I've lost my appetite. Haley doesn't move much.

"This is fun," Maddie eventually says. "Just the way a family meal should be."

This loosens things up a bit. Without words, seemingly all is forgiven. And, that's how it should be. Right?

<u>Maddie</u>

I can say without any doubt that I love both of my older sisters. I've always admired them. They're smart and charming and cool as shit. But, lately, their dislike for one another has begun to annoy me.

Here's it simply put: Jess showed up drunk at Katie's birthday. Mel, rightfully, got upset, and things happened. Now, she won't allow her daughter to speak with her aunt. It drives me nuts thinking about this nonsense. If Jess and Mel are done with one another, that's fine, but they aren't the only ones in this family. I won't be in the middle of this anymore. I say as much to Jess before I leave a really nice dinner she prepared for me and Haley. She seems to want things to get back to normal. We'll see. I'm happy she's trying to put her life back together, as best she can. It must be so hard. I can't even imagine.

I feel stupid that turning thirty is a constant in the back of my mind. Even when I'm relieving stress in the shower, it's there. I just can't help it.

Work seems to help a little, though. Being able to read manuscripts, doing my best to find errors and make notes page after page after page, is a great way to take one's mind off things. I totally recommend editing a 400-page novel. That said, the best use of my time is either hanging out with friends or family.

Angie's been my friend since high school. We actually managed to keep in touch all four years of college, and when I moved back, we moved in together. Things didn't go south. We had fun and spent most of our twenties side by side. Eventually, though, my work began to overtake most of my free time. Soon, Angie and I got our own places. Still, we saw each other at least twice a week. Now, ever since what happened to Thomas and Jess, I've begun to change my priorities a little. I still work my ass off – just less often.

For instance, a few weeks before my dreaded birthday, I pull an all-nighter and then go see Angie at the bookstore.

She tells me she's hired someone to help with customer service.

"An employee, huh?"

"Yeah, I know. I'm such an adult now."

"Are you going to be a cool, laidback boss, or are you going to be a hard ass?"

"I'll be whatever's needed. So far, Hebah's doing a solid job. If anything, she gave a hell of an interview."

"I'm assuming a lot of people do. How else do you explain how some people have jobs when they clearly can't do it or don't want to be there?"

"I hear that, G," she tells me, wandering away to her office in the back. I assume she'll return, as she didn't add anything else to suggest otherwise. After a minute or so, I turn to walk to the back of the store to see what's going on when a girl sporting a backpack with patches and buttons all over it walks in. She removes a pair of wireless Bose headphones from her ears and gives me a smile before walking past me to the back area. *That's Hebah*, I say to myself. She looks around Haley's age, maybe slightly older. Another minute passes and a new song begins. Eventually, Angie does return and, as if her absence never happened, simply introduces Hebah to me. We shake hands, and I realize I need to start doing something with my life.

"Am I your only friend?" Angie asks, both feigning concern and being playful, once we're both behind the counter eating lunch.

"Yep. You're just too awesome. I don't need anybody else."

"Finally, you admit it. But, seriously, as much as I love seeing you, why aren't you working or hanging out with someone else?"

"'Cause I want to be here."

"Okay. Um. Don't take this the wrong way, but I think – just maybe – you need a life."

"What do you mean?"

"You know. Maybe get a hobby."

"I don't have time for a hobby."

"Says the girl eating pot stickers at her friend's bookstore in the middle of the week."

"I'm living the dream."

"I know you are, honey, but come on. This isn't a life. Don't you want to be out there doing stuff? I know I do. If I had what you have…."

"What do I have?"

"How much do you owe in loans?"

I try to say that's nothing, but she keeps going.

"How much does your job pay? How much do you have in the bank?"

"Alright, I get that *financially* I'm -."

"How often do you see your family? How many of them actually *want* to be around you for extended periods of time?"

"Right," I say, quietly.

"And so on and so on."

"Okay. So. A few points. I'll give you those."

She smiles, a bit satisfied with herself.

"So, what should I do? What would *you* do if you were in my shoes right now?"

"One sec." She takes care of a customer with such kindness and efficient-ness. I'm impressed. Once the woman is out of earshot, she turns back to me. "I'd get out of here. Just for a few weeks or so."

"Travel."

"Yeah. I've always wanted to go to New York or San Francisco. I know you have your list of places. Like England, maybe."

"Going to Jane Austen's house would be cool. Or 221B Baker Street."

"See. You're halfway there."

"But I can't just leave my life for a few weeks."

"Why not?"

"Well, I mean, I got my job. I got…." *Huh*, I think. *Touché*. I look at her. She's smirking. "Oh, you're so satisfied."

"I am."

I sigh. "You're a good friend, you know that?"

"I am. And I do."

I begin making arrangements that night.

The plan is to leave for England the day after my birthday. I tell everyone about my plans, and they're all happy for me. I mean, Mel *seems* happy for me. But it's always hard to tell whether she's happy or proud or if she's judging someone for whatever reason. Being that I'm almost thirty and clearly an adult who refuses to take shit from her older sister, I call her out on it during lunch at her place when I tell her about my plans.

"Mm-hmm," she says, after I tell her about the trip. No follow-up question or anything. She doesn't even look at me, focusing instead on her salad.

"Why do you do that?" I blurt out.

She looks up at me, clearly taken aback by my tone. "Why do I do what?"

"I've told everyone about my travel plans, and I chose you last. You want to know why that is?"

She nods and says, "I'm sure you're going to tell me."

"Because you judge people. I can see it in your eyes right now."

She smiles, sits back, and shakes her head, looking away.

"You have something to say about this. It's not enough that doing this will make me feel good. There's some nonsense reason about why I shouldn't be doing this."

"Well," she says, looking back at me. "There's your job."

"Told them. They're glad I'm finally taking a vacation. They were worried I was going to burn myself out. Next?"

She shakes her head again.

"What?!"

"Would you lower your voice?"

"What is your problem? All my life you've been on my ass. Why is that?"

"Well, with Mom and Dad divorcing and Jess off doing whatever the hell she wanted, someone had to watch you."

"No. Someone didn't. I could – and can – take care of myself."

"Jesus. What is this? Did everyone get together and decide this is the year to just gang up on Melanie? What the *hell* did I do to *you*?"

"You make me feel bad! That's what you do, Mel! Always. Nothing I do is worth less than a judgmental look or comment. It's hurts."

"Well, I hate to break it to you, but that's not what I'm doing. I think you project your own insecurities onto what I say or do, and that's *your* problem. That's something *you* have to deal with."

"You're full of it."

She nods now, wiping her mouth and hands. She's clearly done here.

"Okay," she says, steady. "Thank you for coming. You can let yourself

out." She gets up and leaves. I want so desperately to follow her and ask

why she's not as warm as she used to be. I mean, she's always been

herself, but for the past few years, she seems to have taken her anger

towards Jess out on the rest of us, whether she knows it or not. At least,

that's the way *I* see it. Instead, though, I wipe my hands, gather my stuff,

and leave, making sure to lock the door with the key she gave me the day

she moved into this place, my anger dissipating and my guilt rising.

"I can't believe you're actually going to Europe," Haley tells me. "I'm

so jealous." We're in my bedroom, and I'm packing for the trip. She's on

my bed, one of my throw pillows in her lap.

"You're more than welcome to join me."

"I really want to, but Mom's making me get a part time job."

"You're nineteen, right?"

"She still tells me what to do. And I still do it. Most of it, anyway."

"If it helps, I can see if Angie can give you something for a few hours a

week."

"Oh, that'd be awesome. Thanks."

"No problemo." I hold out a floral dress, matched with a jean jacket. "How's this?"

She gives the "okay" hand signal.

"Yeah?" I give it one last look and put it with the rest I'm taking, which actually isn't much. "So. Summer's about halfway over."

"God, I know. I feel like I'm just wasting time."

"That sounds like being young to me."

"What did *you* do when you came home from college?"

"During the summer?" She nods. "I usually interned somewhere. That's how I got my job at Anton & Brock."

"I feel like a slacker."

"Wrong generation."

She plops down on my bed, a whiny face replacing her normal one. I sit down beside her. "You okay?"

"No. And it's your fault."

"*My* fault?"

She sits up. "Why did you have to tell me about Dani?"

"Dani?"

She doesn't say anything, but her face says it all.

"You mean that first night you were back?"

She lies down again and covers her face with the pillow.

"That's still bothering you?"

"Well, I'm clearly not over her," she says, muffled.

"Really? Even after she dumped you?"

"A person can't just change how they feel."

"Fair enough." I push some of my stuff that's cluttering my bed aside and lay beside her. "Have you tried texting or calling? Or going to see her?"

She removes the pillow. "No. No. Yes."

"Really? When was this?"

"A few weeks ago. Before Aunt Greta's birthday. I went to her place. She wasn't home. No one was."

I rub her arm. "You okay?"

She nods. "I think so. It's just hard to not think about her. I mean, I've done so well with that over the past year. But then you brought her up."

"I thought maybe it'd be good to know how she's doing."

"Did she look good?"

"Oh. Yeah. I'd say so."

"Really?"

"Yeah."

"That's cool. Good for her."

"Yeah. I ran into her at Whole Foods. It was a quick thing, you know. I haven't seen her since."

"Right." She considers something and then says, "I wonder if she's going to do it. Make that movie."

"Maybe."

"I hope so. It's what she wanted."

"What do *you* want?"

"I don't know."

"That also sounds like being young to me."

"Do *you* know? What *you* want?"

She gets me there, even if she doesn't mean to. I consider this. Before Angie got me to pursue this out-of-the-country vacation, I didn't know. Even now – even with a fairly detailed plan – I'm still not sure. What will happen when I return? Go back to how things were?

"Maybe I'll meet a guy over there, and I'll fall head over heels for him."

"Really?" she says, totally skeptical.

"No. Unfortunately, that's not how things really work. But we'll see." I roll over onto my back. We lie there for a moment, in completely comfortable silence, staring at the ceiling.

"It would be cool if you married a prince, though."

"Yeah," I say, without much enthusiasm. To each her own, but that's not the story I want for my life.

Mom throws my birthday party at her house, and she's nailed it again. This time, it's inside, and it's very literary, right up to the kind of cake she had made. It's of that classic Shakespeare portrait everyone uses. It's also buttercream, which is just heaven.

Mel shows up, and after awkward pleasantries, she hands me a gift, and we enjoy the evening together with everyone. It's nice, but I find myself – periodically, throughout the night – checking to see if Jess is on her way. I know she won't be. Not if Mel is here. I'm hurt, but I also know how things are now. Tomorrow, I'll see her, and that'll be good.

Haley stops dinner midway and makes a toast.

"To Maddie. You've always been a bit of a role model to me, even if I find your job super boring." There are some chuckles, and I think to myself: *Gee, thanks, Haley.* "But you're opinionated without being rude. You're strong without making others feel weak. And you're beautiful without being stuck up. Everyone in the family is important to one another. And I see your friends here tonight. Angie's cool. Haven't seen

Marie in ages. I guess I just want to say, we all belong to one another. As older sisters, you and Mel did a good job. I love you both. But, since today's Maddie's day, I just wanted to spotlight you a bit. So. Finally. From your little sis, here's to you, Mad." She lifts her glass, and everyone follows. There are a few "awws" and some clapping. Haley looks like she believes what she's just done is stupid. Thankfully, she's sitting next to me, so I take her hand in mind. She turns to me.

"That was great, Hales."

"That was rambling."

"No, it wasn't."

"It kind of was," Mel says.

"Thank you, Mel," I tell her. "Thank you for that."

"Oh, I'm kidding, obviously."

"Don't listen to her. I like when you talk in public. You should do it more often."

"Yeah. That'd be the day."

Later that night, Angie and Marie take me for drinks at an old spot we haven't been to since college. Thankfully, it's still summer, so there are only a handful of young people here. When the shots arrive, Marie hands them out and says, "All right. We're not kids anymore. Officially."

"Officially?" I asked.

"Shh. One shot and that'll be it. I don't feel like puking on the sidewalk."

"Oh, God," Angie says, putting her forehead on my arm. "I totally remember that."

"A toast. To our birthday girl. We did it. We're all thirty."

"Cheers!"

The shot glasses clink and seconds later, the clear liquid is burning our throats.

"Whew!" Angie says.

"Ugh!" Marie follows.

"Yuck," I say.

"Yeah. Yuck. What was I thinking?"

"Either way, thanks."

"No problem."

"It's good to see you."

"No, shit," Angie says. "Where've you been? I'm not on Facebook anymore. I can't follow your exploits."

"Well, I'm on Instagram."

"Really?" Angie takes out her phone to search her.

"Yeah. It's been a crazy few years, but I think I got enough to finish my book."

"Good for you," I say, really meaning it.

"And, yes. I met someone."

"Is he hot?" Angie asks.

"Look at my personal Instagram and see for yourself."

After a few moments, Angie's eyes narrow. "Damn, girl."

"Thank you. And, yes, he's fantastic."

I take a look and see a fit Marie at a beach wearing a barely-there bikini, arms wrapped around an insanely attractive guy. It's not surprising. Marie has always been a beacon for attention, male or female. "What's his name?" I ask.

"Rico."

"Rico," I repeat. "So, he knows what he's doing, huh?"

"Oh, definitely," she says, a mischievous smile on her face. I'm almost jealous. Almost.

According to Dani's Instagram, she's scouting locations for her ultra-low budget horror movie, the title of which is apparently "under wraps." I roll my eyes and make plans to visit the set whenever production starts. Unless I'm back at school by that point. In which case I'll probably just end up stalking her account. God. She is looking *good* – especially given that it's summer, so yeah, there's a bit of skin showing here and there.

To get her out of my mind, I go by Angie's store to see if she needs any help – that maybe I can just help stock stuff for free if Hebah's busy. She doesn't want the liability, apparently, but she does let me hang around. After about an hour, though, boredom begins to rear its ugly head, and I'm off to the movies to see *Dark Phoenix*. I debate buying popcorn and soda and end up getting nothing. The movie isn't as bad as everyone's saying. Once it's over, though, I'm hungry, so I drive to Melanie's for a quick bite, realizing halfway there that she's at work.

I end up at Mom's. She's babysitting Katie.

"Yo, what up, Kate?" I say when she answers the door.

"Wassup, Hale?"

We do our own personal handshake, complete with a little booty shake at the end. I enter.

"Where's my mom?"

"Bathroom." She closes and locks up. "What are you doing here?"

"Nothing. You know, you shouldn't be answering the door by yourself."

"I know…."

I decide to not take this further and tell her, "I'm bored. Wanna play a game?"

"Nah, I'm good."

"No problem. How about a movie?"

"Can we see *Dirty Dancing*?"

"I think that's rated R."

"So?"

"So, your mom will literally murder me if I show you an R-rated movie."

"Okay," she says, sounding disappointed. I sit on the couch beside her. "Well," she begins, perking herself back up. "How about you tell me a story?"

"A story?"

"Yeah. Can you tell me about Mom when she was younger?"

"Mel? You want to know about your mom?"

"Yeah."

"Okay. Okay." I get comfortable. "I remember this one time, Maddie threatened to beat up this girl who was picking on me."

"How old were you?"

"I was in fourth, so…nine? Ten? Somewhere around there."

"So, she was *twenty*?"

"Yep. I know. Insane. But the girl backed off. Then, it turns out she told her mom, and everyone found out. I thought your mom was gonna go ballistic on Maddie."

"What did she do?"

"She took her out and bought her a jacket."

"Huh?"

"She was actually proud of her. I mean, ultimately, she was sticking up for her little sister the way good big sisters do. She bought her the jacket and made her promise to never do anything like that again. Maddie's been pretty mellow ever since."

"So that's it?"

"Well. Maybe you had to be there."

"I was hoping for a story where my mom did something wild and crazy."

"Oh, you'd have to ask Jess for a story like that." Mom comes in and sits next to me. I shoulder-bump her. "Or your grandma."

"What are you bringing me into?" she asks.

"Do you know any stories about my mom being irresponsible?"

Mom gives me a look and then smiles at Katie. "I'm not sure. That was a long time ago."

"You have to remember *something*."

"Why are you so interested?"

Katie shrugs. "I don't know. My mom's so responsible. I was just wondering if she's always been like that."

I raise my eyebrows, asking my mom, "Well?"

She takes a deep breath and sighs. "Okay. There's this *one*. I'm pretty certain it's appropriate for what you're asking."

"What is it?" Katie asks.

"Well. Your mom was fifteen. She wanted to go to this concert. I forget who it was. Some rock band. Maybe Smashing Pumpkins."

"Nice," I find myself saying.

"She kept asking me to either buy her tickets or give her the money. From what I know, Jess wanted to get a part-time job to pay for them, but your mother didn't want to work."

"Really?" Katie asks.

"Oh, she *hated* working."

Already, my mind is being blown. How do I not know this side of my older sister?

"Jess was actually the more responsible of the two. In fact, that's how I found out what happened. Jess told me."

"I bet my mom was mad," Katie says, looking like she feels bad about that.

"Your mom never found out. When I confronted her, I told her that *I* figured it out. Jess never said anything either from what I gather."

"Wait – so what happened?"

"Well, your mom did a few things. One, she stole the money from me. Two, she lied about where she was the night she went to the concert. Three, Jess covered for her, because she wanted to stay. Didn't want to get into trouble."

"Wow," I say. "Jess was kind of lame."

"She was a sweetie." *Uh-huh*, I think. "Fourth. Your mother didn't come home until seven the next day."

"I bet you were angry."

"I was. But I didn't yell at her. She showed up, clearly guilty, and when our eyes met as she closed the front door, she knew she was in trouble. I grounded her for the rest of that year."

"Damn, Mom."

"She never went that far again. At the very least, she never *stole* from me again."

"What did Jess do?" I ask.

"She stayed home to keep Melanie company."

"Really?" Katie asks, looking proud of her aunt.

"She did," Mom says, wistfully. "She was already eighteen at that point. But, she loved her little sister."

I wake up one Saturday morning in late July, after Maddie's left on her European adventure, or whatever, and I find a stupid pimple on my back, near my shoulder. And it hurts. "Ow," I say, trying to pick at it. Where do things like that even come from? I shower before bed almost every night. At least my chest acne's gone away since high school.

I shower, get dressed, and head on over to Mel's.

She greets me with brunch, which cheers me up. Dani on the brain is not a good thing. Frankly, I feel more and more pathetic as the days pass. I think about talking to Mel about it but think better of it. Instead, I want to know more about her. I find it odd and fascinating that there's so much I don't actually know about my sister.

I tear a piece off a buttery croissant, and say, "Can I ask you something?"

"Sure."

"Wh – well, before I ask. Can you promise me you won't get mad?"

"No."

"No?"

"No. You can ask your question, but I might get mad."

"Okay. Um." I shift in my seat a bit. I expected as much. "That's…fair. Um." I swallow hard. "I was just wondering about how you were when you were *my* age."

"Is that the question?"

"Sorta."

"Okay. You want to know how I was like when I was twenty or so?"

"Yeah."

"Alright. I was…hesitant – a lot. It was hard for me to make any real decisions."

"Why?"

"I was…am…not very talented at much."

"That's not true."

"Well, not compared to Jess."

"Oh, this is about Jess."

"Of course, it is."

"You were…jealous?"

"I think so. I mean, I was undeclared for the first two years I went to UT. She went in pre-med. Who was *I* compared to my older sister who had already graduated by the time I was your age?"

"But things turned out well."

"Why? Because I got a business degree?"

"Because you have a family. Stephen's great. Katie's awesome. Plus, your job -."

"Ugh."

"Well, it pays well."

She nods – her way of saying, "Fair enough."

"I look up to you. You know. I don't like to say it out loud, because I'm afraid it won't happen, and then people will start to ask why it isn't happening. But. I'd like a family. I'd *love* to have a wife and a kid. That sounds great to me."

"Really?" she asks, *really* meaning it.

"Absolutely."

She nods, and I'm struck by the revelation of just how incredibly similar I am to Mel. Never would I have thought so, and I hate myself for thinking that. But then I consider how Mel is now. She's not the most emotionally open person in the world. Not lately anyway. That is apparently a change that occurred. Will that happen to me, too? I decide this is the time to ask about Jess, to get down to why things are the way they are in this family.

"Are you mad that Jess never apologized?"

"What?" she asks, a bit blindsided by my sudden question.

"Is that why you're angry at her? Did she do or say something and then never apologized?

She considers this. "She apologized," she then tells me.

"She did?"

"Yeah. A lot of times."

"And you didn't accept?"

"No."

"Why not?"

"Why should I?"

"Because she apologized?"

"That doesn't mean I need to automatically accept it."

"Isn't that how it works, though? She apologizes. You accept. We all move on. That's how it works, right?"

"No. That's not how it works."

"So, you're never going to forgive her for whatever she did or said?"

"I don't know."

"Well, I think you should."

"No offense, but you don't know what you're talking about."

"You could tell me."

"Can we drop this?"

"Why?"

"Because I don't," she begins, loudly. She stops herself, clears her throat, and continues at her previous register, "I don't want to talk about it. It's between me and her." I can tell that it's suddenly difficult for her to look at me.

"Okay," I tell her.

We eat in silence for a few minutes. I decide to do the right thing and apologize – sort of. "This is delicious, by the way." Close enough.

"Thanks," she says, looking at me again. "I like your hair. It's cute short."

This warms me. I touch my hair and smile to myself. Mel doesn't tell me things like that all that often. After that, we finish brunch, talk some more, and even crack a few jokes. She is capable of forgiveness. I wonder, then, *just what happened.* Seriously. At the same time, though, I make the decision to drop it.

Besides, it's time I paid someone a visit.

I walk up to Sasha, who's producing on a deserted street corner in a nondescript neighborhood, making sure the sound guy is picking everything up clearly, referencing the day before where that didn't happen. He says he's on it. When that's over, she looks around, noting Dani with two actors about a dozen feet away and then me. She smiles.

"Haley."

"Hey."

We give each other a quick hug.

"What's up? Whatcha doing here?"

"I'm here to see -." I point to Dani, who still hasn't seen me. She's focused, which I like.

"Ah. Gotcha."

"So, what's going on today?"

"Plot stuff. This is before everything goes to shit. We're still getting to know our characters."

"No blood-and-guts today?"

"This afternoon. Should be fun."

I nod. "Coolio."

"Hey!" I hear Dani call. I turn, and she's on her way to us, beaming. "What are you doing here?"

"I, uh – came to see you, actually."

"Yeah? Okay. Can you stick around? We got a few set-ups to take care of for this scene, then it's lunch."

"Sure. I can watch?"

"Yeah."

"I don't see why not," Sasha adds.

"Okay. I'll just be here."

"Cool." She's off to stand next to the camera. Things get as quiet as they can get, and then she says, "Action." I watch the scene play out in its entirety three times. Then, the camera is moved, and the scene happens again two more times. Then, one last time from a third position. It's interesting and not very exciting at the same time.

The scene goes like this:

Two characters, one female and one male, are walking home from an all-night party. It's an overcast day, but they're happy it's not raining. The girl can't wait for her car to get out of the shop, and the guy apologizes for not having a renewed license. Then, there's apparently a sound that'll be added later (Dani makes a "BOOM!" sound), and the two halt. They are confused and a little scared. They look all around and see nothing. With that, they decide to head to their destination by running instead of walking.

I wonder how it'll play in the finished movie, whenever that happens.

Dani takes me out to lunch, while Sasha stays behind to eat a snack and make sure the next location is ready to go. I tell Dani how impressed I am with Sasha's producing skills, and she agrees.

"She's a total badass. Of course, it doesn't hurt that she co-wrote the thing."

"Kind of wants to make sure the movie's as good as the script."

"Mm-hmm. Even better."

"Well, it looks good – from what I saw earlier anyway."

"We're trying. So, what's up with you? How was school? How was…being away?"

I'm sitting on a hard-plastic seat inside of Carl's Jr., trying to keep my thoughts and feelings together and doing a crap-job with that. On the one hand, I feel hurt just being here a mere three feet from her. On the other, I find I'm still quite a bit head over heels for Dani – smile, skin, smell, voice, and all. I want to hate her, but I don't and maybe can't. "It was…okay. I guess."

"You missed it here."

"Yeah. I think so."

"Well, you've got a good family that misses you, I'm sure. Hell, *I* missed you."

"Did you?"

"Of course. I mean, I know how I ended it. I'm not gonna pretend that didn't happen. It was stupid. And…I'm sorry."

"Wow," I say, a little to her and a little to myself. "I didn't expect an apology."

"Yeah. Didn't expect I'd be giving one. But it's true. So, yeah – I'm sorry."

I shrug. "It is what it is." What else am I supposed to say? That I gave serious thought to walking into traffic after she broke up with me? That I cried like a girly-girl every night for nearly three months? That my roommate at college bonded with me over heartbreaks? Does she want to know any of that? The Dani I knew was sensitive and sweet, but maybe that was never her. Maybe I just projected, because that's what people do. We build people up and then get upset when they're not the person we expected them to be. "But I'm good," I say.

She considers something for a brief moment and then says, "Wanna be in the movie?"

I'm surprised and don't bother to hide it. "Really?"

"Yeah. There's still a few parts we haven't cast, yet. I think you'd be really good as one of them."

"Okay," I find myself saying, not disagreeing with the decision. The summer might actually end on the right note. Maybe I can find some closure to this and go back to school ready to move on. Maybe.

Katie

My mom can be really nice sometimes. Like when we're out at the store, she always wants to buy me something. Usually, it's the kid who asks for stuff from the parent. In my life, it's the other way around. Now, I'm not saying she always gets me the thing she wants to get me, but she always lets me know her intentions. This one time, we were passing by the Disney Store, and she saw something through the window. We went in, and she asked me who my favorite Disney character was. I was going to say Violet from *The Incredibles*, but she added, "Favorite princess, I mean." That was a fair question, so I answered truthfully, which didn't take much effort. "Belle," I told her. Belle, specifically, at the *beginning* of the movie. I like her blue and white dress. I love how much she loves to read and her brown hair and brown eyes. She's really nice, too. Not that she changes by the end. I'm just not a big fan of her in the yellow gown.

Mom smiled when I said this and told me she'd be on the lookout for something that fit my description. A few days later, I came home, and on my bed was a t-shirt with Belle in the blue and white dress. I love that t-shirt. Not only because of Belle, though. I love it because my mom looked so happy when she saw it on me.

She's also nice when we're alone in the car, letting me listen to pretty much whatever I want, "within reason," she always reminds me. That means no swear words or dirty stuff. I have to wait until I'm a teenager before all of that. I get to watch a lot of TV and movies, but always after I've done any school work. My mom gets on me a lot, but at the same time, she gives me so much freedom. I may be only ten, but I know that's something to be thankful for.

One afternoon in late July, I go to my bedroom and open a package from aunt Maddie. She's sent me a big, pink hardcover book with a short note that says:

Katie,

I'm having an amazing time here. I'll be home soon with souvenirs and whatnot, but I thought I'd send you a little something before then. Love you!

- Maddie

I smile wide, tear off the book's cellophane wrapping, and open it. It's filled with pictures and writing – it's crazy and I love it. I wonder if Mom will be cool with me having this. I decide to maybe not tell her.

Thankfully, Aunt Haley's watching me, and she's the one who opened the door to receive it. She handed it to me and allowed me to go to my bedroom and close the door. I decide it's okay if she sees it.

"You think Mom will let me keep this?"

Haley flips through it. "Well, it's filled with a lot of inspiring stuff, even if it is for older girls. Still, you're a bit of an old soul, so I'd let you keep it. And clearly, Maddie thinks it's appropriate for you." She hands it back. "But maybe don't let your mom see it right away."

I nod. Secrets aren't necessarily a bad thing. At least, that's what Aunt Maddie says.

"So, how's Dani's movie?" I ask. Haley's been going to see her ex a lot lately, but she hasn't been all that open about talking about it. I figure maybe I can get something out of her since I'm apparently an "old soul."

"It's cool. Did I tell you I'm in it?"

"No way."

"Yep. I play this college student who comes home right before these creatures show up and start terrorizing the town. I kick a little butt – just sayin'."

"Cool."

"Yeah, it's pretty awesome."

"Can you take me to the set sometime?"

"I'll ask your mom."

I nod, trying to figure out a way to keep this going. I try for the straight-forward approach. "Are you back together with Dani?"

"What? No."

"Oh."

"Is that what you thought?"

I shrug. "I don't know. You seem to still like her, and you've been spending a lot of time with her."

"Yeah, but we're just friends."

"Okay, but…you seem a lot…happier since you started seeing her again."

"Really?"

"Yeah. You can't tell?"

"No."

"Well, you are. Mom can tell, too. In fact, she thinks you're seeing Dani again, even if it's not a good idea."

"She said that?"

"Yeah."

"Well, your mom's a smart lady. She's probably right. Which is *why* I'm not getting back together with Dani."

"But you'd like to."

She smiles. "Aren't you intuitive."

"What's that?"

"Another way to say you're a girl. You pick up on things."

"I guess I do that."

"Katie, the thing about having feelings like love is that they're instinctual. Like laughing. It just happens whether you want it to or not. Haven't you ever laughed at something you weren't supposed to?"

"Oh, yeah."

"There you go. I might still have strong feelings for Dani. I can't help that. What I *can* help is how I go about living my life with those feelings. We're just friends, and that's how it's going to stay."

"I just want you to be happy."

"Well, I am. Can't you tell?" She smirks.

I smile. We decide to have lunch and watch some episodes of *New Girl*.

CeCe comes over a little bit later, just before my mom and dad get home from work. Her real name is Cecelia, but everyone calls her CeCe. She's the coolest person my age, and for some reason, she likes to hang out with me. Haley makes us some homemade mini-pizzas while we listen to these bands with weird names like Bikini Kill and Sleater-Kinney.

"Your aunt is so cool," CeCe whispers to me, as Haley begins to take out the mini-pizzas from the oven.

"*All* my aunts are cool."

"You're *so* lucky."

"I know."

"What are you two whispering about?" Haley asks, a slight smirk on her face.

"Nothing," we both say in unison.

Before we eat, Dad arrives. He comes into the kitchen, says hi, compliments Haley on the food and asks for one of his own, and then leaves to "get out of this suit."

As we chow down, Haley begins to question CeCe about me.

"So. CeCe. How's Katie in school? She being a good girl?"

"Mom says good girls don't get things done," I tell her.

"I think she's talking about not following the rules established by the patriarchy, but fair enough."

"She's really nice," CeCe answers.

"So, she doesn't talk back to teachers or sneak around and do things she shouldn't be doing?"

"No."

"Good girl, Katie."

"We usually finish before everyone, so the teacher gives us time to do stuff together."

"Really? Like what?"

We tell her about this story we've been working on since Christmas about this warring family on an alien planet. Haley looks impressed and intrigued, so we continue. We tell her about Queen Kira and her two daughters who go to war when the mother dies. We explain how we're trying to make sure that both princesses are heroes who shouldn't be fighting one another. We also explain that we don't have an ending quite yet. She asks if she can read it once it's done. We tell her it's a plan.

Once Mom shows up, I ask her if CeCe can stay over. I'm anticipating her saying no, so I've already asked Haley if she can take her home. She's agreed, but then Mom actually says, "Yes."

"Really?" I ask.

"Well, don't be so shocked. CeCe, you're always welcomed."

"Thank you, Mrs. Prescott."

When Mom leaves, I tell CeCe, "If I'd known that, I would've had you over all summer." I love my mom, and she can be really nice, but she's also a bit strict and doesn't let me do things like have friends over for sleepovers. This is new to me. And I like it.

When Maddie returns, we all gather at Greta's. Apparently, she has an announcement. Jess isn't there, like always, but she sends a message through Haley. "She told me to tell you that she has a few things from medical school that you can have if you're still thinking about being a doctor." I am, so I pretty excitedly tell Haley to bring it all whenever she can and that I'll do my best to hide it. Like my lip gloss, which I now realize has been between my bed and box spring for months.

After dinner, we all end up in the living room. Mom and Dad talk and joke around with Aunt Maddie and grandma. That leaves Haley to look after me. "You know, you don't always have to chill with me," I tell her.

"I know. I want to."

"Why?"

"Why not?"

"Because I'm *ten*."

"I'm ten years older than you. But Maddie is ten years older than *me*. You don't think Maddie likes to hang out with me?"

"Not really."

This makes Haley laugh. She calls Maddie over and asks, "Mads, you like hanging out with me, right?"

"God, no. You're so annoying."

I laugh.

"Seriously."

"Seriously. I can't stand you."

I laugh harder.

"I'm trying to prove a point to Katie."

"What? That I secretly hate you?"

I continue to laugh.

"Maddie," Haley says in the same way I do when I start to get upset. I guess adults do that, too, sometimes.

"Okay. Katie, I love my sister, and I love spending time with her." She adds a wink at the end. I try to hold in more laughter.

"Did you just wink?" Haley asks.

"Um, no." Maddie winks at me again.

"I can see you."

"Uhh – okay." Another wink.

This time, we both burst out laughing. Haley wants to leave. I can tell. But before anything happens, Greta taps her glass with a spoon and gets everyone's attention.

"Wow," she says. "Okay. Everyone's looking at me. I suppose that means it's time to tell you all. Which means, now, it's real." She swallows and clears her throat. "I am selling this place and using the money from the sale to travel the world. For about a year."

None of us say anything. Not at first. Then, to no one's surprise, I'm sure, Maddie is the first to react, and she does it loudly. "Hell yeah!" she yells, lifting her glass. That seems to snap everyone else out of it. There's some clapping and a "Way to go!" from Haley. Grandma walks up to Greta, holds her face in her hands, and hugs her sister. It's sweet. Soon, most are offering congratulations of some sort.

Then, Mom speaks up. "But you can't just sell the house and leave. You have work."

"Mel," Maddie says in that tone where you want someone to stop talking.

"No, it's okay. Melanie. Don't worry about me. This isn't something I've just decided. I've considered this for weeks. And, it's not going to happen overnight. It'll be a few months before anything major occurs. And, when I return, we'll see what happens with teaching."

"Well, what are you going to do after?" Mom asks.

"I don't know. Maybe get an apartment."

"Maybe move in with me," grandma says.

"Maybe."

Mom shakes her head. She looks like she can't believe what's going on. Greta walks up to her and puts a hand on her cheek. Mom looks…vulnerable. "It's okay, sweetie. I'm okay."

Maddie claps her on the back and says, "Yeah, you are." Like always, she lightens the mood. She gives her a bear hug, nearly spilling her drink. Dad takes Mom away from everyone. Haley gets down to my level.

"Pretty cool, huh?"

I'm trying to keep an eye on my parents, who are now in the kitchen.

"Katie?"

"Why is my mom upset?"

Haley sighs. "Your mom's very…emotional about things. And, there's nothing wrong with that, by the way."

I see Dad with his hands on her shoulders. They're whispering. She seems like she's calming down a bit, nodding her head at whatever he's saying. I want to go over and hug her. But I don't.

"Katie, you okay?"

I turn to Haley, who looks very concerned.

I nod.

"Okay," she says. "Come on. Let's get some chips. I think they have bar-b-que."

She takes my hand and leads me away to a corner of the room where I can't see my parents anymore. This makes me feel better for some reason. I decide to put my attention towards the chips, which are really good.

"I wish Aunt Jess were here," I find myself saying.

Haley nods. "Me, too. But, hey, how about tomorrow we take a field trip to see her?"

I brighten up and say, "Yeah."

"She's *what*?"

"Selling and travelling."

"That's pretty baller."

Haley's just told Aunt Jess about the big news from the night before. We're at her place, and a part of me is worried that mom will get angry at me. The last I heard, I'm not supposed to see or talk to Aunt Jess. Yet, another part of me *wants* to do this simply *because* I shouldn't. What's that all about?

"I think it's pretty cool," I say, mimicking the words Haley used last night.

"Well, if you say it, it must be true," Jess says, adding a smile afterwards. She doesn't always smile, but when she does, I always notice how big it is. It's almost like she saves it for so long and when it finally comes out, it's like a volcano.

Later, when I'm supposed to be watching *Gravity Falls*, I overhear a little bit of a conversation between the two. As far as I can make out, Haley's starting to have feelings for Dani again and wants advice for how to deal with it. Aunt Jess tells her to do whatever feels right but that she doesn't agree with her going back to someone who hurt her. I silently agree and then laugh at Mabel who's just declared that she's "legalizing everything!"

It's a weird thing to overhear adults who don't realize I'm listening. At school, I hear teachers who seem to have the same problems everyone has. Every now and then, they even swear at each other. At home, Mom and Dad whisper so I can't hear, but sometimes I do. I don't know why they can't all just be upfront about everything. Why keep it all away from me? What's the point? Sooner or later, I'll find out on my own or they'll simply tell me.

It's because I'm a kid. It's because they're adults.

Yeah. Being ten years old in a family of adults sucks sometimes.

Part Three: Same as It Ever Was

<u>Katie</u>

I'm alone with Haley on the way home from Aunt Jess', so I take my opportunity to ask about what they were talking about. I launch right into it and say, "I heard you and Jess."

"Oh?" she says, clearly caught.

"Yep. I heard you say you're starting to like Dani again, even though you told me you weren't going to."

"And like I said before, you can't control these things. Besides, I talked with Jess. She was right. Getting back together with her would be a *huge* mistake. Plus, I'm headed back to school soon."

"Whatever helps you sleep at night."

She gives me a funny look but doesn't say anything.

After moving on from a stoplight, she readjusts her glasses and says, "You ever think about just how similar Jess and your mom are?"

"Oh, yeah. All the time. Except Mom's way more strict then Aunt Jess."

"Well, that's because she's your mom."

"I guess."

"It's just interesting to me. The way they talk is sometimes uncannily similar. Like sometimes, your mom sounds so different than her but other times exactly the same."

"Yeah. And they wear their hair similar, too."

"Oh my God, they totally do."

We laugh.

"And their laugh is the same, too. Even though Jess' voice is a little deeper, it's basically the same laugh."

"It is, isn't it?"

"And their smile."

"Yeah."

"I was thinking earlier how Aunt Jess' smile is so big, but Mom's smile can be big, too."

"Yeah. It's true."

We drive in silence the rest of the way, but it's more comforting than awkward. Haley pushes up her glasses again, which keep sliding down her nose as we drive on. It happens every now and then when she wears them. Apparently, she loves wearing her glasses, but for some reason, she feels self-conscious when she wears them. She told me that basically means she feels like everyone's looking at her. That's why she wears contacts most of the time.

"You should wear your glasses more," I tell her. "You look cool in them."

She looks embarrassed, but she tells me, "Thanks." I can also tell she took the compliment, though. A few seconds later, she adds, "You're the first person to tell me I look cool in my glasses."

"I am?"

"Yeah."

We sing along to whatever comes on Haley's playlist the rest of the way home.

Maddie comes over and brings me a few souvenirs from her time in England. She also shows photos and video while telling us stories. Nothing too dramatic happened during her trip, other than long waits at baggage claim and checking in at her hotel, but she doesn't seem all that disappointed. In fact, she appears more lively than ever. I noticed this the night Greta made her announcement. Maddie's always been funny and playful, but she always seemed a bit exhausted. Mom would tell me it was because of all the reading and responsibility she had concerning her job.

As it turns out, even though she's back home, she hasn't returned to work quite yet.

"Are you *allowed* to take such a long vacation?" Haley asks her. It's just the three of us. Mom and Dad are still at work.

"Not really. But, apparently, and I didn't pay attention to this when I took the vacation, I have a shit-load – sorry Katie – of sick days. They piled up, and I must have said I was using all of them. I've been away for over two weeks. I still have about two weeks more."

"Nice."

"Right?"

I hold up a snow globe with Buckingham Palace inside and shake it.

"I'm sure I came across like an American tourist idiot buying that, but it was too pretty to not buy."

"I love it," I say.

"Oh," she says, remembering something. She reaches into her purse and pulls out an envelope. It's from Aunt Jess. "Here you go."

I hold it carefully in my hands.

"I'm so over their whole feud-thing," Maddie says to no one in particular.

"Amen," says Haley.

Later, I read the letter, reading it aloud, the way Jess speaks, so I can pretend she's here. "Hey, kid," I read. "Make sure you hide this from your mom. One day, maybe, we'll actually be able to talk again. I hate we have to do this, but I also have to remind myself that this is my fault. I did what I did, and I should've known better. For that, I am forever sorry. I miss you, Katie. It's one thing to look at photos and video on my phone of the two of us, but it's another to be with you, whether it's playing poker – never tell your mom about that! – or just sitting around watching old shows from the '90s. Just remember that I'm here for you. Always. I'm even here for your mom. Let her know that from time to time. You don't have to say that I said that. In fact, don't tell her, because that might give it away. Just, if she's ever feeling down, let her know she can call or text, or even come over and see me. She's my sister, and I love her. Regardless of how she feels. Anyway, until then, I love you, and I'll write again. Please feel free to write me, too, if you want. Jess."

I carefully fold it up, place it back in the envelope, and place it in between my mattress and bed spring, next to my lip gloss.

Once Mom and Dad are home, Maddie joins me, Mom, Dad, and Haley for movie night. It's Haley's choice, so she decides to show us a film called *Frances Ha,* which is about this really awesome woman who wants to be a dancer but can't quite figure her life out. Throughout the entire thing, I can see from the corner of my eye that Haley keeps looking at us. Meanwhile, Maddie and Dad seem into it. Mom looks like she's thinking the entire time.

When it ends, Haley – all smiles – turns to us and asks, "So?"

"I liked it," I say, making sure she knows how much I really did enjoy it.

Maddie says, "Yeah. It was pretty sweet. What's it called again?"

"*Frances Ha,*" Haley says.

"Hmm. Well, Greta Gerwig's awesome."

"I agree," Dad says.

I turn to Mom and ask, "What did you think?"

She sits forward, hands on her lap, and thinks before she says something. When she does, it's this: "It was good."

There's a slight pause. We don't know what to say to that. It's so simple, but it's positive. Eventually, Haley says, "Awesome." Maddie and I look at her. She nods. "Awesome."

We finish the night without another word about the film.

However, when I see Haley on Monday, I let her know how much I loved it. She tells me how much she loves movies, and how that love has been "rekindled" since being a part of Dani's movie.

"I was accepted to film school, you know," she tells me.

"Really?"

"Yep. At NYU."

"No way."

She nods.

"What happened?" I ask. "Why didn't you go?"

"A few reasons. Money. Family. Dani. Personal nonsense." She shrugs. "It is what it is. Time hasn't made me regretful, though. Not yet, anyway."

"So, you're okay with where you are now?"

"I think so. I like studying English. Reading and writing are fun to me."

"I like reading. Writing drives me nuts."

"I'm sure you're good at it, though."

"I don't know. I see you and Maddie, and you guys are into reading and writing and all of that. Jess is a doctor. That sounds cool. Even though I'd like to do research, rather than deal with patients all day. Dad's a lawyer. Mom works in an office dealing with numbers. You think things will happen between now and when I'm your age that'll change what I want to do?"

"It's possible. But, Katie, this was ultimately *my* choice. Life didn't really get in the way. It just forced me to have more options. I chose this one."

"And, you don't regret your choice?"

She shakes her head. "Like I said. Not yet."

I open myself to her and say something that causes my voice to shake. "I just don't want to grow up and end up regretting things. I want to be able to do things."

"You can do that. Eventually, you'll be old enough. But enjoy your time now. Someday, you'll miss it. You'll miss being able to have your mom and dad look out for you."

"Unless I stay here forever."

"Well, there is that, I suppose."

We share a smile.

"I say this as someone who was ten once. You're too young to be thinking about regrets. It's a fine motivator and all, but you need to just focus on being you *right now*." She leans in close, like we're conspiring over something. "You're capable of that, right?" She smirks.

I smile and nod. "Yeah, I can do that."

A few nights later, Mom comes home early. She makes dinner for Haley and me, and once Haley's gone, we clean up together, washing dishes and putting away leftovers for Dad. As we begin drying the dishes, she asks me, "Katie?"

"Yeah."

"I won't be mad if you are – I promise. But have you been talking with Aunt Jess?"

I think about lying and decide to give an answer that technically isn't lying: "No." Of course not. We've been writing.

"Because if you are it's okay. I think maybe it was too much to forbid you two from talking."

"We haven't been talking."

"Okay." She brings me close to her and kisses me on the top of my head. "So, are you ready to go back to school?"

"Not really."

"Why not?"

"School's kind of boring."

"Is it?"

"Yeah. Plus, it's full of kids."

She sort of laughs and then asks, "Well, what about your friends?"

"Well, my friends are cool, especially CeCe, but everyone else is just loud and rude."

"That's not good."

"No, it isn't."

"Well, we can't home school you, so you'll just have to stick it out. Who knows? Maybe fifth grade will be different."

"Maybe. Can I ask *you* something?"

"Sure." She leans on the counter and gives me her full attention, doing that thing where she crosses her arms.

I bite my lip and quickly regret asking if I can ask a question. "Never mind," I tell her.

"Whoa. I don't think so. Katie? What's going on? What is it?"

"It's nothing serious. I'm just curious about something."

"Okay," she says, sounding concerned. I've already told her what I want to ask isn't serious, but it's like she didn't hear me. "What are you curious about?"

"It's not about Aunt Jess."

"I didn't think it was."

I'm really kicking myself now. I don't say anything, which I know is definitely not better than saying anything.

"Katie," she says, sounding like she's getting angry at me for no reason. "What is it?"

"I, um…."

She comes up to me and gets down on her knees, her hands now on my shoulders. "Katie, I'm getting worried now."

"I told you it wasn't serious."

"Then why can't you ask it?"

"Because it's about *you*."

After a brief pause, she asks, "What about me?"

I take a deep breath. "Were you always this way?"

"What?"

"Never mind," I say, getting free from her. She grabs my arm, but not harshly – just to stop me from walking away.

"No, Katie. I'm not angry. I'm not *anything* right now. I just want to know what you're asking."

"I just…. I've been talking with everyone this summer."

"Uh-huh."

"It's just – after what happened at my birthday party…." She looks down, apparently still not comfortable with what happened. "I don't know, I started asking about you and Aunt Jess. And I guess I'm wondering if it's true."

She looks back to me and waits for me to ask my question.

"Did you used to be different?"

"Different, like how?"

I shrug. "Just…different."

"Katie, I'm strict because I love you." I begin nodding. I know that. "You *know* that, right?"

"Yeah."

"I'm doing the best I can. I *really* am. If it doesn't seem like that…Katie, I'm *so* sorry."

"No, I'm sorry for asking. I just heard stories, and…I don't know."

"I was reckless when I was younger. Right up until you were born, I…but I'm your mom, and I would do absolutely anything for you. Now and forever."

"I know."

She hugs me tightly. I return it. Why did I have to be so stupid and ask that question? All I wanted to know was this: people change, but why?

I leave for school tomorrow, but Dani's movie probably won't be done until October. She wants me to come over and watch a few of the edited scenes that I'm in. I tell myself that nothing will happen past that, no matter how cute she looks. Thankfully, Sasha's there when I arrive.

"Come in," a voice from inside the apartment calls out after I knock. I open the unlocked door, enter, close the door, and immediately lock it, wondering just how insane these two are leaving a door unlocked.

"No."

"I'm telling you, there's a shot that needs to be placed between this…and this."

I walk into a bedroom that is their "editing suite," as Dani calls it. It's dark in here. The windows are covered by thick curtains and nothing adorns the darkly painted walls. "Just give us a sec'," Dani tells me, as Sasha offers a courtesy smile. They're arguing about the pacing of a certain scene, and I beg the movie gods to not allow them to bring me into it.

"Well, we can grab something quickly tomorrow, but we can't waste time on it. We barely have any money left as it is."

"Yes," Dani says, triumphant.

"Producing sucks."

I stifle some laughter. Sasha turns to me and says, "For real, though. I'm just lucky that I wrote -."

"Co-wrote."

"Co-wrote the damn thing. Otherwise, I would have quitted weeks a lot."

"Quit," I say.

"Huh?"

"It's 'quit,' not 'quitted."

"Is it?" She turns to Dani who shrugs. "I gotta look that up later."

Dani smiles at me and shakes her head.

"Anyway. I gotta go to work. Even though I feel like I've been working all day." Sasha gets up and gathers her bag and keys.

"You're not staying?" I ask.

"I wish I could. I really wanted to see your reaction to this stuff, but someone's gotta pay the bills around here."

"I got a job," Dani chimes in.

"Right. You work less than twenty hours a week at minimum wage."

"Screw you. You're a manager at Forever 21."

"Ugh. Don't remind me." She turns to me. "See ya."

"See ya," I say back.

"Bye!" Dani calls out as Sasha exits the room. Seconds later, the door is unlocked, opened, and then closed. I don't hear a lock, so I leave the room with Dani shouting, "Hey, where're you going?"

"Locking your door," I answer.

"Oh, nothing's gonna happen," she tells me.

"Anything can happen," I say, coming back in and sitting down. "Why make it easier for weirdos and pyschos?"

She giggles and then pats the open seat next to her. "Sit."

I do what she says, and she proceeds to show me the first half of the movie, minus opening credits, finished effects, and sound and music. I die halfway, so I essentially see right up to my death, which is over-the-top gruesome in the best way. I think of Bob's death from season two of *Stranger Things*. Unlike me, when I show others stuff I'm interested in, she never once looks my way as we're watching. When it's over, she turns to me and asks, "Well?"

I'm honest. "It's incredible." Well, a little honest. It's a small movie, and at times looks like one, but she and Dani have created something that looks far better than what their budget was. Incredible? Maybe incredible in that they're going to pull it off. I'm happy for them.

She eyes me for a moment or two, and then this funny little smirk appears. "No, it's not."

"What?"

"You're lying."

"I'm not."

"Yeah, you are. Tell me the truth. Is it good? Bad?"

"I like it. I like it a lot."

"Warmer. But not quite. Come on – you know me. Tell the truth. I can take it."

I decide to be honest. "It looks good for what it is. And, I think you could've found someone better than me to play my part."

She smiles, wide. I nearly melt. "There you go." She sits back and crosses her arms and then her legs. She's so hot. "You're right. I mean, obviously you are. We had – what? – a few grand to make it." She pauses for a moment. I wonder if she actually feels bad about my honesty. "I love you in the movie, by the way. I think you're really good. Sasha thinks so, too. Everybody, really."

"Serious?" This surprises me. I felt like wincing every time I showed up on screen.

"Yeah. Of course." She smiles again, that great smile. If she's hurt, she's not showing it. "I'm hungry," she suddenly says. "Let's get some lunch."

On the way, she plays Smashing Pumpkins' "Disarm" and sings along to it. She keeps her focus on the road the whole time, occasionally asking me questions about returning to school. It isn't until we're seated at a table that we really start *talking* again.

By the time our food arrives, we're in a debate over whether *Gentleman Broncos* is a great movie. It obviously is, but I allow Dani to have her say from time to time. Things are going great, and I realize that being friends with this person isn't something impossible.

"Well, agree to disagree," she says, bringing the debate to an end.

"Fair enough," I say.

"Hey, I, uh…never said anything to you about Jess, and, um, I'm sorry about that. Is everything okay with her?"

"Yeah. Yeah, she's been okay for a good while now. She doesn't seem like she's going to do anything, you know."

"Right. I mean, stuff like that's hard to see sometimes. Even for her."

"What do you mean?"

"I mean, even though Jess may seem like she's okay, and may actually believe it herself, she might not actually be."

"Shit. I hadn't thought of that before."

"I'm not saying it's true. I'm just saying to watch out for anything."

"Yeah, well, I'm leaving tomorrow, but I'll let Maddie and Mom know to keep a closer eye on her."

"It doesn't hurt."

I nod and say, "Thanks."

"No problem. I mean, 1 like your family. Even your mean older sister."

"Mel's not mean."

"Come on."

"She's not. She's just a little strict sometimes. Maybe a little uptight on occasion." I'm defending the woman I called a "bitch" not that long ago. I wonder if I really mean what I'm saying or it's that thing where *I* can say something about my family, but no one else can. Or, it's both. "But, she's a good mom, and I'm assuming, a good wife."

"Okay, okay," Dani says, putting up her hands in surrender.

"She's not mean."

"Okay. Sorry I said it." Things get awkward and stay that way until we get back to her place. I try to find the right words to say before I get back into my car and drive away. It'll be months before I see her again, and I find I'm going to miss her far more than I did when I left the first time.

"So," I say.

"So," she repeats. "You know, I'm…really sorry about what I said. I just remember you always complaining about Mel. And, we were getting along so well, so I thought I'd say something that you'd agree with. It was stupid. I'm sorry."

"It's okay."

"Yeah?"

"Yeah. I mean, why leave it any other way?"

"You mean because once you leave it'll be another year before I get to see you again?"

"We can see one another during Christmas break. Or, we can text or video chat."

"True."

"I'm gonna miss you," I say. And, why not? I mean it.

"I'm gonna miss you, too," she says back, sincerely. I want to kiss her, but I don't. Instead, we awkwardly hug, say our goodbyes, and about a minute later I'm in my car pulling away, trying not to tear up and wishing I had the guts to wear my glasses around her. Tears and contacts don't mix well.

"Well that sucks," Maddie says when I tell her about my morning with Dani. "See, this is why you stay away from exes."

"Oh, really?" I ask. "Is that why?"

"Hey, don't get pissy with me."

"Sorry." I'm at Maddie's place, in her office specifically, trying to decompress every emotion I felt this morning. She's in the middle of reading a manuscript, and I'm amazed at how she's able to hold her side of the conversation well without sacrificing that red pen of hers, which seems to be working overtime. I'm suddenly aware of something.

"I thought you didn't go back to work for another week."

"Working from home. I found out, after going to England, that I grew up to be a pretty boring adult who actually likes a) her job, b) staying home instead of going out dancing or whatever, and c) going to bed before 10:00."

"I feel like I'm supposed to think that's sad, but it actually seems like goals to me."

She lifts up her hand for a high-five, which I give, without taking her eyes off the page. She circles something and writes "awk" next to it.

"What's awkward about that?" I ask.

"Read it out loud," she says, pointing to the sentence.

I do, and she's right; it's awkward. "Huh."

I take a good look around, realizing that this room is the opposite of the rest of Maddie's apartment, filled with photos and prints, toys and collectibles, and three hard-wood shelves filled with hundreds of books. I go up to one shelf and find I'm unable to decipher the order she's put them in.

"Hey, why don't you have a structure to your books?"

"That's too obvious for me."

"Well, look who's a millennial."

"I like having to find something to read, rather than knowing I'm going to find Stephen King or Roxanne Gay in specific places."

I pull out a worn copy of Mary Shelley's *Frankenstein*. Compared to the four other versions near it, this one actually looks like it's been read. I flip through it and find hundreds of annotations throughout, but the writing doesn't appear to be Maddie's. "Hey."

"Yeah?"

"Who wrote on this?"

She looks up and takes a look at the book in my hand. She goes back to the manuscript and then answers, "Dad."

I look back, unsure of how to feel. "Dad?"

"Mm-hmm."

"He annotate anything else?"

"Yeah, uh…*Catcher in the Rye, Cat's Cradle*, and, uh…*Little Women*."

"*Little Women*. Really?"

"Yup."

"You know, Greta Gerwig's directing an adaptation of that."

No answer.

"It comes out on Christmas."

Still no answer.

I get the feeling she doesn't want to talk about this, whether it be because it's Dad we're talking about or because I've been interrupting her work with my lack of a love life; either way, I decide to drop it. I put *Frankenstein* back and look around some more. I see her favorite book and pull it out. When I open it, a letter falls out. As I bend down to pick it up, I realize Maddie's quickly gotten up and beaten me to it.

"Whoa," I say.

She takes the book from me. "Is there a reason you're still here?"

"Hey, don't get pissy with *me*."

"I'm sorry. I'm just in the middle of *work* right now."

"I know. I'm sorry. I just – I wanted someone to talk to, and I'm leaving for school tomorrow."

"I know." She puts her hands in her pockets. She's at a loss for words, it seems like. This throws me for a loop. I want to ask about the letter, but I think better of it. It obviously triggered something. I decide to make the best of it and hug her. She hugs me back. "Be safe," she says.

"I will."

I leave soon after, still wondering about her not wanting to talk about Dad as well as the letter. Maybe they're connected. If so, I want to know what he wrote. Is it addressed to her *specifically*? I suppose, no matter what, it's none of my business unless she lets me in.

I have dinner at Mel's with her, Stephen, Katie, and Mom. Stephen's cooked my favorite, baked ziti with Italian sausage. It's delicious. We talk about random stuff for the most part, occasionally coming back to the fact that I'm headed back to school. Every now and then, I catch Mel looking at me. I can't be sure, but she looks genuinely happy. We end up alone later in the kitchen, doing dishes since she hates using a dishwasher, and I catch her again.

"Can I help you?" I ask, playfully.

"Nothing."

"Something you want to say?"

"If you want me to."

"I want you to."

She smiles, her focus on scrubbing the dish in her hands. "I'm proud of you."

I smile, inside and out. "Thanks."

"You don't have a little sister, so you don't really know this, but watching you grow up from the littlest baby ever to a grown woman who's starting her second year of college. It's amazing."

"You felt like this with Maddie?"

"What kind of question is that? Of course, I did."

"Just asking. I mean, I know you helped raise her."

"I had to. After Dad left the state, I had to do something. Jess was starting her own life in college, before she moved back. I didn't want Mom to have to do it all alone. So, I helped raise Maddie. A little, anyway."

"You helped raise me, too."

"Well, I think we kinda all did. You're this amalgam of all of us. Hopefully, mostly the best of us."

"I'll keep making you proud."

"I know you will. But whatever you do – anything at all – you do it for you and no one else. You hear?"

"Yeah."

Later, before I head back to Jess', I say my goodbyes. Hugs all around, of course. We're a family of huggers. I promise to keep in touch, like always. Mom cries, which almost makes *me* cry. Katie and I do our special goodbye handshake, which we're still working on. Laughs abound. Stephen gives me a hug, and I note that I'm happy that Mel found such a great guy.

She walks me to my car, hands me an envelope, which feels like it has a gift card inside, and tells me not to open it until later. We say our goodbyes and then I'm gone. Again, missing these people more this time than I did last year.

Jess and I watch a double feature of John Waters' *Serial Mom* and Kevin Smith's *Clerks* and laugh our asses off. We're in sweats, eating crap from plastic bowls, drinking sugar, and makeup-free, our shiny faces be damned. Around midnight, she begins to yawn.

"You should go to sleep," I tell her.

"I'm fine," she says.

I look at her. I see a pale face and red hair. I see full lips and dark eyes. I see a woman I wanted to be when I was younger. Do I *still* want to be her? Perhaps. But would that mean taking on everything that comes with her?

She catches me looking, possibly giving me the same look I gave Mel earlier. "Yes?"

"Nothing."

"Doesn't look like nothing," she says, sitting up and hugging the pillow she was resting on. "What's up?"

I try to find the right words, but she does it for me.

"Are you still worried about me?"

All I can do is raise my shoulders.

"Hmm. We're a family of huggers and shruggers," she says.

I manage a small smile.

"I'm fine. I'm always fine. This isn't like what happened with Thomas. What I did, I did…because I was sad."

"Had you ever thought of doing that before?"

"No," she answers pretty definitively.

"I'm sorry."

"For what?"

"Not being here," I say, feeling embarrassed that I'm choking myself up.

"Hey," she says, comfortingly. She rubs my arm. "This isn't your responsibility. *I'm* in charge of taking care of myself. No one else is. Okay?"

I nod as light tears fall from my blinking.

She kisses my forehead. "I love you."

"I love you, too."

"You know, I think we all know that about each other. But we still say it. Constantly. Long before this ever happened."

"Do you still love Mel?"

Again, definitively, she answers, "Yeah. Always."

I swallow hard, the tears subsiding.

She leans in and says, "I want you to go back to school and forget all of this. Don't worry about me. At all. As your big sis, I command it. Okay?"

I nod and sniffle. "Okay."

"And, with that, I *am* tired." She grabs her pillow and gets up. "I'll see you off tomorrow, so wake me up if I sleep in."

"I will."

I barely sleep. So many thoughts run through my mind. There's Mom. There's Jess and Mel. Mel and Katie and Stephen. There's Aunt Greta.

There's Maddie. There's Dani. I count myself lucky to have so many people in my life. So many I can honestly say that I love. Some don't even have one. No family is perfect, but that's because people aren't perfect. I asked Mom once what love was, and she said, "Love is wanting to be around someone no matter what." I like that, because if it's true, Jess and Mel *will* make up one day. I can tell they miss one another.

I also know I love Dani, because even though she broke my heart, I still want to be around her. Maybe that makes me a sucker, but I don't care. We ended things well enough. And, I'll be back soon.

In the morning, a groggy Jess waves goodbye as I drive away. I came home with guilt, but I get to leave with closure. Bring it on, college. I got this.

Maddie

Dad wrote me a letter before he left for California. He put it in a copy of one of his favorite novels. It was about a year before I opened it.

I had my issues with him, but things were said a long time ago. We're in a decent place now, but there's a reason I rarely speak with him. When we do, I'm as cordial as possible, but the truth is he left my mom, and I'll never forgive that. Haley, on the other hand, has a pretty solid relationship with him. I'm happy for her.

The thing is, when she opened his old copy of *Middlemarch*, the letter fell out, and I nearly lost it. Thankfully, she didn't press the situation, and we were able to quickly move on. Still, it was kind of a shock that I reacted the way I did.

I didn't get much sleep that night.

Sitting in my cubicle, a manuscript on my desk, I stare straight ahead at the photo of me in high school dressed as Joan Didion for Halloween. I was such a nerd. How did anyone ever make out with me? I shake my head. Why the hell do I have this thing, and why do I have it among the other paraphernalia hanging on or thumbtacked to my walls?

"Already bored?" Sydney asks.

I swivel to face her. "Just thinking."

"So not bored?"

Sydney's my neighbor and a pretty good editor in her own right. She's drinking water, which she says she prefers to caffeine.

"It's about a boat."

"Oh. Shit. Sounds like Pen or Pulitzer material to me."

"Well, they can't all be winners."

"But, shouldn't they be? Shouldn't *everything* we read be decent, at the very least?"

"Well, it's all personal taste."

"Yeah, but our personal taste rules."

"The title's *There She Blows*."

"Are you goddamn kidding me?"

"I am. It's actually called *The Boat*."

"Well, that's just lazy."

I smile, lean back, and rock myself. I bite my lip a little and ask her, "Is this what you wanted to do?"

She considers the question for the briefest of moments, and then says, "No. I did *not* want to read other people's stuff."

"Right?"

She nods.

"How the hell did we end up here?"

"I don't know. Money's good. We get to read and get paid for it. It's a pretty sweet job when you think about it."

"You know what's better? Being a writer."

"Yeah. Well. We have steadier income than the writers whose stuff comes by our desks."

"Good point. Maybe we're just whiners."

"Yeah. But it's fun to complain about things. It's like if you're dating a guy with a big…you know. Eventually you'd complain about it. Find some reason."

"Like what?"

"Hell, I don't know. Sounds like win-win scenario, actually. Forget I brought that up."

It's a few more minutes before we're back to our work, and I can't believe it, but I'm starting to hate my job. I want to quit, but I remind myself I have bills to pay. And that's why we do what we do. Right?

"Wow. Must be nice to complain about getting paid to just read."

"We do more than just read, you know. We make notes and suggestions. We talk with the writers. We…I don't know."

"So, quit."

"I can't do that."

"Sure, you can."

I never thought my mom would ever encourage me to quit anything, let alone a job. We're in her kitchen, and it smells great. I've never been much of a cook. That's always been a Jess thing. She can do it all.

"I mean, *technically* I can."

"So, what's the problem?"

"The problem is I took a month off work, and I didn't do anything. London was cool and all, but all I wanted to do was to get back to work. And once I was back, I kind of hated it."

"So. Quit."

I put my hand through my hair and scratch my head. I need to wash it. It's getting gross, even if it still *looks* good. "Mom. I know you mean well. I just -."

"What?"

"I. I just…." She waits for me to finish my thought. I find I don't have anything. "Shit."

"Exactly."

"What? Shit?" I say, playfully.

"Yeah. Exactly that. Shit. Or get off the pot."

"Shit or get off the pot. Those are my options, huh?"

"Yep. Keep doing what you're doing, reading work by other people, or…."

Oh, shit, I think. "Write something."

She gives me a knowing look.

"Thanks, Mom."

I give it some time. Over the next week, I consider things. I have decent money saved up. Plus, I can move back in with Mom. Or, maybe Jess would like a roommate. I actually consider Mel for a while. She's my other big sis, and I'd like to think she and Stephen would be open to me moving in, but that would obviously mean telling her that I'm going to quit my job in order to write. She'd lose it, no doubt. Then I'd feel bad. Hell, even as I think about it, I feel bad. Why does she have that power over me?

I think about what would happen, if after a few years nothing gets noticed by an agent or nothing gets published. What if I'm just not that good? Would I be able to go back to work? I highly doubt I'd be welcomed back to my old place with open arms. Could I find another job? Questions and more questions. They all freak me out. I decide to actually talk about it with someone. Haley, God bless her, is a bit too young. She'd probably be all for it. Mom's already in. Aunt Greta probably will be, too.

Mel? Well, I'll get there when I get there.

Jess it is. I take a day off without calling in and drive to her place. Kris is there, and I find out that they're in the process of getting rid of stuff.

"You're throwing all this out?" I ask.

"No," Jess tells me. "We're giving it to Goodwill."

"After cherry-picking, of course," Kris adds. "Want in?"

I give a glance to the pile of cute tops a few feet away but decide my big life choice is more important. "Actually, I just need to talk to you," I tell Jess.

"Okay."

She leads me to her bedroom, where there's more stuff on her bed. I note that it's all *her* stuff. I see the bodycon she wore to my birthday a few years ago. So help me, I find myself picking it up. "You're giving this away?"

"Unless you want it," she says, moving some boxes to the side so she can sit.

I put it up to my body and turn to her.

"Looks good," she tells me.

"I don't know."

"Come on. Every woman can pull off black."

"This looked so good on you."

"I'm sure you'll look hot in it. Take it."

"Okay." I lay it back down, carefully.

"So, what brings you by?"

I take a deep breath. "I have a decision to make."

"Are you pregnant?"

"God, no. I haven't had sex in months."

"What about that guy from London?"

"Oh, yeah. I forgot about him."

She stifles a yeah.

"Wow," I say, adding, "He was really good, too." We share a brief laugh. "Wow. Yeah, anyway. Not pregnant. I've had my period since."

"So, what is it?"

"Well, I…I want to be a writer."

"So be a writer."

"No. Not like that. I mean. I want to quit my job, so I can write full time."

"Where?"

"Nowhere. I just want to write a novel. Like I've always wanted."

"Oh. That's great."

"You think I should do it?"

"I think if you want to, you should."

"Yeah?"

She smiles. "Why do you want *my* opinion?"

"Because...I don't know."

"You're afraid to tell Mel."

"A little – yeah."

"She'll support you."

"How do you know?"

"Because she believes in you. I mean, I may not have spent much time with her recently, but up until the incident, we talked about you a lot."

"Really?"

"Yeah. We both wanted you to write something. It's all you ever talked about until college. Thomas even wanted to swap books with you. He'd read yours and you'd read his. He was *waiting* for your novel."

"Huh."

"What?"

"I think I'm just now realizing the weird feeling I've had about turning thirty had to do with this. I really *want* this, don't I?"

"Looks like it."

Then I guess I'm doing it.

I go to work the next day to formally let my boss know that I'm leaving. She reads over the letter I've presented to her that explains everything, as I sit in an uncomfortable chair in front of her desk. I've sat here before many times, but I find myself taking everything in. I note that there are a lot of framed pictures of her doing things, all over the walls. There's one with her fishing, climbing a mountain (I think), hiking in a forest; a few of them are with a guy. They look happy. I smile to myself.

"Well," she says, putting the sheet of paper down on her desk and bringing my attention to her. "Good for you."

"You're not mad?"

"Of course not. With all due respect, Madelyn," I cringe at hearing my full name, but she seems not to have noticed, "you're an excellent editor and employee but by no means irreplaceable."

"Huh. Not sure how that makes me feel."

"It's business. Regardless, I do hope that after you finish, you bring it to us. We'd be happy to publish your novel."

"Seriously?"

"Well, if it's good."

"Right."

She stands up. "Good luck to you." I stand as well, and as we shake hands, she adds, "Though we both know you won't need it."

I leave and head directly to Sydney's cubicle.

She's warm and excited for me, which makes me feel all the better. I'm not sure what exactly I expected from my boss, but I'm glad I saved Syd for last. She gives me a quick hug, promises to keep in touch, and then hands me the Jane Austen finger puppet that's been hanging from the wall to her right for as long as I've known her. When I get home, it goes on the wall to the left of my desk, next to my framed print of Leslie Knope eating pancakes that Haley got me at Comic Con a few years ago and a thumb-tacked mini-poster of *The Fellowship of the Ring*.

Before I begin writing a single word, I decide to go see Angie.

"Where's Hebah?" I ask, meeting Angie at the counter.

"It's lunchtime. I'm not a monster. She's out having lunch."

"How long do you give her?"

"Thirty minutes."

"You're a good boss."

"I know, I know." Without even taking her eyes off the paperwork in front of her, she adds: "Procrastination, though, I see. You really *are* a writer."

"Hey, I just left my job, okay? I don't need to start right away."

"I mean, it wouldn't hurt."

"I guess."

The place – shocker! – is empty. We talk over the pop music Angie plays regularly now, thanks to a suggestion by none other than my kid sister, not worried about anyone hearing anything potentially embarrassing. I walk over to the reference section that also houses books on writing.

"You have the latest *Writer's Market*?"

"Someone picked it up last week. I ordered a new copy. Still waiting on it."

She's running inventory, maybe? She's behind the counter, bent over before the computer, making notes onto a clipboard. I nod, even though she hasn't looked up much since I walked in. I think that maybe I *am* putting off the inevitable. I should just leave, go straight home, and begin writing. I mean, I *do* have an opening ready to go. It's a good one, too. I think.

"Wanna here my opening?" I ask.

"Why spoil it?"

"Are you sure? It's a good one."

She looks up at me. "You know, I believe in you and all of that, but I really wish you were writing right now. Writing doesn't just happen overnight."

"I know that," I say, getting upset. I guess it's because she's telling me the truth, and that's the last thing I want to here. Less than ten minutes later, I'm gone. But I don't go home. I decide to stop and get some pizza. But I don't take it home. Nope. I eat it there and take my sweet ass time. Crap. I am putting it off.

I'm not sure I can do this.

Jess

I'm turning forty soon, and Sam is far too excited. She wants to throw a party bigger than Aunt Greta's fiftieth, which seems ridiculous to me. I have my family, and I have her and Kris. That's it. I mean, that's nothing to snooze at, but Aunt Greta's party was big because a shit ton of people were not only invited but showed up. She wants to invite some of my former co-workers, but that doesn't interest me. After all, I've only heard from one since that night, the only one who bothered to show up to Thomas' funeral, an intern. I haven't seen or heard from her since.

This gets me thinking about going back to work. Will I even *be* allowed to return? I'm certain a psych evaluation will be necessary and maybe even counseling for a while. It may be worth it, though. I love being a surgeon.

"You should go by and talk to your boss," Sam tells me.

"I don't think I can step foot in that place."

We're on the way to drop off a bunch of stuff of mine at Goodwill. I realized, being in my house so long, that half the stuff I own I don't need *or* want. Sam and Kris helped me pack and organize. Soon, I hope, I'll be able to pack most of Thomas's stuff and donate it all, too. That time will come – as well as cleaning up that corner of my bedroom.

"Why not?" Sam asks me.

"They all know what happened. They even cleaned out my office, I think."

"Really?"

"Yep. Plus, only one person even bothered to see if I was okay after, and I haven't heard from her since."

"Well, so, maybe your former co-workers and boss turned out to be assholes. But that one person might make it all worth it."

I offer a groan that is neither agreement nor disagreement.

"What was her name?"

"Riley. She was an intern."

"*Your* intern?"

"Yeah."

"Well, that's kinda sweet."

"Again. Nothing since the funeral."

"Well, see it from *her* perspective. She's just an intern, and you're this big-time surgeon." I scoff and smirk, but Sam continues like she's heard it all before from me, which she probably has. "She's probably intimidated."

"I do have that effect on people," I say, playfully.

"You kind of do. I remember thinking you were pretty intense when I first met you."

"You did not."

"I did so."

"We were friends, like, right away."

"That's how *you* remember it. I remember it a *little* differently."

"How so?"

"You barely spoke to me the first time we met. I tried so hard that first week. In fact, I can remember giving it serious consideration to request a new dormmate."

"You wanted another dormmate?" I find that I'm actually hurt by this sudden revelation.

"Oh, don't be like that. I said I considered it. I didn't *actually* go through with it, obviously."

"All because I was quiet?"

"It's not just the way you speak. It's more than that. You're very...."

"Intimidating?"

"Yeah. But I grew to like it. I mean, we became best friends. I love you."

"I love you, too."

"See? The whole point of this, though, is to recognize that someone below you at work might be intimidated, not just because you're a surgeon but because you're you."

"I feel like I should be offended."

"Don't be. I'm just...."

"I know what you mean."

"Plus...you were probably sad that day. All of us? We didn't really know what to do for you, and we're friends and family. She's just -."

"An intern," I say, nodding. She's got a damn good point. I decide I'm going to the hospital to talk to head of surgery to see if, and hopefully, when I can return to work. And, maybe visit Riley the Intern to say hello.

My parking spot is still available, which gives me a modicum of hope. I pull into it and breathe a sigh of relief. I grab my badge, which hasn't moved from my glove compartment, and head to the seventh floor to see Glenn.

When the elevator doors open, for a split-second I consider not exiting – just letting the doors close, hitting the button for the lobby, and heading home. From somewhere, I gather just enough courage to enter the white-walled, carpeted hallway. There's no one around. I make my way to Glenn's office and knock on the door.

"Come in," I hear him say from the other side. I take a deep breath and do just that. "Jessica!" he says at top volume, damn-near startling me. "Holy crap," he adds, standing up and walking around his desk to meet me. "How are you?"

"I'm doing good."

"Yeah?"

"Yeah."

"Well, sit." He goes back behind his mahogany desk, and I sit on one of two plush seats, made at eye level with his own chair. "I've been wondering when we'd be hearing from you."

"Yeah, I – uh – wasn't sure if I should call or just come over."

"Well, I'm glad you're here. What's up?"

"Oh. Yeah. Um." I swallow hard and lick my lips. I can do this. "I'd like to come back."

He smiles. "I think we can do that."

I exhale, relaxing. I nearly smile before he continues.

"Of course, we'd need to do a few things."

Here it comes.

"First off, with all due respect – and you know I respect you – but we would need you to complete a psychological evaluation."

"Of course," I say, nodding.

"And, we'd like for you to attend counseling at least once a week."

"Absolutely."

"You're fine with that?"

"I am. Anything you and the board need."

"Okay. There is, of course, one other thing."

I hold my breath, kicking myself that I didn't consider this part.

"You will be on probation for a few months. Hopefully, a lot less. And you won't be leading many surgeries for the time being."

So help me, I actually want to cry. Instead, I swallow hard once again, obliterating the lump in my throat and nod. "Sounds good," I say.

He seems to sense something and changes his tone. "You know, I always thought you were headed for my job one day. Hell. I hope you still are. None of this means we still don't believe in you."

"It's a concern. I understand."

"Are you okay?" He's asking about my mental state, but he's also asking out of genuine concern, it seems. I give him the benefit of the doubt.

"Yeah. I'm fine."

He considers me for a few moments, eventually offering a smile – back to platitudes. "Well, then, let's get you back to your office, shall we?"

He leads me back to, sure enough, my office, which still has my name on the plaque to the left of the door. He opens it and walks in. Most everything is beneath sheets or plastic. "We tried to cover as much as we could so nothing would get dusty." They actually kept my office. I'm so happy I was wrong. I want to cry again, but for an entirely different reason. Tears of joy. Again, I swallow them down. "We knew you'd be back. Plain and simple." I walk to my desk and gently touch the sheet.

"You're a born surgeon, Jessica."

I turn to Glenn, who actually seems happy for me.

"Thank you," I tell him.

"Right. Well. Let's get the paperwork started." And like that, he's out the door. I give the room one last look and follow him back to his office, ready to get back to work.

On the way out, I pass Riley, who is making notes on a chart. I stop and back up, looking at her, trying to get her attention. Finally, she senses someone staring and looks up toward me. There's recognition and then she lights up. "Dr. Bradley."

"Hello, Riley. Er – Dr. Stafford."

Her smile widens.

"You're still here?"

"Yeah. I want to work here once I'm not an intern anymore."

"I'll put in a good word for you," I say, adding, "as much as it's still worth."

"Well, everyone still talks about you."

"Really?"

"Oh, yeah. You're still a total badass around here. It's always like, 'How would Dr. Bradley approach this?'"

"No shit? You're not pulling my leg or trying to make me feel better?"

"No. It's true. I mean, it's not all the time, but it happens every now and then."

"Huh." I smile. "Thanks."

"For what?"

"For telling me that. Made my day."

"Oh. Well. You're welcome."

"You know, you guys might be seeing a lot more of me."

"You're coming back?"

"Looks like it."

"Awesome."

She gets a text and checks it out.

"Duty calls," I say.

"Sorry."

"Go. Be a doctor."

She smiles and puts her phone away. "You look great, by the way." As she walks away, she says, "It was good seeing you."

"Likewise," I call after her.

I head on out, feeling better than I have in months.

"One month away," Sam says.

"Wait, let me do the math," Kris says, miming doing calculations. When she's done, she says, "Yeah. Checks out."

They've come to see me on my break, so we're eating lunch in a nearly empty hospital cafeteria.

"You excited?" Sam asks me.

"A little," I answer.

"Are you going to go all cliché on us?" Kris adds.

"I don't know. What's a cliché for a woman turning forty?"

"I mean…there's gotta be one, right? I mean, maybe you can find a really smokin' hot twenty-year-old who likes to fuck a lot."

Sam smiles, as she continues to eat the bland spaghetti that she says is actually tasty.

"You know, that's a cliché I can get behind," I tell Kris.

Kris tears off a piece from her garlic bread and seems to consider something. Then, it looks as if she's made up her mind, and she asks me, "Are you *ready* for sex?"

Sam begins coughing. We turn to her as she picks up her glass and drinks.

"You okay?" I ask.

She nods, the coughing winding down, and gives me a thumbs up. "I'm okay," she manages, a few more coughs following.

"No, Kris. I don't think I'm ready. I thought we were just messing around."

"No, I know. I was just…if I'm ever insensitive or cross a line -."

"I'll definitely let you know."

"Cool. Cool. You know, instead of a boy-toy, you can always buy a car. I mean, turning forty and buying, like, a Porsche isn't mutually exclusive to just dudes, right?"

"Fair enough. Doesn't seem worth it, though. Plus, I love my car."

Sam clears her throat.

"You dying over there?"

"No," she answers me with a somewhat hoarse voice. She swallows and clears her throat again. "But I do have something to tell you."

"I'm betting it has to do with Melanie."

"How'd you know?"

"Because it seems like something you'd try to do as a birthday present."

"Well, I haven't done it yet."

"Please don't."

"Come on."

"Sam," Kris interjects, "she doesn't want you talking to Mel. Leave it alone."

"I just don't -," she begins but then cuts herself off. She gives a frustrated exhale, moves her food aside, and reaches across the table to me. "You and your sister need to get over this nonsense and become civil again."

"Nonsense?"

"Yes. At this point, it's ridiculous. And, believe me, I know what happened. I was there for each of it, including finding you on the bathroom floor."

I glance at Kris, who has stopped chewing and is now staring at her food. Then, my eyes find my own plate. I can't look at Sam when she gets too earnest.

"I've known the two of you for a *long* time. You *honestly* expect me to believe she isn't hurting over what happened?"

I look up and say, "Then why hasn't she said or done anything other than be an asshole to me?"

"Because she probably feels guilty for not taking your call. And, well, Katie's birthday."

"Yeah – I really blew that, didn't I?"

"Yeah. Well. What's done is done at this point. But maybe we can still rectify all this."

"She's got a point," Kris chimes in. I turn to her. She shrugs. "She used to be your best friend. I mean. *We're* your best friends. Sam probably more than me."

"Kris…"

"It's fine. But Mel? She's your sister, too. If I had a sister, I'd want to talk to her."

Kris has never been one to be all that open about her feelings. Even during the day of the funeral, she didn't say much. She was mostly by my side the entire time, keeping my right hand clammy. I never complained. It was what I needed. While Sam was making sure my world didn't fall apart around me, Kris made sure I kept living in it. I want to tell her how much she means to me, and I nearly do before she says, "Or try to punch her, miss, and fall on top of my niece's birthday cake." She returns to her food and for a moment the statement hangs there before Sam and I look at each other and burst out laughing. Kris smirks.

Mom thinks I need to put Mel out of my mind and just focus on my own life.

"Fair enough," I tell her.

She sips her tea and makes a face. "Why every woman in this family has to shrug everything off by saying 'fair enough' is beyond me."

"I'm pretty sure you and Greta taught all of us to say it," I say while chewing on an insanely buttery croissant. "We're keeping the tradition alive."

"Fair enough."

We're in a nearly-empty and adorable bistro that's just opened up by her place. Seated in the corner, away from any vents (as per Mom's request), we do some catching up. I acknowledge this, knowing full-well that I haven't spent much time with her in many months. Sudden guilt overcomes me. I wipe my mouth, sit back, and finish chewing.

"Something wrong?" she asks.

I swallow and say, "I'm sorry."

"For what?"

"For not being a very good daughter."

"Oh, please," she says, going back to buttering an English muffin.

"No, I'm serious."

"I know you are."

I sit up. "Mom, I'm apologizing for…"

She stops and asks, "For what?"

She's got me there. I decide to be honest, even if it's more about me than about her. "I just feel guilty about not spending time with you recently. I'm sorry."

"Honey, there's no need to apologize. You're a grown woman with your own life. You have things you need to do and friends to spend time with. I'm fine."

"Yeah, but I still feel guilty."

"Have you *always* felt guilty?"

"About what? Not spending time with you?"

"Yes."

"Well, sometimes, yeah."

"Which times?"

"Which times?"

"Which times?"

"Um. Well. There's now."

"Uh-huh."

"And, there was Aunt Greta's birthday. And Maddie's birthday."

"Any times not from this past year?"

"Well, I -. I…." I shake my head.

"Sweetie, you just feel bad because you suddenly find yourself with more time alone."

"Yeah. We used to spend just about every night together."

"And that's not something you just learn to live without."

"No, it isn't."

She wipes her mouth, folds her napkin and sits it on the table, and leans in slightly toward me. "Now, *I* want to apologize."

"For what?"

"For not being there when you needed me."

I shake my head. "No."

"Sweetie -."

"Mom."

"I'm sorry."

I find it difficult to look at her, suddenly; I want to cry. Which pisses me off, because I thought I was done with that. I shake my head again.

"There's nothing to apologize for," I manage to say.

"Please look at me."

It takes quite a lot for me to move my head and eyes and look at my mother. She's smiling, warmly, at me. I don't feel like crying anymore.

"I *am* sorry. I wish I could've been there for you. I wish I could take away all of your pain and sadness. I wish, I wish, I wish. But there's still something I *can* do, which is be your mother. If you want to spend time with me, I'm here. If you don't, that's okay, too. Nothing – absolutely nothing – makes me happier than when my children are happy. You don't need to apologize for wanting time on your own. You don't need to apologize for being sad – or wanting to cry. You have every right to cry. Or scream. Or swear. You can choose to try to make things as close to what they were before. You can even choose to go along with how life moved on. Because life *does* move on. And, yeah, it sucks. But it's also amazing. I mean, can you believe how much Katie has grown this year?"

I smile, realizing I'm actually crying. This makes me laugh.

Mom smiles, her eyes a little glassy. "You're almost forty, baby girl. You do whatever the hell you want. And I will love you."

I want my sister back. That won't happen until she's ready. I decide right then and there that that's okay.

Jessica's fortieth birthday is held in a ballroom at a Hyatt, and it's lovely. Her best friend Sam organized it, and she is beaming every time I look at her throughout the night. Jessica shows up about an hour after everyone's arrived. The lights are low, the DJ is playing what are, in essence, songs from Jessica's life – in no particular order, I'm told. She's wearing loose-fitted jeans, and she strolls in, hands in pockets, looking grateful yet sheepish about the whole thing. I see her make her way through the party, making sure she says hi to everyone – and there are quite a few people. There's immediate family, as well as Sam and Kris, of course. Then, there are co-workers from the hospital, including a young woman who looks honored to have been invited, acquaintances of Thomas', and Maddie friends. All told, I'd say there are about fifty people in attendance, and I think two things:

1) How much did this all cost, and how the heck did Sam pay for it?

2) Jess has a lot of people in her life that care enough about her to come here.

I suppose that's actually three things. I also notice that she's smiling. A *lot.*

Maddie comes over, a glass of sparkling water in her hand. "I need a drink," she says, straight-faced. I know she's playing. Still, I say her name as a warning of sorts. She responds with, "I'm just playing."

"It's a dry party."

"I know. I'm supporting Jess."

"She looks so happy, doesn't she?" I ask.

"She does. Too bad Haley couldn't make it."

"Midterm exams?"

"Yep."

"I'm sure she's thinking of her big sister."

"Aren't we all?"

I see that Jess is giving my own big sister a big hug. I feel uneasy that I'm entertaining the idea that Jess has shown up drunk – based solely on how happy she seems. I shake my head to make the thoughts go away.

"You okay?" Maddie asks.

"I'm fine."

Soon enough, Jess ends her tour with us. After hugs, I take note that I smell no trace of alcohol and put those thoughts to bed. "Quite the party," I manage over the music, which seems like it has increased in volume.

Perhaps, now that the person of the hour is upon us, the party can now truly start.

"I know, right?" Jessica says.

"I forgot your gift," Maddie tells her.

"It's no problem. I don't need gifts anyway. You know that."

"That I do. You think you're better than me?"

"Yes."

I enjoy the banter between the two and feel good that at least one of Jess' sisters is with her tonight.

Later, my sister gives a speech before announcing the appearance of a simple buttercream cake with an overwhelmingly amount of fruit on it. In her remarks, she tells a story about Jess and "her sister," who we all assume is Melanie, and it's one I'm unaware of. It starts when the two of them were in middle school. On New Year's Eve, the two of them dared one another to not pee from nine until midnight, which apparently led to one of them – "Jess," my sister adds – peeing on herself. "Mom," Jess says, flabbergasted, mouth agape – her face turning as red as her hair. "Suffice to say," Sarah continues, "it was a quite the wet New Year." A few giggles and groans follow, with Jess putting her face in her hands and Sam rubbing her back as she tries to hold in her laughter. "I, of course, had to clean up. Little did I know that night's events would end up as a story I would tell on my daughter's fortieth birthday. I love you, sweetie."

"Thanks, Mom," Jess manages.

"Forever and ever. Here's to you." She lifts her glass, as does everyone, and we toast. I see then the first hint of melancholy from my niece. But, soon enough, Kris whispers something in her ear and she's all smiles again. I thank God she has friends as good as these.

The next day, I tell Sarah that there's a buyer and that there's a good chance I'll be selling the house just after Thanksgiving. I'm excited, and because she's the best older sister ever, she's excited, too.

"Now comes the hard part," I say.

"What's the hard part?" she asks.

"Packing."

"Ugh."

"Yep. And getting rid of stuff. I'm betting more than half the crap in this house is junk."

"Well, this is as good a time as any to take stock. Maybe even a better time."

"Yeah. Need a ten-year-old couch?"

"I'm good."

We begin – albeit slowly – that day. We start in the guest rooms, figure out what can be given away and what can be sold, and make our way to Phillip's old office, which I dust regularly, but hasn't seen much use since he passed. I find comfort in this room, which I still consider to be very much his, though he never saw it that way. His door was rarely closed, and I don't need to admit that I miss the sound of him hitting the keys of his word processor. I walk to his desk, remove the processor's clear cover, and run my hand gently over those keys. Sarah begins to make file boxes for whatever it is I'm keeping, which will probably be a lot harder than I thought.

"So," she says, hands on her hips, the first box ready to go. "Where shall we start?"

I look up, first at her and then I scan the room. "The photos."

We make our way to the bookcase he faced while typing. It has five shelves, each with about a dozen framed photos of various sizes of the two of us, me, friends, and family. There's one on our wedding day with him, me, and both of our parents, may they all rest in peace. I pick it up, and Sarah rests her chin on my left shoulder. "Beautiful," she says.

"Amazing how they're all gone."

She rubs my back, kisses my shoulder, and begins carefully placing the photos in the box. "We'll bubble wrap these later," she tells me.

I put the framed photo in the box and pick up one of a much younger me and Sarah. I'm wearing my cheerleading uniform, while Sarah sports a pair of jean shorts.

"Wow. Who are those hotties?" she asks.

I smirk at her. "Not bad, huh?"

"We did all right."

"You miss it?"

"Nah. You?"

I shrug. "Not really."

We move on, and without any effort, we find that we've filled three boxes worth of framed memories. Then, it's lunchtime, which is when I'm told Melanie will be coming over.

"Oh?" I respond.

"Yeah. We've been talking lately about how badly she feels about her reaction to you selling the house."

"Well, with all due respect, that daughter of yours doesn't accept change all that well."

"Very true, but can you necessarily blame her? Within just a few years, her older sister and best friend moved away, her parents got divorced, her father moved half a country away, and Haley was born. God knows I wasn't the best single parent during that first year. To her *and* Maddie. I don't know what I would've done without Melanie."

"And being still in high school at the time."

"That's right. Wow."

"Yeah. She really stepped up during that time."

Sarah nods. "Definitely a change in her. Much more responsible. Quieter, too, maybe."

"You raised some damn good kids, Sarah."

"Thank you. I tried."

"I see the way Melanie's raising Katie, and it's similar to how you raised both Melanie and Jess."

She smiles.

"And, she's got Stephen, which is great."

"Lucky her. I always wished Roger had done more."

Melanie arrives with some plates from an Italian place nearby, and soon, we're munching on calamari, ravioli, and bruschetta.

"Aunt Greta…I, uh – wanted to apologize for my behavior concerning your decision to sell your home."

"Thank you, Melanie. I appreciate that."

"Are we good?"

"Of course."

She seems reassured by that simple – and quite frankly, obvious – fact. I assume it's because she's consciously or unconsciously worried that perhaps Jess will never accept any apology she might offer. This is all crazy, of course. We're a tight-knit family who have disagreements all the time, but we always move past that nonsense.

"Maddie told me about how she quit her job to write a book." She takes a moment before she adds, "And, I wanted to tell her that was irresponsible." She looks at Sarah. "That was my first thought."

"And what did you tell her?"

"I told her that maybe she should've just asked for less stuff to edit, that leaving a well-paying job isn't the smartest thing in the world. And then she got mad at me. And…something happened. I saw myself. And I thought, why wouldn't I be at least a *little* supportive of her decision? I mean, it's her life."

Sarah nods.

"Mom, can I ask you something?"

"Of course," Sarah says. Melanie's proper, etiquette-light persona began around the time of her maturity and has only increased since Katie's birth. It's actually lovely most of the time, but every now and then I find myself contrasting this version of her with the one I knew decades ago, and they appear as if they're different people. But, they're not. They're both Melanie. And, inside, and occasionally on the outside, she's still the same judgmental, brash, and deeply caring human being she's always been. I smile to myself. I truly love the two women seated with me.

"It's about Jess," she says, her hands fiddling with one another, her eyes looking at her plate. Then, she finds the courage to look at her mom.

Sarah has her poker face on. "Mm-hmm."

"I'm, um…do you think I'm wrong?"

"Wrong about what?"

"Not talking to her. Freezing her out of my life."

"Well, you're in charge of your own life. I don't get involved in things like this. You know that."

I squirm a little in my seat. Why is Melanie doing this while I'm here? Should I say something? Should I stay quiet?

"Right. But…do you know what happened? Between us?"

"Yes. She told me."

"She did?"

Sarah nods. "About a year ago. Before Christmas."

"Did you tell her to come talk to me?"

"Of course not. But I'm sure our conversation inspired her to."

"I just…. I don't know why I'm so mad. Like, I don't even know if I'm still mad at her. It's like I have this grudge and I don't want to let it go."

"Why do you think that is?"

"I don't know. What do you think?" She asks that question carefully.

Sarah mulls this over, sits back, and crosses her arm. "It doesn't matter what I think," she says.

"Mom, come on."

"Come on, what? Melanie, you're old enough to figure out your own problems."

"Sarah, she's just asking."

"I know she's 'just asking.' I know. But you're not fooling me, Mel. I know you know *exactly* how you feel."

"You think I'm wrong?"

"It doesn't matter. What do *you* think?"

"I do."

"I know, hun."

Mel takes a deep breath and asks, "Why do I think that? I don't know that part."

Sarah takes a deep breath of her own and sits up, leaning closer to her daughter. "You feel guilty about not taking Jess' call."

I can tell Melanie wants to burst out crying, but she does a hell of a job holding back the tears, even biting her lip.

"You were confident that you were right. Yeah? You freeze Jess out. That punishes her. But then you're punishing you, too. But you rationalized that. After all, what Jess said crossed a line and broke a trust that could never be mended. So much so that when Jess showed up to your house with Christmas presents, acting like the previous two years hadn't happened, you lost it. There was yelling and horrible things said. Still, Jess kept calling, right? Still, you kept pushing her away, right? And then she called you because she was hurting after Thomas died and -."

"Okay!" Melanie yells. She pushes her plate and plants her elbows on the table, her face in her hands. She's crying.

"Sweetie, it's not your fault."

"Yes, it is."

"No, it's not."

"Mel," I say. "It's not. I've talked with Jess about this. She doesn't blame you at all."

I hear snot. She looks up at me, wiping her cheeks. Her eyes ask me, "Really?"

"Really," I answer.

Sarah takes hold of Melanie's head and brings her close to her chest for a hug. Mel seems to be half-crying and half trying to hold it all in. "Don't you ever think that was your fault. You hear me?"

Melanie nods.

Sarah kisses the top of her head. "Shh," she tells her as Mel begins to find it hard to breathe through the sobs.

Family is a complicated thing. It is at once both the easiest thing in the world and the most difficult. It's easier because you can simply be born into one or choose one. It's difficult because you share so much with your family, which makes the hurt all that much more when it happens. Yet, it's family, so you find ways to make it through any and all hard times. Melanie and Jessica have been through a hard time with one another for years now, but I believe it's nearing its end.

Finally. Sometimes, you can choose to live life going backward, which is insanity, because we all know the world keeps moving forward whether we like it or not.

November arrives and so does confirmation. Someone wants to buy the house. The waiting game begins, as does the packing. Most of the furniture is headed to Goodwill, aside from a few things the girls would like. Maddie wants Phillip's desk, which she was careful to ask for. It's more than fine, and I'm happy that it's going to a good home – and that it'll actually see use. I hope her novel is coming along nicely. She's apparently not ready to discuss it yet, which just makes the rest of us more excited.

Haley wants a few bookcases, which will go into storage in Jess' garage until Haley graduates and gets her own place. Melanie's taking a chair she loved to sit in back when she visited when she was young. Jess didn't want anything – at first. Then, after I offered her the set of encyclopedias in my separate office, she requested any and all books I was willing to part with. I decided to give her all of them, except the first edition of *Carrie* that Phillip gifted me on our first wedding anniversary. When Maddie found out, she jokingly said she was hurt, but then remembered she has an entire bedroom in her place that is literally filled with bookshelves and piles of books. "Welcome to the club," she told Jess. Meanwhile, Sarah accepted a rarely used lamp from my bedroom, which Phillip and I bought about a year before he passed.

"Packing kind of sucks, doesn't it?"

"You got that right."

On day one of packing, Maddie and Jess have come to help. We focus on the living room.

"But, don't get me wrong, Aunt Greta. I love it."

"Thank you for lying, Maddie."

"It's what I'm here for."

"There are a *lot* of breakables," Jess observes, offering a quick smile immediately after. I offer one back and tell her, "I know. But, when you believe you're staying put, you don't think about how you'll be packing it later on. A lot of this is heavy, too." I motion around to suggest the entirety of the house. Neither seem all that phased.

"Haley's lucky she's in school. Otherwise, we'd be making her do most of this," Maddie says.

"Oh, Maddie," I tell her.

"What? That's what big sisters are for? Right, Jess?"

"It's true. That's what they're for."

I smirk, scoff, and shake my head, bemused, and I take a filled-box to the kitchen for taping up. I can hear them still playing with one another. I place the box on the table and grab the tape, immediately struck by a sense of déjà vu. I did this exact thing once before. It was when Phillip and I decided to remodel parts of the house. We decided to box-up and give a few things away then, too. I can remember taking a box to this very table, lifting the tape up, and Phillip surprising me by hugging me from behind. I jumped and fell into a fit of laughter at the startle. He kissed my neck. His lips, of course, were dry. I miss that. Without even thinking, my free hand finds that spot and I carefully touch it, as if it will fade away if I'm rough with it.

There's a sense of shame over how much I miss my husband. I was never one to believe that another person could complete anybody. Everyone is capable of living a life on her or his own. Still, I cannot help my feelings. I'm unclear as to what can be in the afterlife, if there is one, but there's a part of me that believes in the soul. At one time, I did consider the very real possibility that Phillip was my soulmate. I find myself entertaining the idea more and more with each passing day. I loved – no, *love* that man. *That*, I can truly say, I feel zero shame over.

Part Four: The World in a Glass Hat

<u>Greta</u>

And like that, Thanksgiving comes around, and there are two family

dinners, surprise, surprise. Everyone, except Jess and Haley, who stayed at

school for the break to study, as well as to, presumably, hang out with

friends, has lunch at Melanie's. She's smart enough to not serve turkey.

Instead, she's made this wonderful pasta; fettuccine, with olive oil,

tomatoes, mushrooms, garlic, and onions. It's absolute heaven. I have

three servings, which I'm not afraid to admit.

"Melanie, sweetie, this is pretty fantastic," I tell her.

"Yeah, really," Maddie agrees. "Where's this side of you been all my

life?"

"Well, it's something I've been working on. As you all know, I'm not

the greatest cook in the world."

"No."

Melanie gives her a look. The two made up. Maddie, Melanie told me,

showed up a few days before with half of her manuscript and gave a little

speech about how much she looks up to her and how she really values her

opinion and how it would be great if she could find the time to read what she's written so far. Without missing much of a beat, Melanie invited her in, took the pages, and they talked about story and character and -

Here we are. I hope that Melanie takes this opportunity to look inward and maybe pay Jess a visit soon. I nod to myself and move on, knowing that's their journey and not mine.

"I assume that Jess is cooking the turkey again this year?" Melanie, of all people, asks Maddie.

"Well, she's a total badass at it. No offense, Mom."

"None taken. I'm glad she's taken that up. As much as I love eating it all, it's such a pain to make."

"Well, all you need is love, right?"

"Ha-ha, daughter."

Maddie blows Sarah a kiss, and we all chuckle.

"So," I turn to Katie, who's seated beside me, "what'd you do this week?"

She's chowing down on a carrot stick, leaving most of her pasta alone.

"We all went to the zoo," she tells me.

"Really?"

"Oh, we have a *ton* of pictures," Stephen says, pulling out his phone. He unlocks it and finds the pictures in no time. "Here," he says, handing it over.

I scroll through the first few of the three of them entering the park. They all look so joyful. "Oh, look at that." Maddie, who's on my other side, looks at the phone, too. "It looks cold. Were any of the animals out?"

"Yeah, actually," Melanie answers. "Most of them."

"Really?"

"Yeah," Katie says, more excited than I've seen her in a while. "We saw this lion that kept yawning – it was so funny."

"It sounds funny," I tell her, stopping at a picture of her being hugged tightly by Melanie, who is also giving her a kiss on the cheek. I look up briefly and see Melanie deep in thought, a funny smile on her face. I look back and begin scrolling again.

"Dang, Stephen," Maddie says, sitting comfortably back in her seat. "You did take a ton of pictures."

"Like I said."

"They mostly look like crap, but…."

He laughs, as Melanie says, "Maddie."

"Oh, shit – sorry. Shit."

Katie laughs. I look to Melanie who genuinely smiles at her and shakes her head. "Not in front of my kid, thank you," she says, sounding like she's holding back laughter.

Maddie leans forward and turns to Katie. "Katie?"

Katie does the same but toward her aunt. "Yeah."

"Don't say shit."

"I won't."

At this, most of the table laughs, with Melanie scoffing and chuckling. I smile at Sarah, who is beaming. She catches my eye and winks.

I'm the last of the guests to leave. Everyone's meeting up at Jess' in a few hours. I plan on heading straight there to offer any help I can. Melanie stops me as I head to the door, putting on my coat.

"Aunt Greta?"

"Yes?"

She seems nervous, something I have not seen from her in years. She looks like a teenager again, worried that her mom will find out she failed an important exam. "I, uh…." She scratches her head. "Can you tell Jess 'Happy Thanksgiving' for me?"

I offer a warm smile and a hug.

"Absolutely."

I arrive to find Sam and Kris are already in the kitchen helping. Well, Sam is. Kris, meanwhile, is working on the cranberry sauce, which amounts to no more than sitting on one of the counter stools and watching *Elf*, while a can of Ocean Spray and a can-opener sit beside the small TV.

"Well, hello, ladies," I tell them.

"Hey," Sam offers, while Kris tells me, "What up, Mrs. Kane?" We high-five. Because – why not? I mime rolling up non-existent sleeves and take a place beside Jess.

"Okay. What can I do?"

She slides over. "You can finish your sis's green bean casserole."

"Okay."

"While I finish up the stuffing."

"Dressing," Kris says.

"What?"

"If you're not stuffing it in the turkey, it's called dressing."

"I don't think that's true."

"It is. I read it somewhere."

"Where?"

"I don't know. But it's true."

"Whatever. I'm calling it stuffing, because that's what my mom called it, and that's what *her* mom called it."

"As your unofficial family motto says, 'Fair enough.'"

Jess curtsies, and we go back to preparing, while Kris goes back to the TV, laughing almost immediately. I look up and see Buddy getting into it with the fake Santa. I smile.

"I love this movie," Kris says.

"No. Really?"

"Jess, you are uber-sarcastic today. And, I love it."

"I'm assuming you two will be here for dinner," I say.

"Not me," replies Sam. "I've got to go home. My mom and dad have been bugging me since summer to visit, and to be fair, it's been a while. Plus, it'd be nice to spend a holiday other than New Year's with them."

"Will you be there for Christmas and New Year's, too?"

"I don't know. We'll see. Travelling at this time of year is a pain in the ass, even if it's ultimately worth it."

Kris says, "*I* will be here, because my family sucks."

"Just because they're conservatives doesn't mean they suck."

"I didn't say they suck because they're conservatives. They suck because they're rotten human beings."

Jess giggles. I don't find that funny. "Kris, you shouldn't say that about your family."

"With all due respect, Mrs. Kane – and I do mean that – my family believes being gay is a choice, that Muslims cannot be trusted, and that giving to charity is for suckers."

"Oh."

"Yep. So, I'll be here with you guys."

"You and Sam are basically my sisters, so as far as I'm concerned, your family is my family, and I'm pretty sure we don't suck."

"Even Mel?"

The three of us seem to stop what we're doing and wait for a response, which actually comes pretty quickly.

"Mel, too."

I see Sam smirk in the corner of my eye.

"Speaking of Melanie," I say, "She told me to tell you 'Happy Thanksgiving.'"

"Really?" Sam asks.

"Yeah."

Jess looks like she's at a loss for words.

"That's cool," Kris adds.

"What do you think, Jess?" I ask. "Should I tell her you said it back?"

She takes a deep breath. "Yeah. Sure." She goes right back to her stuffing, and we all follow suit. I try, every now and then, to get a solid reading from her expression, but I can't make anything out.

When dinner comes around, we video chat with Haley, who's in her dorm, killing time before she's off to have dinner with her roommate and her family. Maddie pretends to feed the small phone-version of Haley mashed potatoes. The semester seems to have been a much less stressful one than either from her first year at college. We all tell her how proud we are of her, and soon, she's gone.

We begin reminiscing about things, tip-toeing around the fact that Melanie, Phillip, and Thomas aren't here.

"You excited about the move?" Maddie asks, breaking me out of my wistful reverie.

"Hmm? Oh, yeah. Definitely."

"You don't sound very excited."

"Well, I'm fifty now. I don't have the physical constitution to be as excited as I was a few months ago."

"Uh-huh."

"I'm sure my sister is excited, but it's a different kind of excited," Sarah tells her.

"Exactly. It's exciting in that I don't know what's coming. But not in a bad way."

"Sounds scary, more than anything," Jess says.

"Perfect," I tell her. "That's it. I'm excited and scared. At the same time."

"Yikes," Maddie says.

I take a sip of wine and say, "There's this quote from Sylvia Plath about a glass hat that I've always loved." I say it and take another sip.

I see Maddie, deep in thought, nodding. Jess seems to be taking this in as well. Sarah smiles at me. Then, she says, "What exactly does that mean?"

We chuckle a little, but I know my sister. She's smart as a whip but has never really had an ear for poetry. I tell her, "It means I'm new to this again."

"To what?"

"This. All of it. I'm starting over. And, I'm scared to mess up. But, I'm excited at the possibilities."

"Huh," she responds. "Well, you could've just said that."

A few more chuckles from the girls.

"What's the fun in that?" I ask.

She tells me, "Fair enough."

I move the final boxes on a Tuesday morning, three days before I sign a bunch of papers and hand over the keys. Things have moved so fast, but there's something cathartic about leaving my home behind and turning it back into a house. I'm also anxious at the idea of my bank account swelling due to the sale. What comes next exactly? I've thought about some things. I've said others out loud. What are my plans? As I make one last walk through the house, I realize I don't have any solid plans beyond staying with Sarah for the foreseeable future. Then, there's the cruise. And my students. But what about after that? Yikes.

My thoughts gently dissolve into light nostalgia and memory. I can still see where every piece of furniture and knickknack went. I can see Phillip on the couch watching old TV shows. I can see Sarah in the kitchen making a dinner I didn't ask for, but because I'm her best friend, she'd come over unannounced and do it. I smile. The bathroom smells like cleaning products, any trace of myself is seemingly gone forever. It's the same with the bedroom, sans the smell of bleach. Phillip's office looks worn and lonely. I see him typing. I see him reading. I see him pacing. He catches me looking and gives me a warm smile. I smile back.

Outside, I give my goodbyes to my garden and all the herbs and vegetables I planted. I look at the uneven but still nice-looking brick work Phillip did here and there. I see him sweating, exhausted after a long day building a wall around my garden that ultimately didn't amount to much. I believe it took him a month and a-whole-lot of money to make the damn thing. I run my hand over it. I love it.

I love it all. But, it's just a yard. It's just a house. It's just things.

Jess' car is visible through the bare living room windows. As I close the patio door, the doorbell rings. I open the door, even though it's unlocked. "Hey," she tells me and gives me a big bear hug. I return it ten-fold. I find I don't want to cry. I don't need to. This is the right thing. I'm okay.

She gives what she can see a once-over and nods. "That's that, huh?"

"Yep."

"Well, okay then."

"Thanks for coming."

"I actually thought I was going to miss you. I wanted to be here."

"Thank you, sweetie." I give her a kiss on the temple, put my arm around her, and we both say our goodbyes to this place.

Soon enough, the door is closed and locked by me one last time. I tell Jess I'll go by her home later to have dinner. She tells me to come by around eight and that she's headed to work. I watch her drive away, turn back to the house, wave goodbye, get into my car, and drive away. The music is upbeat, and I sing along to it.

I'm reminded suddenly of the final words of Kilgore Trout in Kurt Vonnegut's *Breakfast of Champions*. I used to be scared of those words. I never wanted to grow up and have regrets, the kind that make old people want to relive their youth. I've lived a good life, and I intend to keep living it. I just need a plan. Nothing too specific. Maybe I need to revisit my bucket list. I'll talk to Haley about it next month when she comes home for winter break.

<u>Jess</u>

Session nine goes like this:

I'm seated on the couch, my shoes off and my feet on the cushion – comfortable, like I've been since session five. Dr. Amelia Shephard sits across from me, a glass coffee table with nothing on it between us. The room is similar to my own office, in that there's very little clutter, but still personal touches here and there. There are the usual framed photographs of herself and loved ones – I assume – and diplomas. But there are also two Funko Pops on the shelf beside the filing cabinet behind her desk. One is Batgirl from the '60s *Batman* TV show. The other is Jyn Erso from *Rogue One*. Haley would appreciate those touches.

"So, how was your weekend?" she asks me. I'm not positive, but I'm pretty sure she's my age. That makes things easier for me, somehow.

"It was good."

"Thanksgiving."

"Yeah. Had everyone over. Made dinner. It was nice."

"Did Haley make it?"

"No – she stayed and had Thanksgiving with her roommate's parents, I think."

"Did you miss her?"

"I always miss her. She's my kid-sister."

She nods, writes something down, but without missing a beat says, "And, Mel?"

I hesitate, lick my lips, and say, "Nope."

"And how did that make you feel?"

"Bad."

"How bad?"

I take a deep breath. "Ummm…I didn't cry. Sort of got to thinking that this is just how it is now."

"Did thinking that make you feel any better?"

"It did. I was able to move on with the rest of the night because of it."

"That's good."

"Guess we can't control everything, huh?"

"Most of us know this, but actually practicing it? It's difficult."

I nod, not knowing what to say today that hasn't already been covered. I look around the room, and when I finally land on Dr. Shephard, she looks like she's waiting for me to say something.

She smiles.

I smile. This is awkward. "So…," I say.

"So…," she responds.

"Should I…maybe say something?"

"Is there something you want to say?"

"I don't think so."

She leans toward me. "How about your father? Or, your step-mother?

Or, your sister…." She begins to look at her notes.

"Penelope," I say.

"Yes. Penelope."

"No. They weren't there for Thanksgiving."

"No call. No email."

"We don't really do that."

"Understandable."

I want to get up and leave, but I know that would hurt any progress I've

made so far.

"Have you ever thought of calling or emailing *them*?"

"Why would I do that?"

"Because they're your family."

"No, they're not."

"They're not?"

"No."

She nods and leans back. She considers something and then asks, "Why

did you want to become a surgeon?"

"Because it was my dream."

"You never dreamed of doing anything else?"

"No."

"Why not?"

"Because this is what I wanted to do."

"Dreams come from somewhere, Jess."

"Yeah. From our minds."

She forms a small smile. "Did your father support you?"

"Did he support the fact that I wanted to be a surgeon? Yeah."

"How?"

I take another deep breath. "He bought me medical supplies when I was in elementary."

"Like?"

"Like, I don't know – a stethoscope, a lab coat, green scrubs -."

"Do you still have any of that?"

"No."

"What happened?"

"I threw it all out."

"When?"

"When he left my mom," I say, my voice breaking.

"Did you keep *anything* from him? That he gave you?"

"No."

"Nothing? At all?"

"Not one thing."

"Why?"

"Why would I want *any* of that?"

She shrugs. "Because they were gifts."

"Well, I didn't want them anymore."

"So, you *will* keep things you *do* want?"

"Yeah, I guess."

"What do you want?"

"What do I want?"

"Mm-hmm."

I try to find the answer to that, which seems like it'd be easy to answer, but I find it difficult. I decide to say the obvious thing. "Family and friends."

"And, your father, your step-mother, and Penelope don't count."

"That's right."

"Does Mel count?"

"Of course, she does."

She nods. "What about work?"

"What about it?"

"Do you *want* to be here? Do you *want* to continue to work here?"

The answer should be "Yes," but it won't exit my mouth. She seems to notice this.

"You keep the things you want. What *do* you want?" She puts emphasis on that last question, and I find she's actually helped me.

I knock on Glenn's office door and open it. He looks up from his lunch and says, "Oh – hey, Jess. Want some chicken salad? Mia made a ton today."

"I'm good," I say, sitting down. "Rain check."

"No problem. What's up?"

I take a deep breath and decide to not pussyfoot around it. "Glenn…as much as I appreciate being here, when exactly am I going to be allowed to operate again?"

"Well…you're on probation."

"I know. And I've been going to therapy."

"Yes, I know. You've been doing great, I hear."

"That's good."

"Dr. Shephard seems to think you'll be back to work in no time."

"When?"

"I'm sorry?"

"When? When will I be officially back?"

He doesn't say anything. He doesn't have to.

"That's what I figured."

"Jessica -."

"No, I get it. I really do. It's just…operating on people…it was my passion. And now I'm an overpaid assistant. And that's ridiculous for a few reasons. Not the least of which is that I'm still getting paid what I used to and have a nice office."

"Jessica, if you can just wait -."

"Until…?"

"Until it's time."

"I can't wait anymore."

"So, what are you saying?"

"I'm saying that I'm leaving."

"To another hospital?"

"Maybe. Eventually. Right now…I'm not sure."

He gives me a look, like he's trying to figure out the person sitting before him. We used to be close colleagues. Now, I'm a stranger to him.

And, I *do* get it – even if I don't like it. After a few moments, he nods. "Okay."

Well, that's that. I lean forward. "I'd like to recommend intern Riley Stafford. She's going to make a hell of a surgeon. I assume there'll be money for that once I'm gone."

"Indeed."

"She's going to be great. If you still trust my judgment, give her a chance. Don't lose her to another hospital." I stand up.

"Jessica, if I may."

"Yes?"

"You were the best."

"I know. Maybe I'll get there again."

He stands and holds out his hand. "Good luck to you, Jessica," he tells me.

"Thank you," I say, shaking it. "And, just so you know, I have a lot of crap in my office, so there's a good chance we'll see each other a few times before I'm actually gone."

"Need any help?"

"I think I got it."

Sam genuinely cannot believe what's happened when I tell her. She's come over to look through my old things from grade school, hoping to find something that she wants to put in a scrapbook she's making for me. "You're insane. You know what you're giving up?"

"I do. For the past few months, I've basically been an OR nurse, which there's nothing wrong with, but I'm a surgeon. I should be operating on people."

"So, what are you gonna do now?"

"Beats me. All I know is I wanted out. Now, I'm dreading everyone asking me that question."

"Sorry."

"No, it's a fair question. I just don't *know*."

"You're not just going to be staying home all the time, are you?"

"What's wrong with that?"

"I mean…I don't know. Boredom?"

She's talking about how I was this past spring. I don't blame her. "Sam, I'm not going to start drinking."

"How can you know that?"

"I don't. But I can honestly say I haven't wanted a drink in a long time. And that's thanks to *you*, by the way."

"I just worry about you."

"Don't. I'm fine."

"But you're not."

"What do you mean? Of course, I am."

"On the surface everything looks fine. You might even feel fine. But you still have Thomas's picture in the corner of your bedroom. You haven't bothered to clean that up."

"That's…true. I haven't."

"And, that's okay, I think. I'm just saying I'm worried."

"And, I'm just saying that I'm fine."

"Okay. I believe you."

"Thank you."

"Well, it's time to go hunting." She heads to my bedroom.

"Have fun, Indiana Joanie," I call out to her.

About twenty minutes later, my doorbell rings. I answer it, and I my heart nearly stops. Mel stands on my porch, holding a grocery bag in her right hand. She looks nervous. We don't say anything. I wait for her to say something, but I'm pretty sure she's waiting for *me*. I decide to be the first to speak. "Come in," I tell her. I move aside, and she enters.

I close the door, lock it, and turn toward her. She's almost shaking.

"Jess, do you have anything where you used paints or something?" Sam asks, entering the room. She quickly slows down, unsure of the scene she's just walked into. "Hey, Mel."

"Hey," she says to Sam, quietly.

"Long time. Since Katie's party, I guess."

"Yeah."

"You look good."

"You, too."

"Right. Well. I was just leaving." I don't say anything. I just let Sam gather her purse and keys and walk past us to the door. "I'll see you tomorrow, Jess."

"Yeah," I respond.

"See ya, Mel."

"See ya."

Once the door's been closed, I lock it again and turn back to my sister who hasn't moved much since she's been here.

"I love my daughter," she says suddenly.

I immediately know what she's referring to, and my stomach drops slightly. "I know you do," I say.

"I mean, I know what I almost did, but I didn't do it. And if I had, that would've been my choice, but I didn't do it, so…. I would *never* hurt her."

"I know, Mel," I tell her, softly, nearly a whisper. I'm so ashamed of myself.

"I hated you for what you said."

"I know."

"Did you hate *me*?"

"Why would I?"

"Because I cut you off. Because I didn't take your call that night. Because I rubbed it in your face that you don't have children."

"I don't hate you. I've never *not* loved you."

She begins breathing quickly. I sense that tears are on the way, but they don't come. I'm almost relieved by that. "I'm sorry."

I cannot believe what I've heard. It's not right. I have to correct it. I say, "*I'm* sorry."

For the second time, I make the first move and walk up to Mel, throwing my arms around her. She responds instantly, and we hug for the first time in nearly three years. "Oh, God," I say. It feels amazing. She lets out a long sigh. The air suddenly feels easier to breathe. "Wow. You *have* been

working out," I tell her, which gets a laugh, and slowly, the shakes
dissipate.

"You, too," she says, and we both laugh.

We part and look at each other. We haven't been this close in so long.
We smile. Of course, we do. We never stopped being sisters, but this is the
first time in a long time that it feels like we actually are.

She's brought two pints of ice cream, including my favorite, strawberry.
I provide the spoons, and soon, we're on my couch watching old episodes
of *Dawson's Creek*.

"So, I hear you're back at the hospital."

"That was a while back."

"Oh, shit. Sorry."

"No, it's fine. Funny, actually."

"Why?"

"I quit today."

"You *quit*? Why?"

"They had me on probation, and I just couldn't handle the fact that I
probably couldn't be trusted the way I used to."

She nods.

"So?" I ask her.

"So?" she asks back, playfully.

"You're not going to ask me?"

"Ask you what?"

"What I plan to do now?"

"Oh, I know you don't have a plan."

"How do you figure?"

"Jess, I've known you literally my entire life. You've always wanted to be a surgeon. If you're not doing that, I don't know *what* you're doing. And, if *I* don't know what you're doing, neither do *you*."

"Geez, it's like we have twin telepathy going, except we're not twins."

She stifles a laugh, and then asks, "Do you get to keep your white coat and stethoscope?"

"Yeah, that's all mine."

"That's cool." After a moment, she's turns away from the TV, toward me, and asks, "Did you ever…play dress up with Thomas?"

"What do you mean?" I ask, intrigued.

"Well, Stephen wants to dress up and do some roleplay."

"He does not."

"Yeah."

"Oh my God."

"Yeah."

"Jesus. Well. Me and Thomas used to play doctor."

"Shut up."

"We did. I'd put on my scrubs and my white coat."

"And, what was he?"

"A patient."

"Oh, that's naughty."

"Oh, yeah. I'd take my stethoscope, and I'd -."

"I don't want to know!" she blurts.

We both burst out laughing, and it's great. I have not been this happy in a *long* time. That makes me feel a little bad, because it's not that Mel is the only one who can make me truly happy. It's just that she's been missing from my life for too long. And, now she's back, and I'm never letting her go.

We make a plan to tell Katie first. The rest of the family will come soon after. We'll arrive like it's no big deal and try to keep our faces straight while everyone gives us looks of shock and confusion.

I'm enthusiastic about being back in Mel's home, properly. Being able to hug and hold Katie, the way it should be, without knowing I shouldn't be there. Being able to talk with Stephen. He's such a decent guy. Mel got incredibly lucky when she found him.

We get to Mel's place a good half hour before she's got to go pick up Katie, so we nonverbally decide to hang out some more. She begins showing me around the house, and it really is as if I'm showing up here for the first time. Because it's been so long, there are so many new things everywhere. She starts by pointing out the living room set, which she says they got last summer. When we get to the hallway that leads to the bedrooms, she presents what has to be the centerpiece of the entire house. About two dozen framed-photos line the walls. More than half of them are for things I wasn't around for, like Katie in her school's production of *Beauty and the Beast*. She played Belle for one night, when the lead got sick and couldn't sing. Mel promises she'll show me the video of the performance.

There are two pictures of Mel, Katie, and Stephen at Universal Studios, looking as happy as ever. There is one of Haley in her graduation gown, holding up her diploma in victory. Maddie standing in front of the building where her publishing house was located – most likely her first day of work. I wasn't there, if memory serves. I was most likely in hour three of a surgery. There's Mom and Aunt Greta. I see birthdays and holidays. The more I look, the more down it gets me. I'm apparently nowhere to be seen, until I get to the end, and I see one of me with everybody. It's from Mom's 60th. Mel and I were civil that night, not really making much eye contact with one another and saying anything of value besides, "Hey," and, "See ya." One would never know that based on the faces in this picture. Still, I understand now just how apart I was from my sister's life. I want to leave right then and there, to be alone and process this, but Mel taps my shoulder.

I turn around.

"Come on," she says, gesturing me to enter a room. I follow her into what looks like half office space and half storage. She walks to a desk on one side. It's hers, obviously. Stephen's is on the other side and doesn't really look like it gets used much. Hers is filled with papers, post-it notes, and toys and trinkets. There are photos here, too, which she points out with a smile. "In case you were wondering where I keep you."

Sure enough, there are four photos of me hanging above and beside her computer. There's one of me holding Katie the day she was born. There's one of me on my wedding day. Thomas looks so handsome. There's another of me – maybe in high school – mid-laugh, trying to put a Cheeto in my mouth. I don't remember it, but I love the idea that Mel not only took the picture and kept it, but that she has it framed and hanging at her workspace.

The fourth one is of me and her, sitting on the grass, our arms holding our legs in, heads resting on one another's, smiling softly into the camera. I know this picture. Thomas took it for Mel. She wanted one of us that day, because she said we looked really cute. And we do. That was the day Mel told us she was pregnant with Katie. I remember hating myself because I was jealous. For reasons, we couldn't conceive. It was something I eventually came to accept, but at that point in my life – let's just say, I wanted to walk away, cry, and then come back and yell at her. I wanted to say, "How dare you?! How dare you have a kid?! Why would you rub this in my face?!" Even now, thinking about it, I find myself shaking my head.

"What's wrong?" Mel asks.

I decide to lie. It makes sense to. What point would it possibly serve to tell the truth? Besides, there's another thought that's entered my head. "I'm in here."

"Yeah, I know. The truth is, I removed you from the wall when…. I'd just started at that point, so I figured it was easy enough to just remove you. But then I realized just how much I love looking at you. So, I put you here. I'm in here a lot when Stephen and Katie aren't home. I love that picture." She points to the one of us side by side. "We look so happy. Like at peace, or something."

"Yeah, we do."

"It'd be cool to take a picture like that again one day."

"It's a plan," I say.

When Katie finally comes home, she abruptly stops the second she sees me in the kitchen. She looks apprehensive. Mel's led her in here. She looks to her. Mel smiles and nods. In one movement, she turns back toward me, drops her book bag, and runs to me, spreading her arms. I stand up and kneel, meeting her in an embrace.

It's different than the one I had with Mel. That was a long time coming. I've been hugging Katie all along. Well, except for those few months earlier this year. Regardless, what makes this special is that I'm able to do it openly, with my little sis here, and I realize for the first time in a long time, that I actually have a loving family who I love and who loves me in return.

"I missed you," she tells me.

"Oh, sweetie. Me, too."

We mean it. Even though we've kept touch on the down low, it wasn't *this*. The afternoon, inevitably, becomes the night, and when Stephen comes home, the four of us have dinner and watch a movie. Katie has school, but unsurprisingly, she finds it difficult to fall asleep. I sit with her, and we watch another movie on Mel's iPad. Soon, she drifts off, and I spend another hour with Mel and Stephen. We talk about nothing in particular, but I savor it all nonetheless.

Maddie

I feel relief when I arrive at Mom's for dinner and see Mel and Jess sitting next to one another and – so help me – laughing. But, apparently, my body feels differently, because I come to a slow stop and take in the scene before me. They turn to me, giving looks as if nothing big has happened.

"What?" Mel says, actually joking. For the briefest moment, a lump forms in my throat, as I realize just how much I've missed Mel. The person she's been for the past few years has *not* been her. I thought she was gone. She was just in emotional hibernation. At least from my perspective, which I grant isn't always reliable given my mixed feelings toward her. Maybe she never changed. Maybe she was right. Maybe I do just project onto her. I make a note to apologize for this sometime in the near future.

"Nothing," I finally say.

"Well, come in," Mom tells me, entering the dining room from the kitchen. "The food's ready. Jess and Mel brought Japanese."

"Yum," I say, taking my seat.

"I like your hair short," Jess tells me.

"Thanks. I thought Haley looked cute with it short, so I thought I'd try it."

"Maybe try not dyeing it anymore," Mel offers. *There she is*, I think.

"Oh, totally," Jess agrees. *What?!* "I like your dirty blonde hair."

"But -," I begin to say.

"I mean, there's nothing wrong with it like this. You're really pretty as a blonde…," Mel adds.

"We just like the way you look. No coloring. No makeup. Just you."

I turn to Mom who looks to be holding in laughter. *Great*, I think. "I think I liked it better when you two were fighting."

They all laugh, and even though I want to turn into mush and crawl away, I'm thankful that things are relatively back to normal.

So, yeah. I got my hair cut. Shoulder length. And, sure, Haley inspired it. But, so did my writer's block. Seriously – writing's tough. Getting started is fun, but over one hundred pages in…I can't stand what I'm coming up with. Over the past few weeks, ever since Mel read over what I wrote, actually said she liked it, and gave a few notes (all of which were spot on), I've been stuck on one particular chapter. It involves the moment Matt tells Jen that he loves her and that he's always loved her. It's not necessarily difficult. It's more that every time I write the scene it feels cliched. Which then causes me to continually re-evaluate what I've written and come to the conclusion that it's all shit. Mel notwithstanding, I'm probably right.

Or, maybe not.

I feel like I'm in the middle of the episode of *Stella*, where Michael, Michael, and David write a novel about three guys named Michael, Michael, and Craig. We get to see them writing during a hilarious, and hilariously true, montage which features them frustrated, ripping out pieces of pages, hating what they've written, declaring that the ideas have stopped flowing. True. All true.

I visit Angie during day six of this madness, and the first thing she asks me is, "How often do you write?"

"Every day," I tell her.

"No – how often *every day*?"

"Oh. Um. A few hours."

"How much do you get done?"

I shrug. "I don't know. I guess it depends."

"Depends on what."

"It depends on what I got going on that day."

"Maddie, you quit your job to write full-time. What the hell are you talking about? What else do you *do*?"

"I spend a lot of my time formulating my ideas."

"Uh-huh. Translation?"

"I spend it watching movies and TV."

"Oh my God." She takes a box of books from a stack beside her desk and leaves her office. I follow.

"I'm still working out. It's not like I'm living on my couch."

"Jesus."

"What?"

She sits the box down on the floor behind the front counter. "I could care less if you work out. Your body's not going anywhere anytime soon."

"For the record, I *have* gained about seven pounds."

"Heaven help you," she says sarcastically, heading back to her office.

"Alright, fine. Whatever. I'm dodging. Don't you want to know why I'm here?"

"You have writer's block."

"Right."

"Did I miss anything?"

"No."

She picks up another box. "So go home and write." She leaves her office again, and I follow – again.

"But I can't get past myself."

She puts the box down, sighing. Turning toward me, she says, "Why come to me?"

"Because I value your insight."

"You act like I can't spot your bullshit." She's off to her office once more. "Why are you *here*? Why *me*?"

I shrug again, following her. "Because I know you can, maybe, provide insight into what the characters are going through."

"You want to mine my experiences?"

"If you don't mind."

"Jesus, Mads. *Lead* with that." She picks up the last box, and I follow her to behind the counter one final time.

"I feel guilty. And not just of asking you about past stuff. I feel guilty all the time now. I mean, I write, and I hang around my place. All day. Every day. And it's great."

"Well, you've earned a chance to do this."

"I know. Still feel guilty, though. And now that I have this block…." I shake my head. "It's ridiculous."

She leans against one of the counters. "So, what do you need to know?"

I take a deep breath. "Promise you won't get mad."

"Sure."

"Promise."

She rolls her eyes. "Fine. Promise."

"Okay. I have a character who…I need to know what it's like to tell someone you love them – romantically – and not have them say it back or feel the same way you do."

"Oh. Okay."

"I'm sorry."

"No. It's cool. It's just – it's been awhile since I've thought about all that."

She doesn't say anything for a minute, seemingly putting together her thoughts and emotions. Someone comes in, and I greet her. Angie finally says something after the door has closed. She stands straight and looks at me. "It was like my entire body was sore and my mind was exhausted."

I don't know what to say. I swallow and manage, "Okay then."

"I loved him. More than I thought I ever could. And it *was* love. I know that. And when he told me that he didn't see me that way, that I'd always be his friend, I hated myself. I didn't hate *him*. I wanted to be someone else entirely. Someone he *could* love. And I hated that, too."

"Man…."

"Yeah. Hate piled on hate, piled on love. And like that, we weren't friends anymore."

"I never asked, but…what *did* happen with you two?"

"I stopped wanting to hang out with him. I made it weird, and I ruined it. He was actually a pretty good guy. Did his best to spare my feelings."

"Do you still love him?"

She smiles, sad. "Yeah, I think so."

"I'm sorry."

She shrugs. "It's okay. Interesting to know that's still a part of me."

Later, after we've talked more, and I've left knowing her spirits were back up where they belong, I make my way to see Mel – we have lunch in her office. I've brought Panera. As she tears into her sandwich, I take a look around, still impressed she has her own office and not a cubicle. I'm jealous in the best way.

"This office is so cool."

"Can't complain."

As I unwrap my own sandwich, I say, "I wanted to ask something."

"Mm-hmm," she tells me, chewing.

"I went to Angie earlier and got her to sort of relive something I know was painful for her. It's for my book. I mean, she said she was fine telling me. But, then, when she actually told me, she looked really bad. I think I made her feel better, but I can't help I've brought things up I shouldn't have. And for a stupid book nonetheless."

"Well, I don't think your book's stupid. Otherwise, why spend your time on it? And, as for Angie, she's a big girl. She'll be fine."

"I mean, I know she *will* be. That's not the problem."

"Guilt?"

"Yeah."

She nods. "It happens. Decent people feel guilty."

"Good to know I'm – at the very least – decent."

"Well, nobody's perfect," she tells me, barely able to contain her smile.

"Can I just say it's nice to see you…relaxed?"

"You mean, you're happy that me reuniting with Jess has made me happier. That I'm back to myself again."

"Well, not in so many words."

"I'm not dumb. I know how I've been. I hated it. But my stupid pride, or whatever the hell it was, prevented me from just accepting Jess' stupid apology."

"Man, I tell you. Sometimes I think back to Katie's birthday party…."

"Please don't."

"Can you imagine if Jess' punch had landed?"

"Well, it would've been a sucker punch, and I probably would've gone down."

"Would you have gotten back up?"

"And fought her?"

"I'm just asking."

She considers this for a brief moment and then: "I don't know. Probably."

"Wow. You were really angry."

"I was holding on to the anger and hurt I felt years ago. It wasn't healthy. And I don't need Mom's psychiatrist-expertise to tell me that."

"Well, I'll stop bringing it all up." I pick up my lemonade and raise. "A toast." She lifts her sweet tea. "To sisters." She smiles. We toast.

"So, what did you want to see me about exactly?"

"Oh, just wanted to hang out. Being out of work has given me quite a bit of time, and although I know I should be working, I'm also taking advantage."

"Good girl. As long as you have your priorities laid out."

"I do. Mom."

She gives me a look, tempered by the smirk on her lips.

"Sorry," I tell her.

"I know, I know. I'm not Mom."

"I like it. From my point of view, that's just you being my sister. It's the only version of you I've ever really known. I have vague memories of you before Dad left, but they don't seem all that different than the ones after. Except maybe you were more of an 'adult.'"

"I've always seen you and Haley as kids. Just like a mom would, I guess."

"You think Jess sees you that way?"

She shrugs. "I don't know. I don't think so."

I nod. "I always thought you two were best friends."

"Yeah. It's weird, though, you know. How we all have our own specific relationships with one another."

"Yeah, weird but…kinda cool."

"I'll second that."

We toast for good measure. She goes back to her food, and without a second thought I suddenly tell her, "I'm sorry about how I acted at the hospital." She looks up at me, her face the complete opposite of just a few seconds ago. "I didn't mean what I said."

She swallows. "It's okay."

"It isn't," I say, almost at a whisper.

"You were upset about Jess. We all were."

"Yeah, but that doesn't excuse -."

"Well, how about how I grabbed your arm and -."

"Okay," I say, realizing I'm not too eager to relive anything from that night. I take a deep breath and add, "Fair enough."

Mel puts a hand on one of mine and lifts her glass again with the other, saying something that catches me a little off guard. "To your book," she says earnestly.

I don't say anything, which she seems to find amusing, a smirk slowly forming on her lips. I lift my glass to meet hers. She clinks it and says, "Cheers."

We drink, and I know right then that Mel and I are going to be all right.

I take Angie to go see *Band of Outsiders* at the Paramount. Haley loves the movie. I think it's okay. Afterward, Angie can't stop talking about the "dance sequence," as she calls it. She seems to be in good spirits.

"Hey, I wanted to thank you for earlier," she tells me once I've pulled out of the parking lot.

"Really?"

"Yeah. I mean, it could've happened at a better time than while I was at work, but…I don't know. It made me feel better."

"Huh. Well. You're welcome."

We end up at a small Italian place. Angie recommended it, and I'm glad. The food rocks, and I make a note to bring Jess here, because I know she'd appreciate it.

"It's weird how we move on – or we think we've moved on. You know?" I say.

She nods.

"I think about my dad every now and then. Most days I don't. With no effort, really. I just don't think about him. But when I do – I don't know – I feel all of these emotions. But I get through it, and – yeah – I guess I do feel better."

"We were loved and left."

"I suppose so. I honestly have no idea how Jess and Mel and my mom deal with it."

She finishes her water and looks around for the waiter.

I consider something I haven't thought about before, but I feel the urge to bring it up without much thought. "You ever think of hiring someone to take care of your store?"

"What do you mean?"

"Well, like today. We had our usual hang-out at the bookstore. But we could've had it elsewhere. If you had someone there."

"I don't want anyone else there."

"Well, maybe not now, but eventually you're gonna get tired of it. Aren't you?"

She seems to shrug without actually doing it. "I don't think so."

"Really?"

"Yeah. I love it."

I'm not sure what to think or do at that precise moment. I see that she's telling the truth and that she's peaceful. The waiter comes by and fills her glass. I'm having tea, so he goes to get it. When he's gone, Angie says, "You okay?"

"Hmm?"

"You're staring off into space. Deep in thought?"

"Um. Yeah."

"About what?"

"How can you be so sure you're doing what you want to do?"

"Well, because even when I have a bad day, it feels good to still be doing it. That bookstore – even if I'm forced to close it one day due to bad sales – I'm gonna love it."

"That's awesome."

"You feel that way about your writing?"

I think about the novel I'm currently writing. It's been fun, but it's also been a bit safe. Truth be told, there's another novel I want to write, but for whatever reason, I'm scared to do it. Maybe it's too personal. I don't know. "Sometimes," I say.

"Why sometimes?"

"Because sometimes I'm not writing what I really want to."

"That's silly. You quit your job to write. You should write what you want."

"Even if it ends up being a waste of time and doesn't sell?"

"Yeah. Whether it wins the Pen Award or ends up inspiring over a hundred rejected query letters. If that happens, you go back to work. You pay the bills. But you can always write. And when you do, you write what you want to write."

"That's happiness, huh?"

"It could be," she says. "What's happiness to you?"

I feel like I should know the answer. But I don't.

Haley

Finals aren't even here, but they're already kicking my ass. Plus, I'm pretty sure my Chemistry professor hates me. Serves me right for taking

246

Chemistry in the first place. I should've taken Geology, like Nicole did. She told me to take it, too. But Jess went off this past summer, talking about how much she loved it and that I should give it a shot. I'll be lucky to get a C. Thanks, sis!

In fairness, I was interested. It's not like anyone forced me to take the class. Still, sitting here in this library desk-slash-cubicle thing-y, studying for this final, is making me re-think my entire existence. Never mind that I probably knocked my English and Political Science finals out the park. This one is going to be the end of me. At least I had the good sense to take Music Appreciation this semester. Learning about Rock n' Roll was kind of fun, and the final exam is going to be 25 multiple choice questions. I should do fine.

But this class. This final exam. Ugh.

I take a break and send Dani a text, asking her what's going on. She replies a few minutes later, after I've gotten something to eat, and I'm now seated on this bench beneath a tree, hoping no birds poop on me or my sandwich. "thinking of u," she writes back. I blush, knowing it's bullshit, but liking Dani's playfulness. I write back, "I'm thinking of u too."

She sends me back a picture of her blowing a kiss to me, her eyes closed, and lips puckered. She has blue streaks in her hair now. They look good. I consider sending her a picture of me here but know there's no way

I can pull off her natural charisma. Instead, I write, "cutie. Is it weird that I

miss u?"

"it'd be weird if u didn't," she replies. ":)…when are u coming home?"

"I'll be home in about a week and a half."

"that's too long. can I come and see u tomorrow?"

I freeze. Is she serious? All semester long, we've texted a few times a

week, but nothing like her visiting has ever been suggested by either of us.

I'm unsure how to reply. I mean, maybe she's joking. I take too long, and

she eventually writes, "I want to say I'm joking but im not."

I take a deep breath. *Yes or no?* I ask myself. I write, "yes."

She writes back, "see u tomorrow afternoon ;)"

What the hell have I done?

I'm in love with the girl who broke my heart. Dani and I met at the start

of junior year in AP English. We'd seen each other around but had never

spoken a word to one another. During the first week of class, Monique –

the student council president and first in our class – approached me as I

waited for my mom to pick me up after school one day. She suggested that

I join one of the after-school clubs to meet new people. Being as persuasive as she was, I told her I'd join the Spirit Committee. When I arrived the following day, no one seemed to want to acknowledge my existence. Still, I tried my best to help out with a banner. When it seemed like I was just kidding myself, I gathered my things and left. The next day, Monique asked why I'd left, and I told her the truth. "One more day," she told me. That afternoon, I tried again.

She was there this time, along with a girl named Danielle. I managed to actually help a little, but I soon let Monique know that this wasn't for me. "We're always here," she told me. I never attended another after-school club again.

On that Friday, my AP English teacher got us to get in groups of three. Dani asked me if I wanted to join her and her friend Jim's group. I figured, why not? Instantly, she acted like we were good friends. Jim seemed to follow her lead. We wouldn't talk much before or after class, but he was always nice to me. Dani, though, for whatever reason, *did* hang out with me. Not that I didn't have other friends, all whom I'd find out were friends with her. "How did we never meet before now?" she asked me a few weeks into our friendship. It was a question neither of us ever found an answer to.

Dani was an extrovert, which seemed to blend with my introverted personality. She got me to speak up more, attend the Homecoming football game, and go out on the weekends, instead of watching movies alone in my room.

"Favorite movie?" I asked her one day.

"Hmm. I like a lot of different stuff."

Me too, I thought.

"I guess my favorites would be *Say Anything…*, *Scarface*, *The Usual Suspects*, *The Godfather*, and *Akira*."

Who *was* this girl?

Just before the start of Christmas break, she gave me a gift – a book of movie bloopers, which I loved – and a kiss on the cheek. We both knew the other liked girls, but I'd never really considered going with someone like her. Because here's the thing: I'm not unattractive. I have a good-looking family. But Dani is a dream girl. She has olive skin, blue-green eyes, dark brown hair that changes slightly when it's sunny outside, a great butt, and a stomach that's…yeah. Well, that's the superficial stuff. She's also incredibly eclectic. Her taste in movies isn't a fluke. She loves to read, listens to all kinds of music, likes to go out and dance, talks to everyone, seemingly always has a job to do, was eighth in our class, and –

at that time – had a girlfriend, who was in college. Still, when she gave me that kiss, I realized I wanted more from our relationship.

I wrote her a note explaining my feelings, wondering if she felt the same. I gave it to her, as well as an awkward kiss on the cheek, which made her laugh. I felt dumb having done it. She texted me that night. Even though that phone is long gone, I still have the screenshot. This is what she wrote:

"haley you're the coolest person I've ever met. I never knew you felt this way. I guess I never told you that me and Ronnie broke up almost two weeks ago. It hurt but I guess I'm too good at hiding my feelings. anyway yeah we should do something before Christmas don't you think? text me an idea. I think maybe we should try it." It was followed by a kiss emoji.

We ended up going to see a movie. Afterward, we kissed. Nothing was ever "official," but we were a couple. And we did couple things. And she was the one I lost my virginity to. And she was the one I took to prom. And she was the one I said "I love you" to for the first time to anyone outside my family. She was the one.

And then we weren't together. And then I went to college. And then I came back home and played a part in her and Sasha's movie. And now we've reconnected. And now she's coming to see me.

I love this girl. Always will. But what the hell am I going to do?

"You should get ready. Shave or wax, maybe buy a new underwear, -."

"Whoa – we're not having sex."

"Sure."

"We're not. She's just coming here to see me."

"And have sex." Before I can think of something to say, Nicole continues, passing me by and patting me on the shoulder as she heads for the dresser. "But don't worry. I'll sleep at Myra's tonight." She's packing stuff for an overnight stay. It's blowing my mind. Sex was not something that was on my radar concerning Dani's visit.

"Holy shit," I realize. "We're gonna have sex."

She stifles a laugh. "Well, not if you don't want to."

"Oh, I want to."

She laughs.

"Oh, man. I was just thinking she wanted to see me." I sit on my bed carefully. "What do I do? I mean, it's *her*."

"I don't know. Just don't do it on my bed, please. It's more cushion-y, but don't let that motivate you to do it there." She's playing around, but it feels like shit is getting real. Of course, it's entirely possible and plausible that Dani really *is* just visiting – nothing more. But if sex is implied, and I would definitely be up for it, well, that complicates things, doesn't it? I mean, would being with her mean we're back together? Does *she* want to get back together? Do *I*?

I go ahead and take a hot shower so I can shave as best I can. It's not waxing, but it's the best I can do for my time and money. Then it's onto my underwear, which I'll have to settle for in lieu of lingerie, which I don't have. I decide on a set of white and lavender that I've only worn a couple of times. I put it all on and adjust. *I look good*, I think. I don't overdo it on the hair and makeup and end up wearing jeans and a sweatshirt. Screw it. I like the way I look in this. I can pull it off.

"I'm here," she texts, nearly a half-hour early. I anticipated this. Dani is a lot of things, but she's not someone who shows up late. It's mostly a good thing, though it can suck when you've thrown her an eighteenth birthday party and a few people show up at the last minute, meaning that they show up long after we've yelled, "Surprise!"

I meet her outside and bring her in. It's still afternoon, so visitors are more than welcome to be in the building. I point out a few things to her as we make our way to the fourth floor. As I unlock the door to my dorm, she sniffs my hair. "Yum," she says. "I like cucumber." We enter, and I close the door and lock it.

She tosses her bag on my bed and flops down on it, taking a deep breath. "Ah. You smell good," she says rubbing her face on my comforter.

"Thanks," I respond.

Dani turns to her side and holds her head up with her right arm, posing almost. She gives the room a quick look around and nods. "Nice. A lot smaller than I thought it'd be."

I nod.

She lies down on her back. Neither of us say anything for about a minute. And then, she turns my way and says, "I'm hungry. Wanna get something to eat?"

I'm not prepared for that. The panties I'm currently wearing aren't really the most practical outside of wanting someone to see you in them. They're clearly made to be worn for a few minutes and then removed, spending most of their life on the floor or in a drawer. But food actually sounds great. And, I want to spend time with Dani, more than anything really. We go to the food court, which is being set up for Open-Mic Night. There are about a dozen people there.

"Have you seen the trailer to *Portrait of a Lady on Fire*?" she asks me.

"Oh, *hell* yeah. Looks freakin' good."

"Sucks we have to wait until February, but whatever."

I smile in agreement.

"I just finished reading *Frankenstein*, by the way. Oh my God, it's so good."

"Told you."

"It's so much better than any of the movies." I'm going to say something, but she says it for me. "Except for *Bride of Frankenstein*."

"Of course," I agree.

"Seen anything good lately?" she asks, as we get our food.

"Well, there's this film club here. We meet once a week and watch something and then talk about it. Last year we watched Ingmar Bergman's best. This year, we're watching the *Sight & Sound* top ten."

"Oh, nice."

"Yeah. A lot of them I've only seen once, so it's cool seeing some of that stuff projected onto a big screen."

"We should watch something."

"Sure. What do you want to watch?"

She motions to the makeshift stage at the far end and asks, "What's that?"

"Open-Mic Night."

"Ever done it?"

"*Hell* no."

"Oh, come on. I know you play some guitar."

"No thanks."

"For me?" she asks.

I'm not feeling it, but I say, "We'll see."

That's good enough for her. Dani takes a bite from her burger, confident enough to not care as her hands get messy. I, on the other hand, hate eating in front of people. I'm too self-conscious. I carefully eat my own burger, plain of course, and Dani snickers.

"I like the way you eat," she says.

I cover my mouth and respond. "The way I eat?"

She laughs. "You're so freaking cute."

"What?"

She mimics covering her own mouth and says, "What?" She laughs some more.

I smile. "Whatever."

"I do, though. I like the way you eat."

"I like the way you laugh."

She gives me a wink.

After we've eaten our fast food, I go to the bathroom. When I return, Dani's beaming. "What?" I ask.

"Please welcome to the stage, Haley B."

There's light applause. My mouth slowly drops open, and I look at Dani, who raises her eyebrows, basically saying to me, "Well?" I manage to stand and make my way to the stage. I pick up a guitar that sits next to a few instruments meant for anyone who comes up here and then sit on a stool that's been placed in front of the mic.

"Hey," I say into it. It's weird hearing my dumb voice. I want to scream and run, but I see Dani in the back, who's now standing, hands in her pockets. I look back to the guitar and quickly tune it as best I can. "Okay. So. This is one of the few songs I know how to play. Hopefully, it's not God-awful."

"Whoo!" Dani calls out from the back. This makes me smile, even as a few in the audience, which has grown since earlier, look back to see who made the sound.

"Okay," I sigh. Then, I begin to play David Bowie's "Absolute Beginners." I sing it to Dani, and it's pretty damn romantic. When I'm done, there's more applause than before. I get off stage as fast as I can without seeming like a dork.

"Can I be your groupie?" Dani asks me.

"Shut up."

We take showers, and she gets comfortable. I do, too…a little. I feel uncomfortable in the bra now. It's meant to enhance my boobs, since I have c-cups that don't even look like c-cups. It's tight and it's pushing things up that aren't really made to be pushed up. I want to just take it off, but I put it and the matching panties back on after the shower just in case.

On comes the movie. Dani takes the bed, which is more than okay. I sit on the front side, my butt resting on a pillow, my back against the bed. I have to look up and to the left whenever I want to face her. I notice right away that even from this angle she's gorgeous. I mean, even with a pimple below her chin that's really only visible from this angle she's great looking.

"Oh, I bet Felicity Jones smells so good," she says.

I want to laugh. "What?"

"Look at her. She looks so soft. Don't you want to hug her and smell her?"

"I guess," I say, sort of getting it.

She gets the remote and puts the volume down, and then gets off the bed and sits beside me. "Where's your roommate?"

"She's staying at a friend's place."

"Oh yeah?"

"Yeah."

"We're alone all night?"

"Yeah. Why?"

She shrugs and looks back at the TV.

"Really?"

"What?" she asks, oh-so-innocent.

I scoff and shake my head. We both turn our attention back to the movie. Dani turns the volume back up. We actually finish it. As the credits roll, she stands, pulling her yoga pants up as she does. I can't help but to check her out.

"Like the view?"

I look up, and she's smirking at me.

She holds out a hand, and I take it.

"Hi," she says, not more than three inches from me.

"Hey," I manage. She just keeps looking at me. After a few moments, she smiles wide, bright. We move in for a kiss.

It's amazing. There are no fireworks. That's past. This kiss is familiar. Like home. We pull away, each looking at the other, trying our best to decipher what that meant. I kiss her again, this time more passionately, and she reciprocates. We begin to undress ourselves and then each other. Within seconds we're on my bed, though it doesn't feel like we're rushing it. Dani has completely undressed me. We kiss, but I stop the momentum to remove the rest of Dani's clothes. This has happened so fast I want to laugh at myself for spending the time I did on my underwear. Dani is on top of me, her upper thigh between my legs. We somehow finish before the credits end. I pull her closer. It's never been that good. Even when we were together. She delicately pushes the hair away from my face.

"I love your eyes," she tells me.

"I love your everything," I say.

We do it a few more times and fall asleep side by side.

In the morning, I wake up, having come to my senses a little. I look to my right and Dani's still asleep, her visible breasts rising and falling. I cover them up and try to get out of bed, so I can pop in the contacts I took out when she wasn't looking last night before we fell asleep together, but I just end up slipping and falling on her.

"Oh, shit," I say.

She giggles. "Good morning."

"Sorry."

"Not a bad way to wake up." She gives me a quick kiss before I lie back down. We don't say anything, completely comfortable in the silence.

A question looms. One I've wanted to ask for so long. And now that we're growing close again, I need to know. So, I roll onto my side and ask it. "Why did you break up with me?"

For a brief moment, she's caught off guard, but she recovers, probably because she knows the answer. "Because you were going to leave me."

What? I think. "I wasn't leaving you."

"Yes, you were. You were going to college, and you were leaving town and by extension me."

"I didn't...Dani, I didn't know."

"Well, you were so excited."

"I was."

"It's okay. I get it now. It wasn't about me. When I dumped you...that was selfish. I'm sorry."

I've wanted an apology for so long, but having finally gotten it, it doesn't feel all that good. I return to lying on my back.

"Should I leave?" she asks. She sounds hurt.

"If you want to." *Why the hell did I just say that?* I think. She looks at me, visibly shocked, and then throws the covers off. "Wait. I didn't mean that."

She begins to dress. "Oh, what did you mean?"

"I don't know. Not that, though. Please stay."

I watch her put on her pants and then her bra. As she's putting on her shirt, I say, "Dani." The shirt comes down, and she gives me a look of apprehension, almost as if she wants me to keep talking. I don't know what to say. Eventually, I just end up saying, "Stay," again.

She sits down, her eyes looking down at her hands, which play with one another. She sighs. I move next to her, wanting so bad to see her face. She looks up and me, her eyes smiling. We kiss.

"Let's get some breakfast."

She nods. "Sounds good."

On the way out, I try to grab my contact case from my desk and end up knocking some stuff over, revealing my glasses. Dani sees them, and for a moment seems to think they're Nicole's, but I can see her putting things together. This is clearly *my* desk and *my* stuff that's been knocked over. As she picks up the glasses, I hold my breath, trying to figure out what to say when she asks about them.

But she doesn't say anything. She puts them on me, very carefully, lightly pushing them up my nose once the arms are behind my ears. She nods, as if now they're back where they belong. I want to float away from this world with her.

I'm in love with this girl. And, I'm pretty sure she's in love with me. And she makes me feel like I can do anything. I'm happy she stayed.

Katie

Mom's been in a good mood lately. Aunt Maddie tells me it's because Aunt Jess is in the picture again, and I agree. Jess actually hangs out here a lot more now, like she used to. She even picks me up a few times a week when Mom and Dad are too busy. She was over to help decorate for Christmas a few days ago. Now that I'm off on break, I get to see her every day. One day, while my mom's on her way home, we decide to watch an old episode of *Grey's Anatomy*. "Don't tell your mom," Jess tells me. She's awesome like that. The thing is, when I ask her if she can maybe take me to work, I think she's going to say that she has to ask Mom, but instead she says, "I don't think so, hun."

"Why not?" I ask. I'm confused. She said that one day she'd take me to see her office and show me around. Now that I'm ten and her and Mom are talking again, isn't that the perfect time? "Mom would let me go."

"No," she says like she wants to say more. She's not looking at me anymore and seems a little sad all of the sudden.

"She could come with us."

"It's not that."

"Then what?"

She takes a deep breath and finally looks at me. "I don't work at the hospital anymore."

"You got fired?"

"No. I quit."

"Why?"

"Because…I wasn't happy there anymore."

I don't want Aunt Jess to be unhappy. It makes me worried. "Are you sad?"

"Well, not right now," she says, getting happy. "I'm with you."

"But sometimes?"

Her smile slowly goes away. She nods. "Sometimes." She starts to play with my hair. "But everybody feels sad sometimes. Don't you?"

"I guess."

"It doesn't necessarily mean anything. Besides, I don't work there anymore. So, I'm no longer sad when I go to work – because I don't have a job."

"But don't you *want* a job?"

"Um…huh. I don't know. I know what I love. I love slicing people open and helping them. I also love making food and reading. I love spending time with *you*. And friends. And the rest of the family – obviously." She says that last part super-close to me, which always makes me laugh. "I'll find work again. Right now, I just want to focus on the things that make me happy. I'm lucky."

"Do you miss Uncle Thomas?

"I do. Every single day."

"Does it make you sad that he's gone?"

She sits up and really seems to think this over. She's treating my question seriously, which makes me feel good about asking it.

"Sometimes."

"But not right now?"

"Not right now."

Mom and I go shopping for last minute gifts, "before Haley arrives and the family starts hanging out so much that it becomes more difficult to get shopping like this gone," she tells me. We go through the mall, doing our best to buy clothes for Haley.

"Your youngest aunt doesn't really like buying clothes. So, we're getting her some for Christmas."

"I don't like doing it either."

"Well, we all need clothes. You're not going to walk around in public naked, are you?"

"Gross."

"Exactly. Plus, she doesn't have a whole lot of money. She's got scholarships and grants, and we help her out, but she doesn't have cash to just spend on new clothes. Knowing her, she's been wearing the same pair of jeans all semester."

"So, we're buying her new jeans?"

"New jeans, a few t-shirts, and a nice dress."

"Haley looks nice when she dresses up."

"Everyone does."

We go to Forever 21, which is so cool, but Mom seems to want to get out of there quickly. We buy a pair of cute jeans and move on.

"Mom?"

"Mm-hmm?"

"When you turned 21, what did you do?"

"21? Well, I was probably babysitting Haley while your grandmother was working late trying to provide for us."

"Because grandpa left?"

"That's right."

"That sucks."

"It wasn't so bad."

"So, you didn't go out and party or something?"

"At that point, I was sort of over that kind of thing."

"But you just turned 21."

"That's right."

"So, you were *just* old enough to start drinking."

"Oh – um…well…uh – you can party without drinking. I meant that I was over leaving the house and partying with friends. I didn't drink until I was 21."

"Right." I drop it as we decide to try a department store for the dress.

Haley's not the tallest person in the family. She's also not the shortest if you count me. She's 5'2" and likes wearing sneakers. She has pretty nice legs when she feels like showing them off, but as Mom points out, a short dress isn't something up Haley's alley, whatever that means.

"But, obviously, it can't be long, because I doubt she'd want that either."

"Not too tight, too."

"That's right. Haley hates body-cons."

I spot a light summer dress and walk up to it. I run the soft fabric between my fingers and then step back to get a good look of it. The dress isn't really Haley's style, but I like it. I wonder if maybe Mom could buy it for me for the future.

"Katie?" I hear her call.

"I'm here," I say, raising my hand. She comes over and stands beside me, holding a nice black dress.

"Cute," she says.

"I like it a *lot*."

"It suits you."

"I wish I could wear it."

"We can find something for you."

"I wish I was taller."

"Then you'd be older than you are now."

"Then I want to be older."

"No, you don't."

"Well, I want to be taller."

"Sweetie, you're only ten. You have plenty of time to grow."

"What age were *you* when you stopped growing?"

"I guess…sixteen?"

"And Haley?"

She hesitates and then says, "Fifteen."

"I have five years."

"What's wrong with not being tall? The tallest woman in our family is Maddie, and she's only 5'10"."

"Maddie looks like a model."

"Oh, I'll be sure to mention *that* to her," she says, sounding amused, I think.

"I don't like being shorter than everyone else."

"Are you being bullied?"

I sigh hard. "No, Mom."

"Because you can *always* tell me," she says, as I walk away from the dress to see what else this store has.

"I'm not being bullied. I just don't like being short. I look like I'm eight."

"Oh-*kay*."

"That's a difference!"

"Of course. You're right. It is."

My shoulders slump. She doesn't get it.

"Come on. I found your aunt something." I mentally say goodbye to the dress and walk away with Mom to the registers. She holds up the dress. "Like it? It's simple. It's black."

"She'll love it."

We pay and end up in the food court. As I begin to dig into my waffle fries, Mom puts her shoulders on her side of the table and says, "Sorry for earlier."

"For what?" I ask, confused.

"I worry about you. Sorry – but I'm your mom. I'm always going to worry about you. So, I jumped to you being bullied. I wasn't really listening. But while we were waiting in line, I got to thinking about what you said. You think you're short."

"I am."

"For a ten-year-old?"

"For my age, yeah."

"I was your height when I was eleven."

"You were not."

"Mm-hmm. Ask Jess or grandma. I was a short, scrawny little thing until eighth grade. And then I grew to be taller than my older sister."

"Dad's tall, too."

"Exactly. It's in your genes. Just give it some time. You'll grow."

"I hope so."

"And, so, what if you don't? You think Maddie's had a better life than Haley just because she's almost a foot taller than her?"

I don't know how to answer that. It must look like it, too, because Mom continues without me answering.

"She hasn't. Right now, Maddie is thirty. She quit her job that she was really good at to see if she could do what she actually loves. Haley isn't really sure what she wants to do with her life. No one has it any better than anybody else."

"Fair enough," I say. Mom smirks.

"I should also apologize for the past few years."

"What do you mean?"

"Katie, if I've ever been mean or cold or anything but loving to you, I'm sorry. If I ever made you feel anything but loved, I'm sorry." Her voice breaks, and she looks down at her food, pretending to sort it out.

"Mom," I tell her, not knowing how to continue.

"No." She shakes her head and looks back at me. "It's okay. It really is. This whole mess with your Aunt Jess. I hope it didn't hurt my relationship *you*."

"It didn't."

"I hope so."

"Mom, I know you love me."

She smiles, her eyes getting watery. I feel like I want to cry, too, but neither of us do. She reaches across the table, and we intertwine our fingers. Her hands are so much bigger than mine. "I will *always* love you," she says.

I know that. I *knew* that. But I can't help but feel annoyed with her sometimes. Or bored. Other times, I want her around. Period. I don't know why I feel these different things, but I do. I guess it *could* be a part of growing up. I make a note to ask Haley and Maddie about it.

When Aunt Haley comes home a few days later, everyone acts like it's no big deal that Aunt Jess is here. When she comes in, Mom and Jess pretend to laugh at a nonexistent joke. I hold in my laughter as best I can and watch to see what happens. Haley – who's wearing her glasses now, which she looks cute in – freezes, unsure of what to do.

Then, someone else enters the kitchen. A pretty girl who bounces in, all smiles. "Hey," she says with a wave.

I look at everyone at the table – Mom, Aunt Jess, Aunt Maddie, grandma, and Greta – and they all freeze like Haley did. I have no idea what's going on until Maddie speaks up.

"Hi, Dani," she says.

Everyone's pleasant with everyone, but there's this real awkwardness in the air. I remember the family talking about Dani a while back. I know she used to go out with aunt Haley until she broke her heart. But then why is she here? Maybe *that's* why the family doesn't know what to do or say, other than things like "please" and "thank you."

Mom starts things off by asking about school. Haley tells her that finals went pretty well and that she's sure she at least got B's in every class, except Chemistry.

"Oh, really?" asks aunt Jess. "I *loved* Chemistry."

Dani smiles. She has the biggest dimples I've ever seen. "I was telling her that grades are important, but ultimately, it's what you get out of a class that matters."

"This coming from someone not in college," Haley adds.

Dani playfully bumps her and says, "I went to school. I had teachers. I took classes."

"She's right," my mom tells Aunt Haley. "I had this one professor who never gave me an A, even though I loved his classes. He'd always say, 'I'm not an easy A, but I am an easy B.' Or, my favorite, 'I don't give grades. You earn 'em.' I kept taking his classes because I learned so much and he was cool."

"Well, *this* professor was *not* cool. She was cold and distant. I was never able to talk to her about anything. Her office hours were crap – sorry, Katie – and she never answered my emails. Frankly, I'm amazed I'll be getting a C."

"So, no Chemistry?" Jess asks.

"Sorry, sis. Not for me. Guess I'm still technically and literally undeclared."

"You'll find it," grandma tells her. "Take your time. You're not even twenty yet."

A few whoops and hollers from most of the family immediately follow. Dani smiles again and puts a hand on Haley's shoulder, who looks embarrassed. "Someone's almost not a teenager anymore," Aunt Maddie yells.

"Yeah, yeah," Haley says, sheepishly.

Dani kisses her on the cheek.

Haley points to her and says, "Oh, yeah. We're back together."

"Well, congratulations!" Maddie yells over a new batch of sounds from everyone.

Mom doesn't look as happy as everyone else, but she joins in, eventually relaxing. She catches me looking and gives me a wink. I'm happier that my mom's my mom than I've ever been, and I hold onto that feeling for as long as I can, until it's time for ice cream.

As the evening begins to die down, grandma says she's got an announcement. When she says it, I see different reactions from everybody. Mom gets quiet. Jess looks angry, almost. Maddie looks a little unsure. Haley looks almost like she's waiting for something. Greta looks sad.

Grandma's got her poker face on. Dani looks around, confused. She turns to Haley and asks, "What's wrong?"

Jess wipes her mouth and throws her napkin on her empty plate.

Mom tells me the problem before I go to bed later that night.

Part Five: Christmas with Dad

<u>Katie</u>

Mom's dad is coming to have dinner with the family on Christmas Eve. She's been quiet. Dad talked to me about it a little. Grandpa wants to have dinner. With his family. I'm, apparently, not invited. Dad told me that it's for the best. Grandpa's not the most reliable person, and Mom's still hurting from him leaving when she was seventeen after he and Grandma got divorced. A few months after Haley turned one.

A few days after Haley's winter homecoming, I ask Dad if Jess is okay. I'm worried about her, because she was so sad after Uncle Thomas died. If *Mom's* acting like this, I'm sure Aunt Jess is, too. He tells me to video chat with her and see, so I do.

Jess is hanging out with Haley, and things look to be good.

"I hope Grandpa's not getting you down."

"Oh, forget about that. I am. No worries, 'kay, Katie?"

"Okay."

She blows me a kiss and turns her phone to Haley who waves wildly. I giggle.

After the call, I'm feeling much better, but I go to Mom to see if I can cheer her up. The second she sees me, she brightens up. "Hey."

I sit down next to her on the couch. She's been watching a lot of TV after work, but when I look at her, she doesn't seem to be paying attention to whatever show is on.

"Are you okay?"

"Of course, I am."

"Not really. You've looked sad the past few days."

"I'm just tired, is all."

"Are you sure?"

"Yes. No worries."

"You're not upset about Grandpa coming?"

She gets quiet again and her glow lessens. "Maybe a little. We don't...get along all that well."

"Because he left Grandma and you guys?"

Mom turns toward the kitchen where Dad's doing the dishes. She seems to be thinking of something. Nothing is said, and she turns back to me. "Yeah."

"Is that why Maddie sometimes calls you 'mom'? Because you helped raise her?"

"Yeah. I think so."

"That's kinda cute."

"It is. I like it."

I nod and ask something that's been on my mind for a day or so. "How many times have I met Grandpa?"

Mom looks like she wants to cry but doesn't. She swallows and tells me, "Twice."

"Just twice?"

"Well, he lives across the country. It's not like he has a private jet and can just come see us whenever he wants."

"Was he here when I was born?"

"Um…no. But he was here when you turned one. And a few years ago. Around your fifth birthday."

Oh, yeah, I think.

"You remember that."

"Yeah. He had a beard."

"That's right."

I feel weird. There's two parts of me. One wants to see him. The other doesn't like him and wants to avoid him at all costs. I wonder if Mom feels the same.

Mom takes me to Angie's bookstore and tells me I can get two books for an early Christmas. When we go in, we say "hi" to Hebah, who is so cool. Like Aunt Jess and Aunt Maddie, sort of, but she has pretty skin like Dani's. She's arranging a special "Christmas Table," so I go off searching, browsing beyond the children's section, venturing into young adult and the sci-fi/fantasy section. Mom goes up to the counter and talks with Angie. A few minutes later, Aunt Maddie arrives, and after saying hi to me and ruffling my hair, to my amusement, she and Mom go into the non-fiction section and talk. They're not whispering or talking low – I can make out tones, mostly. Maddie seems upset, and Mom nods a lot, eventually cutting her off by saying something that seems to surprise – or maybe hurt? – Maddie. I see Mom put her hands on Maddie's shoulders; she's the one nodding now.

"Hey, come on," Angie tells me. She's right next to me, and I was so into watching the scene on the other side of the store unfold that I didn't even noticed her walk up. "That's grown up stuff. Nothing to worry about."

"Is Maddie okay?"

Angie takes a quick look and sees what I see. Mom's still talking to her. Maddie seems to really be listening to whatever it is she's telling her.

Angie turns back and begins to guide me to the performing arts section, which is in a spot where I can no longer see what's happening. "She's fine. It's about your grandpa."

"I want to see," I tell her.

"It's not a good thing right now."

"Why not?"

"I'm sure your mom will tell you."

"I doubt it."

"Hey," Angie says, getting down to my eye level. "I'm sure your mom will tell you if you just ask. Your mom's cool like that."

"Yeah," I say. Angie leaves me to meet someone at the counter. Apparently, someone called in to have a book put on hold. I quietly make my way back to my previous spot and see my mom coming toward me and hear the store's front door open and close.

"Well, that was fun," she says sarcastically.

"What happened?"

Mom takes a deep breath and says, "Everybody's a bit emotional about your grandpa coming to visit."

"Is Maddie okay?"

She begins to walk to another section of the store, and I follow beside her. "She feels guilty," she tells me.

"About what?" I ask.

"About being excited to see him. She tends to get along with him."

"Well, what about Jess? Or Haley?"

"Haley – forget it. She's always known him to be absent but also caring. He emails her a lot. All of that. Jess?" She nods to herself. I wonder what she's thinking. "She doesn't want to see him. But, to be fair, she never wants to see him."

"Is she going to be okay?"

"She's going to be fine. Believe me. Just because she doesn't want to see him, it doesn't mean that she's unhappy."

"Maybe the two of you shouldn't go."

"We have to."

"Why?"

"Because he's our father, and even though we feel the way we feel, seeing him is a good thing." Mom sounds like she's just saying things, not like she actually believes it.

"Okay."

With Christmas only a few days away, and Mom preoccupied with family stuff, Dad and I spend the afternoon wrapping presents, though I'm still not allowed to see mine.

He's actually really good at it. Apparently, I've inherited both Mom's lack of folding clean corners and using too much tape. Dad doesn't seem to mind, though.

"Dad?"

"Yeah?"

"Have you ever met Grandpa?"

"Of course, I have. He walked your mom down the aisle at our wedding."

"I know that. I guess I meant, how often have you seen him? Mom says I've only met him a few times."

"That's true. He thought you were amazing."

I smile to myself. For some reason, that makes me feel good.

"Let's see. I believe it's been, maybe, five or six times."

"That doesn't seem like a lot."

"What seems like a lot?"

"I don't know. Twenty?"

Dad smirks. "Fair enough," he says.

Frustrated over the wrapping of this stuffed turtle for Mom that I can't seem to complete, I let out a "ugh" and say, "I don't know what I'm doing."

Dad comes over and inspects it. "Doesn't look that bad to me."

"Don't patronize me."

He laughs and goes back to his own perfect wrapping. "Don't overthink it," he tells me.

I look at the two gifts for Mom that I've wrapped and think that she probably won't care that I did a terrible job. This makes me feel better and inspires me to continue on to the next several gifts for the rest of the family – except Dad, obviously. He's right here.

Afterward, we put them under the tree. It's a plastic one, like it's always been. Mom's allergic to pine, which she says sucks because she loves the smell of Christmas trees. I tell her it's better with a fake one. This way, we don't have to see it wither away and have the garbage men toss it into a truck and take it to the dump. We've had this tree for my whole life. It's still sturdy, too. It's not going anywhere. This brings me comfort for some reason.

*   *   *

CeCe comes over on the 23rd to binge the first season of *Stranger Things*, which she's never seen. She'll be staying over, and then I'll be with Greta while my mom is at dinner with Grandpa. I try not to think about any of that while I'm with CeCe, and thankfully, she and the show are entertaining enough to keep me distracted.

"Eleven's so cool," she tells me during episode six. "She's completely pulling off that hair. Maybe I should shave my head."

"Really?" I ask, almost concerned.

She holds in some laughter and says, "No way."

Even though CeCe has darker skin and hair, she reminds me of Aunt Maddie, in that they're both effortlessly cool. Talking about it with Aunt Haley a few months ago, I think maybe it has to do with confidence. I have no idea how CeCe can be so confident at our age, but she is.

Dad pops in and asks if we need anything, and even though a refill on sodas and snacks would be nice, we tell him no. "Alright. Just let me know if you guys need anything."

"Thanks, Dad."

He's gone just as quickly as he came in.

"I like your dad."

"Me, too."

"I wish my dad would leave us alone when you come over."

"He's trying, though."

"I know, but he says the dumbest things. Oh my God, he's so embarrassing sometimes."

"My dad can embarrass me, too."

"Like when?"

"Well, a few weeks ago, we were shopping for a gift for my mom. We were in Macy's, and he starts asking about just about everything he sees. He's asking me if my mom would like any of this, and I look to my right and see a mom and her daughter pretending not to listen. It probably wouldn't have bothered me, but the stuff he was pointing out was just…ugh. I could tell they wanted to laugh. And probably not meanly, but still…I wanted to just run out of the store and never look back."

"Did you end up buying anything?"

I take CeCe to my dad's closet, which is pretty bare – nothing that looks like I shouldn't be looking at it – except for his clothes, shoes, and a few jackets. At the far end, behind his old college graduation gown, I point out the gift. It's nice summer dress, navy blue with small tulips all over. It's button-down in the front. It's the nicest thing he asked about, so I said yes to it immediately.

"Cute," she tells me.

"Right?"

She nods. We leave the room and settle in mine, sitting crisscross apple sauce on my bed. CeCe's brought a cootie catcher her older sister made.

"Pick a number," she tells me.

"Eight."

She moves her fingers eight times and then says, "Pick another number."

"Two."

She moves twice and asks, "Can you give me a short word?"

"Pig."

She snorts, playfully, and moves her fingers three times. "Okay," she says.

"Pick a number." I look down and see eight, five, one, and three. I consider this for a good moment, before deciding on "three."

She lifts the fold and reads, "You will become President of the United States."

"I can do that."

CeCe puts the fold back and hands it to me. "My turn," she says.

We go through the motions, and she ends up picking the number seven. I lift the fold and read the following to her: "You will live a happy life." I smile. "Well, that's a rip-off."

"I'm sure you'll be happy, too, when you're president," she says, taking back the cootie catcher. She begins playing with it as I lie down.

I'm suddenly feeling a little down. Through the corner of my eye, CeCe sees me and lies down beside me. "You okay?" she asks.

"Are you happy?"

"Yeah. Aren't you?"

"Most of the time."

"Yeah. I guess that's true. Sometimes I do feel sad."

"What do you feel sad about?" I asked, genuinely interested.

"I don't know. Things. Sometimes about my mom and dad. Sometimes school. Sometimes the news."

"Yeah. Me, too." I can see Aunt Jess in my mind's eye. We're at Thomas' funeral. She sees me and smiles the saddest smile ever. "I don't want to be sad when I grow up," I say.

"Me, too."

"I see everything that happened this year with my mom and my aunts. I mean, my grandpa's coming for Christmas, but no one seems happy about it."

"I didn't know you had a grandpa."

"I never see him."

"He's your mom's dad?"

"Yeah."

"Well, what about your dad's dad?"

"He's dead. He died before I was born."

"That's a downer. Sorry."

"It's okay. I just find myself worrying a lot now. I'm worried that I'm going to grow up and I'm gonna end up in a job I don't want, or lose the person I love, or not see my family because we're fighting. I'm scared."

"Scared?"

"Yeah. I'm scared that I'll grow up and be alone. That I'll look back and start thinking about all the things I did wrong. All the things I should've done. I'm surrounded by adults most of the time. They talk about things like this sometimes. They talk about regret. And that makes me scared." I take a moment before I continue. I can see CeCe through the corner of my eye. She's looking at me. I find it hard to turn to her. "I just don't want to grow up and regret things I should've done. Or not done. I don't want to make the same mistakes as my family."

"Then don't."

I nod and finally turn her way. "I guess it's that easy, huh?"

"I guess so."

We'll see, I think. *We'll see.*

Haley

Dad's flight arrives in a few hours. He's meeting us at the restaurant, so we'll be seeing him then. I'm excited. It's been a while. I love my dad. Even though he's spent 99.9% of my life in another state, I love him very much. We email one another often, though not as much as Penelope and I do.

He has another family. I met them once. They know all about me and my sisters, though. I exchange Christmas cards with them, and when I graduated a year and a half ago, my dad's wife, Clara, sent me a card and a Barnes & Noble gift card for $500. I still haven't spent all of it. I never told anyone about it, either. I'm not sure how they'd react.

Maddie has a so-so relationship with him. They've corresponded over the years, and I think they're in a good place, but she constantly feels

290

guilty about it all. I feel guilty about not feeling guilty, but I know I should be angry. He hurt my mom and left her to raise the rest of us on her own. Then, he started a new family. It's shitty. I know that.

But I still love him.

Mel's been very quiet. I know she had to pick up the slack when Dad left. I know she helped raise Maddie. And I know she stayed home instead of going to college. She does so much for *me*, too. I'll never be able to thank her enough or repay her. She's still giving to me. She's my role model. Once Mom's practice took off, Mel was able to start her life. She graduated college, met Stephen, had Katie, and found a good job. That's a great life to me. I'd love to marry Dani, have a kid, and work. It may not be what everybody does nowadays, but I don't care. It's what *I* want.

Then there's Jess. She doesn't want to come to dinner, but apparently Mom and Mel talked her into it. She hates Dad. There's no love there anymore, and again, I don't blame her. When he left, she was in college, pre-med. Rather than come home, she stayed away. I know she hates herself for that selfishness, but again, I don't blame her. She earned her way into UT. She was busting her ass and was definitely on her way to med school. I mean, it wasn't a possibility that she'd become a doctor. She was *going* to be one. Why come home?

I get it. I do.

She hates herself. She started drinking heavily in college when Dad left. She was able to control it, but being an alcoholic is a part of her now. I don't think she blames Dad for that, but it was a contributing factor, even if she won't admit it.

Thomas died. Dad didn't come to visit.

She tried to kill herself. Dad didn't come to visit.

I should hate him, too. But I don't.

I'm disappointed. And angry. But I still love him.

And I know why. By the time I was ten, he was back in our lives again. For half my life, he's been there for me – albeit from a distance. He's been my dad. And I was a baby when he left. I have no memory of the aftermath. None of this is an excuse, of course. Just the understanding of why there's no hate in my heart for him. And yet, if it ever came down to Dad or Mom, or Jess, or Mel, or Maddie – I wouldn't choose him. I wouldn't even give it a single thought.

It's Christmas Eve, and Angie is sick of hearing "Feliz Navidad" playing through the speakers in her bookstore.

"Why don't you just take it off the playlist?" I ask her.

"People love it."

"It's a good song."

"Not after the two hundredth time."

"Fair enough."

I'm here to pick up a gift for Dani, and it's nice to see about twenty people browsing. Every now and then, too, I have to move off to the side and lean on the counter so a customer can pay. I've been here about ten minutes, hanging out because Angie pretty much rules, even in this rowdiness. Well, I suppose, as rowdy as a bookstore can get. "Pretty cool, all these people are here," I tell her once she's done with the latest person doing some last-minute shopping.

"Yeah. It's pretty crazy."

"Where's Hebah?"

"Sick. Want a job for the next few hours?"

"Really?"

"Sure. I know you have that dinner tonight, but I'm closing at five anyway. I'll give you fifty bucks and Dani's gift on the house."

"Shit," I say, standing up straight. "What do you need me to do?"

"Come back here," she says, and as I do, she continues, "you see all of that? Those are orders people will be coming in to pick up. Divide them up between who's paid and who hasn't and take care of them when they come in. Also, I need you – when you have the time – to walk around and make sure things are fine. If it ever slows, go around and keep things in order and help out any customer you can. I'm gonna be back here for the rest of the day, I can feel it."

A few hours later, "Feliz Navidad" starts again, and I hear Angie let out a very audible "ugh!" It's slowed down, so I'm running the register while she's in the back working on some things. She's probably taking a break, but I give her the benefit of the doubt. Marie, who I haven't seen in forever, comes in. She sees me right away, smiles, and walks over, softly singing, "Feliz Navidad." At the counter, she tells me, "I love this song."

That makes me smile.

"Where's Ang?"

"In her office."

"Lazy ass." I chuckle. "How're you? I hear Dani's back in the picture."

"It's going good, actually. Really good."

"Mmm. That's nice. Good for you two."

"Thanks."

"Well, I'm gonna head back and see what your boss in up to."

"Okay."

She's disappears into the back office, and I'm back to work with the next customer. I hear my phone receive a text message, and the second after I say, "Have a good afternoon," I pick it up and read it. It's from Mel: "don't forget to dress up. Also, want me to pick you up?"

I let her know that Maddie's giving me a ride, and she responds with "K." I sit my phone down, disappointed that the text wasn't from Dani. I sent her one this morning, but she hasn't replied. I think better of tracking her to see where she's at, sit on the stool beside me, and wait for the next customer.

A few minutes pass with only a few people in the store. I find myself getting anxious, and I wonder if it has to do with Dani, my dad, or some combination of both.

"You okay?" Angie asks.

I must've been deep in thought, because I didn't see her and Marie come from the back office to where I am right now. I'm startled, and they definitely see that.

"Woah. We come in peace."

"Sorry. Didn't see you guys there."

"You okay, sweetie?" Marie asks me. "You look like you need a cookie or something."

"Oh, I just…I haven't eaten since this morning."

"When was that?" Angie asks.

"Nine?"

Angie checks her watch as Marie says, "It's four thirty."

"Is it?" Maybe I *am* hungry.

Angie slams a hundred-dollar bill on the counter. "Beat it, kid. We got this."

I pick up the money and say, "Angie, I -."

"Eh," she says, cutting me off. "Merry Christmas. Go make out with your girlfriend."

I gather my stuff. "Thanks."

"No problem. Don't forget her gift."

"Oh, yeah." I ask Marie, "You coming to my birthday?"

"I'll be here through New Year's."

"Awesome. Well, Merry Christmas, guys."

"Merry Christmas."

Angie gives me a wave, and I'm off. First, a quick bite somewhere. Then, to see Dani. Then, it's time to get ready for that dinner. Just then, I get a text from Mel. "Jess is saying she's not coming to dinner." I decide to eat at Jess'.

On the way there, I listen to the latest episode of *Reading Glasses*, the greatest podcast on the planet, and find myself wondering what Mallory and Brea would do. I'm sure they'd call my dad a "trash baby," but they'd also be strong and confident. I'm sure they'd say something to the effect that Jess has every right to not go, and frankly, they'd be right. I get to Jess' place, and in the back of my mind, I'm still wondering why Dani hasn't texted, or so help me, called. I let myself in, and Mel and Maddie are yelling at each other.

As I make my way to the kitchen, I hear Maddie yell, "You don't know! No – you don't know!"

"I know, Mad. I know!" Mel yells back.

I enter and see Jess seated at the table, her head resting in her hand, elbow propped up on the table. She turns and sees me, smiling the kind of sad smile I hoped had gone away.

"I'm listening! We're *always* listening to you!"

"No, you're not! You keep saying what you think *I'm* saying, and it's bullshit!"

Mel finally sees me and calms at the sight of me. Maddie's back seems to relax a bit, too. She turns around, and I can see tears in her eyes. After a brief moment, Maddie rushes past me.

"Maddie!" Mel calls after her. She follows her out, and I'm unsure what to do. I look to Jess who's lying back in her seat now. She shrugs. I turn and follow.

Mel gets between the front door and Maddie.

"What?! Move!"

"No."

"Move!"

"No."

Maddie turns and moves away, shouting, "FUCK!" at the top of her lungs.

I stand still, questioning my decision to follow them here.

"Maddie, I get it."

"No, you don't. Stop saying that."

"We don't hate you for -."

"Just *stop*!"

Mel walks up to her, carefully. "I know what you mean. I think Jess should come to dinner, too."

Maddie crosses her arms and shakes her head.

"We know you and Haley have great relationships with Dad. We're not upset about that." I feel uneasy, as I'm starting to get a clearer understanding of what this fight is all about.

With her voice shaking, she says, "You're angry with me because you think I'm telling Jess that she needs to forgive Dad."

"That's not what I think. That's not what Jess thinks."

"Yes, it is. Okay. I saw it in your eyes. I know what it looks like when you're angry at me. And disappointed." Maddie looks and sounds like she wants to erupt.

"That's not true," Mel says.

I hear a knock beside me. We all turn to it: Jess. She's leaning against the archway leading into the hall we're in. She has the same expression on her face as before. I want to hug her but think I shouldn't do it at this moment. "Can I say something?"

Maddie shrugs. "It's your house."

Jess walks right up to Maddie and gets in her face. Maddie looks past her, unable to make eye contact, probably a little scared. Jess gently cups her face with her hands and makes Maddie look at her. It blows my mind a little, given how she's a good half-foot taller than Jess, yet Jess seems so much stronger in this moment. Jess doesn't say a word. Seconds go by. Nothing happens. Maddie swallows. "I love you," Jess finally tells her.

Maddie's tears begin to dry up.

"I love you so much, you'll never be able to understand. I watched all three of you grow up. You know how amazing that was? I can't have kids. And it doesn't even hurt that much most of the time. Because it's like you all fill that part of me. And, if that's how I feel, do you really think I give a *shit* if you want a relationship with Dad? Do you really think that's the thing that'll get me to hate you?"

Maddie blinks, unable to do anything.

"Answer me," Jess says, her voice breaking.

"No."

"That's right. So, I'm coming tonight. Not just for you. But for you." She looks at Mel. "And you." She looks at me. "And mom." She looks back Maddie. "But not for him. You understand me?"

Maddie nods.

"I hate him. That's never gonna change. But I would *never* expect you to feel the same way. Yeah?"

Maddie nods.

"Yeah?" Jess asks again, a smile forming.

Maddie begins to smile, too. "Yeah," she answers.

Jess brings her in for a big bear-hug.

My stomach reminds me I'm starving.

Dani shows up unannounced with a classy-looking pink dress. It's hers. She's letting me borrow it. I invite her in, let everyone know she's here, and once we're in my old bedroom, I ask her, "Why didn't you text me back?"

She carefully lays the dress on my bed and says, "I was working on the final cut of the movie."

"What?" Her movie. I'd completely forgotten.

"*Showers*. I was working with Sasha on the mixing. It looks great. She's still over there, but I wanted to see you before the big dinner and bring you this dress. I think it'll look great on you. Blondes look good in pink."

"You going back over there?"

"As soon as you guys leave, I'm headed back, yeah." I sit beside the dress. "Gonna work on it through the night. We're so close. Then, we get to start showing it to people and submitting it to festivals." She takes a deep breath. "It's exciting."

"Wow, you guys really did it."

"Yeah, it looks like it." She sits on the other side of the dress. "You okay?"

I lightly touch it. It's very soft and cotton-y. "This is pretty. I've never seen you in it."

"Yeah, I only wore it once. For graduation."

"Right. We weren't talking then."

"Nope."

I nod.

"Seriously. You good?"

"Yeah. I am."

"Everyone else?"

"Yeah – Dan…I'm so proud of you."

A smile nearly forms on her lips. "Thanks."

"Really. I am. And, it's not like I didn't believe in you guys – it's more…it's what you two always talked about."

"Yeah, well, I didn't want to wait forever. Grow old and end up teaching kids how to make movies, all because we never actually went out and made one."

"Good for you guys. Tell Sasha I'm proud of her, too."

"Will do." She stands up, gets in front of me, and lifts out her hands. I take them, and she lifts me up. We kiss. "Jess okay?"

"I think so."

"Well, text me later. Hell – come by if you want."

"I don't want to get in the way."

"Even if you do, I like having you around." She puts her arms around my waist, and I do the same.

"Same here."

She kisses me and says, "College Girl."

This makes me laugh for whatever reason.

Dani helps me get dressed. Soon, I meet up with my sisters and mom. As I get in Maddie's car, I wave to Dani. She blows me a kiss. I feel good. Maybe tonight won't be the worst thing.

Maddie

She's already told me that she isn't, but I know Jess is angry at me. All I said to her was that she should go to dinner, even though she said she wouldn't, because no matter what, he's our dad, and that's never going to help her move on. I never said anything about her forgiving him or anything like that.

I hate how quiet Jess has been ever since. I also feel pretty ashamed at constantly going off on Mel, even though I know she just wants to help. I guess it's just feeling guilty and knowing that I shouldn't have said anything in the first place. We all get ready at Mom's. I find myself next to Jess at the two-person lavatory in the master bedroom. Jess is wiping off lipstick. "You look nice," I tell her.

"Thanks," she says. I can't read her, so I assume she's still mad.

"Listen, I'm…I'm really sorry for what I said."

"Are we still on this?"

"Well, yeah."

"Maddie," she says, looking at me. "I'm not mad. I'm not anything, quite frankly. I just want this whole thing to be over with."

"I just feel…you know…"

"I know. It's cool. I promise you."

We don't say anything else to each other. Soon, she's in the living room, and I can hear Mel on the phone talking to Katie, promising to bring her leftovers from the steak house Dad chose for us. I take a look at myself. *What else*? I think. I put my hair up, but then think it's maybe bordering on sexy, so I put it back down. I try putting a clip on my right side. It looks good.

By the time I meet up with everyone in the living room, it turns out

Dani's come by. After some pleasantries, we all end up in different cars,

and Haley kisses her girlfriend goodbye. Mel takes me and Haley, while

Jess and Mom get there together. *This is happening*, I think to myself. It's

been years since all of us have been together, and that should be

something to be excited or simply happy about. But it isn't. These

thoughts are still present by the time we take our seats. Dad isn't here yet,

to which Jess says, "Shocker."

I see Mel give her a look, and she responds with a nod. They've always

– for my whole life – been able to communicate with very little. I guess

that's something I could be jealous about, but I'm not. When that happens,

I tend to feel safe, like everything is right and as it should be. And so, it

does just that. I'm relaxed for a moment. It's great. I take in the place,

which is dark and has been decorated with elegant Christmas ephemera

here and there. It's nice.

Then Dad comes in.

He's in better shape than I remember. He shakes the hand of the host,

who shows him to our table, which is nestle in a corner away from the rest

of the restaurant. We all stand up, except for Jess, who sips on her water.

Dad starts with Mom. They politely hug, with smiles after. Then it's me. We hug tightly, and he asks me how I've been. I tell him, "Good," and he nods and moves to Haley. Their hug reminds me of the ones she gives the rest of us after she's been gone a long time at school. He pats her on the back and kisses her temple. "Love you," he tells her. "Love you," she responds. She looks happy to see him.

"Hey, Dad," Mel says as they hug. It's similar to the one I saw Mom give him. It's a hug, but nothing more. "How're you, honey?" he asks. "I'm all right," she tells him. He nods and turns toward Jess, who's seated across from Mel, two empty seats on her right. She's as far as she can be from Dad once he sits down between mom at the head of the table and me. She stands. "Jess," he says, hands at his side. "Dad." There are some curt nods, and then he claps his hands together and asks, "Alright, who's hungry?"

Everyone but me and Jess say something to the effect of "Me!" I look at her, and she seems to be both hurt and contemplating something. As she sits, everyone seems to be talking over one another. I'm joining in while keeping an eye out on Jess, who snaps out of it once Mel gives her drink order to the waiter. "I'll have a vodka tonic, but more tonic than vodka and lots of ice, please."

"Sure," the waiter says.

Mel gives Jess a look I can't quite read. Jess asks her, "What?" quietly. If I hadn't been paying attention, I wouldn't have heard her.

Once orders are done, we begin going through the menu, with occasional comments from Dad, like "Oh, that sounds good. You still eat it medium?" or "Gonna have to ask that they don't put any butter on mine." It's harmless enough. Once the drinks arrive, we go around giving our food orders, and I see Jess quickly downs her drink.

"I'll take the filet, medium, with the twice-baked potato. And, can I have another -?" She points to her glass.

"Got it. Let me know if you guys need anything."

"Thank you," Dad says, around all of us saying some form of thanks.

"So," Dad begins, "Haley, how's college life this year? Nicole still a good roommate?"

"Oh, she's the best. She changed her major from Business to Psychology, and she's been having the time of her life messing around with people."

Dad chuckles. "You know, your sister, Penelope, is already ready for college, and even graduate school." He turns toward the entire table.

"Imagine being seventeen and already knowing the next ten years of your life."

"Well, I wanted to be a surgeon when I was five, but whatever," Jess says.

"I know that. It's wonderful. I'm not saying there's anything wrong with that."

Jess takes a big breath and loudly sighs over Dad's last sentence. I decide to keep things moving and say, "You know, I was going through my library a few months ago and realized I don't own a copy of Dante's *Inferno*."

"How's that possible?" he asks, playfully.

"I think I left it at your house."

"Really?"

"Yeah. I think I sat it on one of your shelves. Hadn't thought about it at all until I had time recently."

"Wow. How long ago was that?"

"I was twenty-two, so eight years ago."

"Jesus. Time goes by doesn't it?"

"And, how is everything in California?" Mom asks.

"As good as can be. As I said, Penelope's *loving* school. She reminds me of *you* a bit, Jess."

"Just the good parts, I'm sure," she says.

"Oh, they were all good parts."

"Were they?"

"Jess," Mel says. Jess turns to her and gets quiet.

"It's okay, Mel. Believe me. I understand. I'm your father, and I'm not around much. I'm sorry for that."

"But what's done is done," Mom interjects. "And we can relive the past over and over or we can move on with the rest of the world. It's going to move on with or without us."

Dad says, "Well said, Sarah." Jess rolls her eyes.

"Dad," Mel says, also seemingly wanting to move on – she reminds me so much of Mom right then and there. "You should think about staying a little longer. I'm sure Katie wants to see you."

"Oh, I would, but I'm sure you know how impossible flights are during this time. Changing one would be insane, and I'd lose even more time to spend with you guys."

I'm not sure that adds up, I think.

"It's cool. She thanks you for her birthday gift, by the way."

"It's the least I could do. How old is she now?"

Mel hesitates before answering, "Ten."

"Wow, she's growing up so fast, isn't she?" He turns to mom. "Crazy how fast time goes when you get older."

"Tell me about it," she says. I look over at Mel, who seems deep in thought. Jess puts a hand over Mel's hand, which wakes her up. She gives Jess a smile and straightens up, doing her best to get back into it. I start to feel butterflies in my stomach. "I was just thinking the other day how crazy it is that this one," she points to Haley, "is going to be *twenty*. How is that possible?"

"No longer in your teens, young lady," he says, trying his best to sound playful.

"I don't feel like I'm turning twenty, though."

"Don't worry about it," I say. "It's overrated. Wait until your twenty-one. That's when the real fun starts."

"Don't give her any ideas," Mel says.

"I wouldn't dream of it," I tell her. Turning to Haley, I say, "We'll talk later."

Mel tries to hit me with her napkin. I dodge it. Most of us relax and let out some laughter. The waiter comes by to check on us. Jess asks for another drink.

"You know, before I forget, and there's a good chance that'll happen," Dad begins, which prompts Jess to chew on her ice and continue to look away from the table. He pulls out a small stack of envelopes. "These are from Clara and Penelope." He hands the stack to me. I take the one with my name on it and pass it on. "Just a little something from them. They wanted to be here, but again, flights this time of year."

I open mine, and it's a nice little Christmas card with a cottage covered in snow on the front. On the inside, beneath the generic Merry Christmas in calligraphy are two different handwriting styles. The first one, clearly from Clara, says, "Madeline, have a good holiday and a Happy New Year!" The other, from Penelope, reads, "Maddie, Wish I could be there. Hope everything's been good. I can't wait to read your novel. Can you send me a copy when you're done? Your Step-Sis, Penelope." I want to ugly-cry all of a sudden. But, maybe more than anything, I want to get up and call Penelope right then and there and talk to her. I hate myself and the fact that I rarely talk to her. She's my sister, step or not. I look up to see everyone else's reactions. Haley's smiling, almost holding in laughter.

Mel looks conflicted. Jess hasn't opened hers. The waiter brings her drink, and she tells him, "Thank you." She doesn't sound drunk yet.

"Oh, that's so sweet," I hear Mom say. I turn to her and Dad. She rubs his shoulder. "I'll call them later tonight to thank them."

"Yeah, me, too," I add.

"Good," Dad says. "I'm sure they'd love to hear from all of you."

"Penelope asked me to ask you about a picture of her from Halloween," Haley says.

"Ah," Dad says, feigning embarrassment. I find myself wanting to roll my eyes as well. "Well…." He takes out his phone, finds the photo, and turns it toward the rest of us, though Mom obviously has to lean over to see. It's of Dad, Clara, and Penelope dressed as the Incredibles family.

"Aw," Haley says. "You guys look so cute."

"Yeah," I say. "I gotta admit. You do."

"How'd Clara convince you to do that?" Mel asks.

"Well, I just figured it was time to start having fun." He searches for another picture and then hands the phone to me. "Here's one of Penelope giving a speech for winning a Student Essay Award for her grade level."

"Oh, was that the one on fossil fuels?" Haley asks.

"That's the one."

"Wow," Jess says. "Penelope sounds awesome. You're pretty lucky you ended up with a daughter like her. I mean – geez – it only took five tries, right?" She takes a big gulp and from the looks of it, the bartender put more vodka than tonic this time.

"Jess, can we speak outside?" Mom asks, putting her napkin on her plate.

"Nah, I'm good."

"Jess," Mom says in a way I haven't heard in a long time.

"I said I'm good. I'm enjoying the meal." She takes the phone from Haley's hand. "See? Wow. Penelope's so awesome. Is she still a cheerleader, too? You know, it's hard to beat a crazy smart cheerleader. Ya done good, Dad." She raises her glass in a toast.

Mom gets up and grabs her arm, trying to pull her out of her seat.

"Jesus," Jess says. She gets up, puts down the glass and phone, and follows mom outside.

There's tension. No one knows what to do, but Mel comes to the rescue and simply moves on without comment. She says, "You know, Maddie's been working on a novel. I've read about – what? Half so far?"

"Oh, um – yeah," I say.

"Really?" Dad asks.

"Yeah, I actually stopped writing that one."

"You did?" Mel asks.

"Why?" Haley adds.

I shrug. "Found something better."

"Well, good for you," Dad tells me. After taking a sip of his tea, he continues, "So tell me about this new one. What's it about?"

"Well. It's about a girl. Or a woman. Well, both, actually. It's sort of this sprawling look at this woman's life. You see, she's talented. She's funny. But she never quite figures out what to do with that. In the meantime, we take this journey from the eighties, through the nineties, up until about 2015."

"What's the story?"

"That. That's the story. It's her life. Meghan. That's her name. The plot is still a bit up in the air, but I'm having a blast writing it, so I don't really care. Except when it comes to thinking about how this is going to make me any kind of money."

Dad nods. "Just make sure you have a back-up plan. At least you're still -."

"I quit my job a few months ago."

"You did?"

"Yeah."

"To write?"

"Yeah. It's what I wanted to do."

"I don't know, Maddie. It just…doesn't seem like you thought this through."

My eyes find the empty bread plate before me. I feel like I want to run away.

"What happens if this thing doesn't work out? Again, do you have a back-up plan of any kind?"

"I can go back to my publishing house. They've left the door open for me."

"Maddie, look at me."

I do it, even though I feel the same way – worse, maybe – than I did when I told Mel all those months ago about going to London.

"You're smarter than this. Now don't get me wrong. You're capable, and I'm sure this book's going to be good. But come on."

I nod and say, "You're right." I suppose he is. It was pretty stupid of me to do this. What the hell was I thinking? I feel like such a fucking idiot. The waiter comes with the bread and lets us know our food should be out shortly. I try my best to mask my feelings, but I'm unsure as to how successful I am.

"Maddie," Mel says. I look to her. "I got your back. Anything you need. *I* believe in you." I smile.

Mom returns without Jess, and my immediate thought is that she left, but then Mom says, "Jess needs a minute."

"Again, I understand," Dad says. He turns to Mel. "I really do. I'm not sure it's worth much, but I mean it, nonetheless. I'm sorry for what I did. I love you all."

"Thanks, Dad," Mel says, even though I can tell she doesn't mean it. I've heard her say things a variety of ways over the years. My smile grows.

Jess returns. "Dad. I'm sorry for being rude. It was rude of me. I shouldn't have been rude. After all, it's Christmas. The end." She obviously doesn't mean a word, and it's also clear that the alcohol is finally catching up with her. As she sits, I glance at Mom, who seems to be ignoring her now. When the waiter stops by to offer refills, Jess asks for a club soda. I feel better for her, but my guilt still hasn't dissipated in the slightest.

Things continue on until the food arrives. Haley asks about the last thing Dad read, and he says this: "Oh, Penelope wrote this article for her school paper. It's fantastic. I have to send it to you all." Out comes his phone, and in no time, he actually sends each of us a link to the article. I look to Jess, who nods, reassuringly – her eyes telling me, "Don't worry about it. Don't listen to him. We got you."

<u>Jess</u>

I've been wasted many times throughout my adult life. I know when I've had too much. The problem is that I know this after I've woken up the next day. You see, if I can remember everything, I didn't drink too much. If there's holes in my memory, well – that's that. I've only ever done the latter fewer than five times in my life. The last time was in college. Although I've been drinking a lot since I lost Thomas, I can say this: I haven't had too much.

Tonight, as I sit at this table, listening to this asshole talk about his other family, I badly want to drink enough to forget this shit. But I also want to be as present as possible. I'm here for Maddie. And Haley. And, yeah, even Mom.

Outside, she rounded on me, asking what the hell my problem was.

317

I shrugged, refusing to look at her, realizing even in that moment how I felt like a teenager again being scolded by her.

"Jessica!" she yelled at me.

I sharply turned to her and yelled back, "Mom!"

She glanced at the people near the entrance doors and then dragged me a few more feet away. "What the *hell* is wrong with you tonight?"

"You know exactly what's wrong," I told her, my voice breaking.

"Oh, you're angry. Get in line. Tonight is not about what happened two decades ago. It's about celebrating Christmas as a family."

"You *gotta* be shitting me."

"Excuse me?"

"He's not my family. I may share blood with him, but that's it. As far as I'm concerned, he's gone the moment I don't see him. And that's the way I like it. And, you know what? The same goes for his wife and daughter."

"You mean your step-mother and biological sister."

"Whatever. They don't mean anything to me."

Mom gave me a look I couldn't quite place. I still can't. "What a horrible thing to say," she said quietly.

I swallowed and doubled down: "I mean it."

She looked at her shoes and nodded. Without giving me another look, she told me, "Apologize when you come back or don't come back." She was already entering when what she said fully hit me. I did entertain the idea of simply calling a Lyft to take me away from here, but instead, I swallowed my damn pride and went in and gave a shitty apology. It was the best I could do. I even ordered a club soda, knowing in the back of my mind that I'd be drunk before the bill came.

But I stay quiet, listening to Haley go on and on about college to him. Every now and then Maddie or Mel make a comment and everybody but me laughs. Mom doesn't acknowledge my existence and that seems fine with me. I chow down on my ribeye, nearly wolfing down the whole thing, plus loaded potatoes.

"So, and I don't want to embarrass you, but seeing as we're all family, how are things going with Dani?"

"Pretty great, actually," Haley says, her face slowly beaming.

"Yeah? Good for you. I hope things work out."

"Me, too."

"And, Maddie. Any guy – or girl – in your life right now?"

"I'm mainly focused on my writing, but I'm open to any possibilities."

"Well, take your time."

She lifts her glass of wine. "Yes, sir," she says playfully, taking a sip after. The waiter picks up a few plates, and I order vodka on the rocks. Fuck it.

Mel gives me a pleading look, but I just stare back, daring her to say or do something. I want a fight. From anybody at this point. Her attention is taken away once he asks her about Stephen. My drink arrives, and I'm happy that there's very little ice. I take several sips, wishing I hadn't come back in. I know I'm about to say something stupid, but maybe I can get through this. Maybe I can. It's possible. There's a way to -.

"I always liked him; you know?" he tells Mel. I have no idea what they've been talking about, of course. I'm so deep into my own thoughts; plus, the alcohol's definitely doing its thing now. "I was happy you two found each other."

"Thanks, Dad."

He actually turns to me and says, "Same with you and Thomas."

I tense up. My mouth agape. I look up at him. I don't see anybody or anything else. "What did you just say to me?"

"Thomas. He was a good man."

"Was," I repeat.

"So," Mel begins, "are we getting dessert?"

"What the *fuck* are you talking about?" I ask him.

"Jess," Mel tells me quietly. I can see her through the corner of my eye. I'm focused on *him*, though.

I'm steady with my words, nearly whispering. I'm in some weird space between anger and depression; crying and screaming; wanting to hit him and run away. "Thomas is dead. That's why you used 'was.' But…he's dead. And you say you liked him. That he was a good man. When was the last time you saw him, Dad?"

I can see mom. Her elbows on the table, forehead in her hands.

"I'm sorry, Jess."

"You keep saying you're sorry. And that you understand how we feel about what you did. But it's never gonna change anything. Right? You left. You found a new wife. Had a new kid. You *stayed* with them. And I hate you. You know I hate you, right?"

He seems to find it hard to look at me now. I can see Maddie, unable to move and speak. "Jess…I know. I messed up. But you have to understand that because of Penelope, I wouldn't change anything. Does that make sense?"

I turn to Haley. She's definitely making an effort to not look at me, and for whatever reason, I find that I don't blame her. Screw Penelope. Haley should be the one with all of her pictures in his phone. He should be telling people stories of *her*. I turn back to him and ask, "Why didn't you call?"

"I'm sorry?"

"When Thomas died, why didn't you call?" My voice breaks again, but I'll be damned if I'm going to cry.

He doesn't say anything.

"Why didn't you call?" I say louder.

Nothing. I sit back and finish my drink. I continue on, this time just looking into space. "You could've at least shown up to the funeral. Thanks for that. Thank you *so* much. You're such a great dad. Thank you, thank you, thank you." I rub my eyes and then return to him. "Oh, and thanks for not coming to the hospital to visit me when I tried to kill myself." The moment I say "hospital," Mel puts her napkin on her plate, and by the time I finish the sentence, she's kneeling beside me.

"Come on. Let's go." She's quiet about it.

"Thanks for not calling that time either."

"Jess, come on." Her voice is still steady.

I decide to leave with her. She helps me up, but before we leave, I tell him loud enough so everyone can hear, "You're a great father. A *great* father."

She gives her ticket to the valet, and I take a deep breath. It's a fairly cool Texan December night. I can see my breath. Soon enough, she's beside me.

"I'm drunk," I tell her.

"I figured," she says. "Wanna see a movie at your place?"

"Yes!" I yell. Finally, something I want to do.

She smiles, and within fifteen minutes, we're pulling into my driveway. Soon enough, I've hit the bathroom, and Mel's helped me change into sweats. We find ourselves on the couch watching *It's a Wonderful Life* on Blu-ray because we missed it on NBC. "You're not gonna change?" I ask her.

"I like the way I am."

"Ha-ha."

She giggles. "I'm fine. Don't worry about it."

"I'm the older one. It's my job." I lie down. She puts my feet on her lap.

"I love you."

"I love you, too."

After a few minutes of just watching the movie, I find myself beginning to drift off, but I have a few things to say first. "Do you remember Haley's first Christmas?"

"Of course, I do."

"I got so drunk that night. Mom yelled at me like she'd never done before – or since."

"I didn't know that. Shit – is that why you went to stay at Sam's?"

I nod.

"Oh, man. I don't know *what* I thought then."

"Mom told me I needed to wake up and grow up. That I needed to stop being a child. She told me not to come back unless I changed things."

"Jesus, Jess. That's why you didn't come back again until summer. Why you never called?"

"I was so angry at her. I don't know why. Honestly, I was trying to figure out what I'd done that was so bad, but I get it. I was drunk and wanted to hold Haley. I nearly got her out of her crib before Mom saw me. That's why I get why you got between me and Katie."

"I overreacted."

"Maybe. But you weren't wrong."

"I think when we get angry, we say horrible shit to each other to win or make the other one feel bad – or both. I'm sorry."

"Don't be. I'm a drunk. Always will be. Even when I can fight it, it's me."

"I don't believe that," Mel tells me. I'm unsure what to say to that. A moment passes, and then she asks, "Did mom say anything else? Except the thing about not coming back?"

I take a deep breath and figure this is as good as any time to say it. "She slapped me after I told her Dad would still be here if it weren't for her."

Mel shifts in her seat, and for a brief moment, I think she's going to leave me. She doesn't. In fact, she sort of massages my feet. "I'm sure she knows you didn't mean it."

"Doesn't matter. I said it. She slapped me. And we didn't really get along until I was in med school."

"Damn…well, that clears up a lot. You know, I resented the fact that you were off at school, completely ignoring us. That *I* had to be the one to help mom with Maddie and Haley."

"I know. I can never take those years back."

"Don't. Don't think that. I have no idea what would've happened to me if I hadn't had to step up. I wouldn't be who I am right now, that's for sure. I probably would've done something stupid and ruined my life."

"Maybe – maybe not."

"Fair enough." She takes a deep breath. "Merry Christmas, big sis."

I truly smile for the first time tonight. "Merry Christmas."

I fall asleep before adult George enters the picture.

In the morning, Sam's there. Jess had to leave to spend Christmas morning with Katie and Stephen. She's made me boiled eggs and coffee. She knows how to cure my hangovers very well. When I enter the kitchen, she's reading the paper.

"Merry Christmas, sunshine."

I put my chin on the top of her head and hug her. She does her best to hug me back. I fix my plate and join her at the table.

"Bad night, I hear."

"Not so great."

"Wanna talk about it?"

"Maybe tomorrow. It's Christmas, you know."

"Fair enough," she says.

I begin eating. "So, what time did Mel leave?"

"About an hour and a half ago."

"Sorry you had to babysit me."

She closes her paper and pats my hand. "Oh, sweetie," she says, getting

up and taking her plate to the sink. "It's not babysitting to me. I love being

around you. Besides, I have dinner with my parents on Christmas *night*.

You know that."

"Where's Kris this year?"

"She told me she was headed to Canada, for whatever reason. You

know, I love that girl, but sometimes, she sort of blows my mind."

"Well, we should all hangout when she gets back."

"No problem."

"We can throw a party. The three of us. Spend New Year's Eve

together." She looks at me like I'm crazy. "What do you say?"

"You're serious? You're being serious right now?"

"Uh-huh."

She smiles wide. "That sounds like a good time."

"Let's do it!"

"Let's do it!" she repeats.

I slam the balls of my fists on the table. "Yeah!" I cry.

She raises her hands in the air and yells, "Yeah!"

We laugh. It's the first time – in a *really* long time – I've felt genuinely happy.

About an hour later, I get a text. It's from Maddie. It says: "can you come outside?"

Maddie's parked on the curb. I walk up to her passenger window, and she rolls it down. "What are you doing? Come inside."

"Can you sit down for a sec?"

Confused and a little cold, I open the door, sit, and close the door. The window goes up, as I wait for her to say something. After a few seconds, she does.

"I wanted to say I was sorry. Or that I *am* sorry. Sorry."

"Three sorry's. Not too shabby."

"You know when you're so focused on yourself or on what you believe others are thinking or going through that you actually miss the truth of what others are thinking and going through?"

I go through her convoluted statement and answer, "Yeah."

"I should've known better, Jessie. I mean, where the hell was *anybody* when Thomas died?"

"I seem to remember a lot of crying between you and Mom."

She closes her eyes. I'm sure that night she and mom came to see me at the hospital is still vivid in her mind. I decide to say something I've wanted to say for months.

"I never apologized to you."

She turns to me, confused.

"I'm sorry for making you and Mom feel the way you did. It was selfish of me."

Her confusion becomes replaced by bafflement.

"Don't *ever* apologize for that," she eventually says.

"Why not? Neither of you -."

"Went through what you went through. Jessie, I've never once considered anything other than you did what you did and that I was so sad for you. And definitely sad for Mom, too."

I nod.

"It was messed up. But I don't want an apology for it. I *have* what I want. You. Here."

I manage a closed-mouth smile.

"And that's something Dad and them won't ever understand. You were right. Dad should've come."

"Penelope texted me."

"What? Really?"

"Yeah. She told me she heard and was sorry she couldn't make it to the funeral. That I could text back if I wanted."

"Did you?"

I shake my head. "Nope."

"Why not?"

"I don't know. Why did I treat Sam like shit when she took care of me every single day after I came home from the hospital?"

"You should text her."

"Eventually."

Maddie looks like she wants to say something, but she holds back. I'm a little thankful for that. "Did Clara…?"

"She called. Left a voicemail. Apparently speaking for both of them. They couldn't make it. They felt bad. Blah-blah-blah."

"Dad should've been here."

"Yeah, well…."

After a moment, Maddie sort of changes the conversation. "Haley is spending Christmas dinner with Dani, because she hates herself right now."

I sigh. "Well, tell her feeling guilty about having a good relationship with Dad is ridiculous."

"She's taken it upon herself that everything that happened is her fault. You and Dad. You and Mom. Dad and everybody, actually."

"That's so dumb."

"I'm sure she knows that."

"Am I supposed to go and talk to her about this, or…?"

"I don't know. She made her announcement to everyone once all the gifts were opened – we missed you this morning, by the way. Mom asked about you."

"She did?"

"Yeah. She hoped you were feeling better."

"Well, we'll see."

"Yeah. Well, anyway, Haley said it was her fault, because apparently, she asked Dad to come to see us for Christmas."

"She asked him to come?"

"Yep."

"Why?"

"I guess you can ask her when you go and talk to her."

"So, that's happening."

"Maybe."

I consider this and then ask, "So, what happened after I left?"

"Everyone was quiet. Things stayed awkward as Dad paid the check. Outside, he hugged us and promised to do a better job keeping in touch. Then Mom drove herself home, and I drove Haley."

"Well, Merry Christmas."

"Amen. Seriously, I'm sorry."

"Eh! Forget it. All of that was between me and Dad. Maybe I need to go back to therapy."

"Maybe."

"We'll see."

We say our goodbyes, and when she's gone, I feel even better than before. Eventually, Sam leaves, and I clean up, both myself and the house. I get dressed to go see Haley at Dani's apartment. As I'm about to put on my shoes, the doorbell rings. When I look through the side window to see who it could be, I see it's none other than Riley the Intern, a wrapped-present in her hands.

When I open the door, she's smiling the kind of smile where the eyes squint.

"Hello," I say, surprised and amused to see her.

"Hi," she says, still nervous around me.

I invite her in, and we end up not much further than the entrance hall. She holds out the gift to me.

"For me?"

"Yeah. Merry Christmas."

"Thank you so much." I unwrap it and see that it's a brand-new stethoscope. I smirk.

"I really didn't know what to get you."

"You didn't have to -."

"Oh, but I wanted to. I also wanted to say thanks. I got the job because of you."

"Well, you deserve it."

"Yeah. Actually, I…kinda always thought you didn't think much of me."

I nod. "I'm told I can be intimidating."

"A little," she says through a nervous giggle.

"I'm nothing special."

"You're amazing, quite frankly. Part of the reason I'm here, apart from saying thanks and giving you a Christmas present…I – uh – wanted to ask something of you."

"Okay," I say, probably a bit apprehensively.

"Would you be my mentor?"

Holy shit. What? I think.

"I mean, I know you're no longer at the hospital, and with your talents, I'm sure you'll find work somewhere again. It's just that…I think the world of you. I sorta…want to *be* you?" She says that last part funny, like she's unsure if she should be saying that to me.

"Wow. That's…that's *not* something I was expecting. Ever."

"I know. Um. Feel free to think it over. Take whatever time you need. I'm sure the last thing you need is some kid hanging around you."

"Yeah. I mean…what am I saying? No. That's not…." I take a deep breath and speak honestly. "That sounds doable to me."

"Really?"

"Yeah. I mean. Why not?"

"Are you sure? Because like I said, you can take time to think about -."

"I don't need to. Because you wouldn't be a waste of my time and effort."

"Wow. This is happening then."

"Looks like it."

"Okay. What now?"

"Now, it's Christmas. I'm having dinner with my family. How about you?"

"My parents live in Connecticut."

"Well, you're free to be my guest at my sister's place tonight."

"Holy crap, really?"

I stifle a laugh. "Yeah, really."

"Okay. Should I come here?"

"I'll text you the address."

"Okay."

We say our goodbyes, and when she's gone, I feel absolutely incredible.

I knock on the door with a Santa on it. Of course Dani would decorate her door. I'm positive her landlord will give her shit about it, but I doubt she cares. Haley found a good one.

Dani answers, sporting a Santa hat. "Hey," she says.

"Haley here?"

"She is," she says, moving aside. Once the door is closed, she tells me she'll get her. I lock the door. She returns about a minute later. "Okay, so, she *wants* to see you, but she also doesn't want to. Or something like that."

"Tell her I'm not mad at all and that I want to spend Christmas with my little sister."

"That's so cute," she says before she's off again. After another minute, she returns; this time, with Haley, who can't even look at me, by her side. "So, I'm gonna give you guys some space." Dani leaves us alone.

"Haley, come on. Have dinner with us."

"Are you still mad at Mom?"

"I was never mad at Mom. We got into a fight because I was acting stupid last night. That's what drunk people do."

"Did Maddie tell you I was the one who invited Dad?"

"Yeah."

"Aren't you mad at me?"

"For what?"

"Last night wouldn't have happened if -."

"Last night proved what I've thought and felt for a long time. It also reminded me of what a shitty older sister I've been to Penelope."

"Yeah, I guess we can all do better on that front."

"You seem to be doing fine."

She smiles. "I like Penelope. She's nice."

"Well, maybe I need to text her sometime."

Haley finally looks at me. "That'd be good."

"Why invite him in the first place?"

She shrugs. "I just thought…it's Christmas. This year was a tough one. Maybe we could all make peace, you know. Move on."

"I know it seems simple enough, but it's not. It just never will be."

"I get it now. As much as I can, anyway."

"So, you're gonna stop this nonsense?"

"Yeah. It's kinda silly, isn't it?"

"I've done silly things, too, you know. So, coming from me, I think you're okay."

"You're a *great* older sister."

I didn't ask Santa for any of this but come on. For Christmas, I woke up with Sam being the best friend in the world. I got a mentee in the form of Riley Stafford. I've strengthened my bonds with Maddie and Haley. I've made the decision to actually be an older sister to Penelope. Tonight, there's dinner with everyone at Mel's, who I'm cool with now. There's Katie, my goddaughter.

There's the memory of Thomas, who will always be there. I go to my bedroom and pick up the picture frame in the corner of the room. I cleared the broken glass a while back, but the frame stayed there. I turn it over. A few shards are loose. I'm careful when I touch the face of the man I'll always love. The photo is of the two of us on our wedding day. We threw a prom at the reception, and that's what this photo is. It's looks like we're at prom. But, most importantly, it looks like we're happy, because we were.

And, you know what? I'm happy again. Whatever that means, I'll take it.

Greta

Sarah comes home, upset. She drops her purse beside her chair and falls into it. "That went about as expected," she says. "No shouting, at least."

I hug her from behind, and she hugs me back. "How are the girls?"

"Well, Mel seems to be taking it best. Maddie looks like she wants to do something but doesn't know what. I don't blame her. Haley stopped talking after Jess left."

"What happened?"

"She called Roger out."

"Well, good for her."

"She was a little drunk. I might have gotten on her a bit too much. Completely disregarded her feelings."

338

"I'm sure that wasn't your intention."

"Doesn't change facts, sis."

"I know." I kiss her on the temple and take a seat on the couch adjacent to her.

"I just wanted tonight to be something of a peace treaty. It's not like we were all going to suddenly be one happy family again. That time's long past. He never even comes to see them. And, let's face it. He can. The asshole's retired now."

"So, is Christmas ruined? Are we calling it off?"

It takes a moment for Sarah to fully register my lame humor, but she reacts with a long laugh that seems to have relaxed her a bit. "Yeah. Call Santa and let him know he can skip us this year."

"Speak for yourself. I want some presents."

Later, Haley comes in, quietly. She nearly jumps when I tell her, "Hi." I let her know it's okay and that her mom's in the shower. We go to her bedroom, and as she takes off her shoes and jacket, I ask her if she's okay. She just nods. I know her body language. I know that face. She wants to cry. She wants to break things. She wants to scream. She wants to run away.

"You want me to stay?" I ask.

After a moment, she nods.

"Okay."

We don't say much. She gets comfortable and washes up. We listen to a record Dani got her for Christmas. It's of a band I'm unfamiliar with, but they're pretty damn good. She ends up falling asleep long before I'm ready to, so I go to find Sarah, who is in the living room watching *It's a Wonderful Life* on DVD.

"It's hard to beat this movie on Christmas Eve, huh?" I say.

"Always good to be reassured that you are, in fact, my sister."

In the morning, we all go to Melanie's place to open presents. She tells us that she left Jess with Sam and that she thought letting her sleep in would be best. We all agree. Maddie's already here, so we commence the ripping open of some carefully wrapped and some not-so-carefully-wrapped gifts. I end up with a lot of gift cards, which suits me just fine.

After, while choking back tears, Haley apologizes and says she invited her father here. We immediately try to tell her she shouldn't feel bad for wanting that, but she tells us she's having dinner with Dani and leaves. Maddie tells us she'll figure something out. Until then, we try to make sure Katie's not caught up in any kind of drama, so we watch some of the

Christmas parade, which we all agree is pretty lame compared to the Thanksgiving one.

"Did you get what you wanted?" I ask Katie, who's seated between me and her mother on the couch.

"I didn't do too bad," she says.

"Well, that's good."

"I wish Aunt Jess were here."

"Well, we'll see her tonight."

"Definitely," Melanie adds.

Whatever Maddie did, it works, because Jess and Haley arrive for dinner, and no one brings up anything. In fact, Maddie does her best to get Haley and Katie laughing, and Jess and Sarah act like nothing happened between them. This is how it's supposed to be. No one did anything more than say things when they were upset, and we've all apologized and said "I love you" enough times to know that those are all just words, ultimately. We all *want* to be here with one another. We're so lucky, because that's certainly not how all families are.

An acquaintance of Jess' shows up a little late, constantly apologizing for it, but she's so sweet it's not hard to love her. Apparently, she's alone for the holiday, so Jess extended an invite. "The more the merrier," Melanie tells her.

Once the evening's over, and everyone begins to slowly leave, Melanie invites me and Sarah to stay the night. We do. Soon, Katie's asleep and it's the four of us seated around the kitchen table. Stephen makes some coffee.

"Thanks, babe," Melanie tells him. He responds by giving her a light but loving kiss.

"Quite a year, huh?" he says, taking his seat.

"Year's not over, yet," she tells him.

"Oh, I know. Little Haley's gonna no longer be a teenager."

"Don't remind my sister," I say.

"Every time one of my girls has turned twenty," she says, "it's been almost incomprehensible. How am I the mother of four girls who are all adults? My God, where did the time go?"

"Should we be cherishing these years with Katie?" Melanie asks Sarah playfully.

"Cherish all of them," she answers.

"Amen, Sarah," Stephen toasts to her.

She lifts her cup in response.

Haley's birthday is in less than a week. She was born on January 1, and every year before, we've always celebrated on New Year's Eve. This time, however, Jess is throwing a party with Sam and Kris. Everyone's invited, but it does seem like it's their own thing, which actually aligns with Katie's own plans. She's been invited to a sleepover that night. She really wanted to go, she confided in me, but she knew it was her aunt's birthday and didn't want to be rude by not being there. Now, she can go.

"You see, the old-slash-recent me would've been upset that Jess made plans on this night, but not anymore. I'm even fine with Katie spending the night at a friend's house. We've only done this for nineteen years. Who needs tradition?"

I'm at Sarah's place with Melanie and Stephen. We're trying our best to begin decorating for Haley's party, which is scheduled to start, for the first time, on the day she was born. Mel is doing her best to not be upset, but if it's something we can count on, it's Mel reacting to sudden change. I can't blame the girl. Sudden change threw her entire life off balance. (Or, perhaps, put it on balance. Hmm.)

Stephen gives me a look. "You know, this is a good thing. We can relax. Actually watch the ball drop, you know? I mean, really, when was the last time we actually did that? I haven't done it since high school. Greta?"

"Oh, geez. It's *definitely* been years and years."

"I guess," Mel says. "Jess could've said something sooner, though."

"She just wants to hang out with friends and colleagues," I say. "We're invited, too."

"Fair enough. I'm actually happy for her." She stops what she's doing, as if she's realizing something. "Yeah. I am. After this year, this is a *great* thing for her. You know, maybe I *will* stop by. Just for an hour or so."

"Am I invited?" Stephen playfully asks.

"Ooh. Sorry. I was planning on showing up without my wedding ring and leaving with a little something. If you catch my drift. I mean, sex."

He feigns being brokenhearted, and then looks around. "What's the theme to this, anyway? I see a lot of different stuff."

"It's something Dani came up with," Mel says. "It's prom on the moon. Apparently, it's based on a script Haley wrote for a short film in high school that never got made."

"Is that right?" I ask.

"Uh-huh. It seems Haley has a treasure trove of stuff she's barely shown anyone. Dani says she's only shown her that script. That she won't let her read anything else."

"Well, at least she's opening up that part of herself to Dani," Stephen says. "It's kinda sweet, actually."

"Yeah, it is."

"I want to do a world premiere for *Showers*. After the party and after Katie's asleep, of course. And, anyone who can't stomach blood and guts and stuff."

Dani's gathered Maddie, Sarah, Mel, and me to discuss the possibility of showing her and Sasha's horror movie after Haley's birthday party.

"Don't forget, she's in it, so it's not just me using the occasion for my own benefit. I think it'd be cool to watch our girl. Plus, it's not just graphic. Sasha and I were going for political subtext, George A. Romero-style. It's really about the Trump administration. Sort of."

"Is she in it much?" Maddie asks, confused.

"She was only meant to be in it a little, but the more she hung around this past summer, the more I wanted her in it, so me and Sasha rewrote another part so she could be a main character. She's really good in it."

"I don't know. How gory is it?"

"Pretty gory. But, not over the top, you know. We don't want people laughing or getting sick. This is about horrifying people."

"Oh, well that changes it."

"You got my vote," says Melanie. Everyone turns to her, and she reacts to everyone's reaction. "What?"

"Seriously?" Maddie asks.

"Yeah. As long as Katie's not watching. It's Haley's twentieth. Dani's her girlfriend. She's *in* the thing. Why not?"

"Huh. Okay. My vote, too."

Dani looks to me. I shrug and say, "Why not?"

Finally, there's Sarah. Dani looks at her, anticipating something positive. Sarah seems to really think this over. After a moment, she asks, "What are your intentions?"

"Huh?" Dani asks.

"With Haley. What are your intentions?"

Maddie stifles a laugh.

"My intentions?"

"Do you love my daughter?" she asks, very seriously.

Dani straightens up and says, "Uh. Yes, ma'am."

Sarah leans in and studies Dani's face. Then, a smile slowly appears across her face. "I always wanted to do that for some reason." She stands up and grabs Dani head, kissing the top of it. "Of course, you can show it," she tells her to her face.

"Well, that wasn't something I was expecting," I tell Sarah after everyone's left.

"I'm feeling pretty good. At the start of the year, the worst thing was that Mel and Jess weren't speaking. Then, it just got worse. But we survived it. So, I'm feeling pretty good right now. Plus, I'm pretty positive that girl got Haley to stop being shy about wearing her glasses. I like her."

In the end, I'm prepared to watch the ball drop in New York with everyone but Jess, Katie, and Haley, who – I assume – will opt to spend the night with Dani. By the time it's the New Year for those of us in the Central Time Zone, I'll barely be awake. We'll all toast and watch fireworks lit by neighbors a few streets away. I'll be asleep by 12:30.

<u>Greta</u>

Sarah and I go to HEB to put in an order for Haley's cake. On the way back, we discuss a bit more about the cruise trip I have planned for Haley and me.

"It sounds amazing," Sarah tells me after I've given her my current plans, which I plan on revising with Haley once she knows.

"It will be."

"Let me know how Notre Dame is doing after that fire."

"I will. But I'm sure Haley's going to want to visit the Louvre most of all."

"Are you sure you want to spend this much?"

"It's for Haley."

"I know."

"It's a big birthday for her."

"It's just…a lot of money."

"I have my retirement coming up in a few years. I have the money from the house. And, I still have plenty from Phillip's life insurance. Plus, I'm going to be your permanent roommate soon. I'll be more than fine."

"Well, okay."

"And, I promise to look after Haley as if she were my own."

"I know you will."

She drops me off at Angie's bookstore so I can meet Maddie for some last-minute shopping.

"She's not here, yet," Angie tells me when I enter.

"No problem," I tell her. The place is empty. "Pretty quiet."

"The dreaded aftermath of the holiday season. Everyone's done shopping for a while. Makes me regret opening this stupid place."

"I'm sure it'll turn around."

"I guess."

"Hey – I'll tell you what. How about I assign a few books this semester that students can pick up here for a discount? Get you a little business."

"Sounds great, actually."

"Okay then."

"How were your students this semester?"

"Good. In one of my classes, a student – Desiree – made me this giant card, which they all signed. I have it hanging in my office."

"Oh my God – that's so sweet."

"It was. They were good kids. I'll miss them."

"What are you teaching this semester?"

"British Literature II and American Lit I and II."

"Oh, damn. That's the good stuff."

"Yeah. For American Lit II, I'm thinking of focusing on the twentieth century."

"Oh, please assign Ursula K. Le Guin or Shirley Jackson. Maybe even *We Have Always Lived in the Castle*."

"I'll think about it. I'll let you know when Haley and I return."

"That's right," she says, leaning on the counter. "You guys are headed to France."

"Correct."

"Oh, you have to go to Shakespeare and Co. I've always wanted to visit."

"I think we can manage that. It's in Paris, right?"

The door opens, as Angie says, "That's right." It's Maddie.

"What's up? What are you guys talking about?"

"You. We're talking about all the things that annoy us about you."

"Must've been pretty difficult."

"It really wasn't."

Maddie sarcastically smiles at her and then turns to me. "So, where we headed?"

"I don't know. Any ideas?"

We end up at Waterloo, digging through crates for anything Haley might be interested in. We both figure she has enough movies. I kick myself for selling my modest collection of a two dozen or so about ten years ago. They would've made a lovely gift.

"I remember getting Mel to drive me around town to look for a record player back when I got my first job," Maddie tells me. "They were pretty expensive. The ones we could find anyway. And, I can remember buying *London Calling* – used – at Half Price Books for ten bucks. An original printing. I was so ahead of my time. And then a quarter of an inch of water came in that year and basically ruined all of them. Well, the packaging anyway."

"I remember. You were so upset."

"It's trivial, I know. But I never started over. I still have the same record player and a few dozen records in plain white sleeves. I rarely listen to them."

"Well, it's up to Haley to keep the tradition of vinyl love in this family alive."

A decision is eventually reached to buy half of the eight albums we found. Once in line, I ask Maddie how her new book is coming along.

"It's fine. For whatever reason I have this recurring motif of 'The Rainbow Connection,' but I'm not even sure that's allowed. I mean, I'm not quoting anything; it just pops in and out throughout – different characters sing it or refer to it. It's a weird choice."

"Have you figured out what to do with the main character?"

"How did you -?"

"Haley."

"Of course. Well. At this point, I just want to get to the finish line. Then, there's going to be quite a bit of research."

"Really?"

"Well, I'm writing about a lot of real-life stuff, so I want to make sure everything adds up properly. Last thing I'd want is an agent rejecting it because of inconsistencies."

"Does that happen?"

"I mean, if something shows enough promise, you can always work with the writer. That's the whole idea. But if the writing's not interesting enough *and* it has problems like that – forget about it."

"Hmm. Do you miss it?"

"Being an editor?"

I nod.

"Sometimes. It was a lot of work, though. I mean, this is actually a lot more work than I thought. I wrote a ton of pages for the first book, which I walked away from. That got me here. It was worth it in that sense, but combined? Jesus. Lots of work."

"Work, work, work."

"Yeah, well, at least I'm not having to work in the sun for ten hours a day for barely any pay. I'm lucky."

"I think we're all pretty lucky in some way."

"We work hard in this family."

"Yes, but you can never overlook luck. After all, you'll put in the hard work and have a finish novel. *But* you'll need the luck of having someone who reads it and actually likes it. I mean, we know the stories. How many times was J.K. Rowling rejected?"

"Fair enough."

Jess makes us lunch and asks what the big deal with vinyl is after we tell her what we got for Haley.

"It sounds better."

She brushes it off.

"No, it does. Aunt Greta?"

"If the record's good, with minimal damage, it sounds wonderful," she offers.

"Well, with all due respect," Jess says, "I'm more than okay listening to Spotify."

I find myself suddenly wondering what Phillip would've thought of things like Spotify. The man loved music. Any and all kinds. I can remember him asking to borrow every single cassette he could so he could copy it and listen to it again and again and again. I went through the few boxes in the garage of things I put away a month or so after he died as I was packing up the house. I found the one with about a hundred tapes, mostly of stuff I've never heard of before. I've been meaning to use Sarah's tape player to go through each one.

"Aunt Greta?" Jess asks, waking me from my reverie.

"Sorry."

"Penny for your thoughts?"

I smile at that. "Just thinking about your uncle. It happens."

"What about?" Maddie asks.

"Music."

Maddie seems to think of something.

"Penny for *your* thoughts, Madelyn?"

"Nothing really. It's just this weird feeling. It's, like, we talk about Phillip like he's gone, because he *is* gone, but…I don't know. Like I said, it's just a weird feeling."

"The Writer, ladies and gentlemen," Jess announces.

Maddie gives her a smirk.

Phillip died before Katie was born. He had a heart attack at the age of 42. It was not something anyone saw coming. After all, he ate right, didn't drink or smoke, and he went on walks multiple times a week. When it happened, I was heartbroken, but I also had bills to pay and a job to go to. He died in April. I still had several more weeks left in the school year. Thankfully, by this point, I not only had Sarah, but there was Jess and Melanie. They all helped when they could. Sarah was with me throughout, of course. She took care of most of it.

I suppose it wasn't until his birthday came along that October that I started the long process of truly moving on. When the date of our anniversary came the following January, I cried, but I also found comfort in remembering the years we spent with one another. As time has passed, I've found that I've only grown to love him more. Thinking about his tapes is a good example of this. I knew of them when he was alive. Only now do they represent something else. In a way, I'm still learning about him.

"I think I'm going to make Haley a mixtape," I say.

"Hmm," Jess responds.

"I like that," Maddie says.

"Yeah," Jess adds. "It's hella thoughtful. Just one question, though. How is she going to play it?"

"Does Melanie have her old Walkman?" I ask.

Through fits of laughter, Haley tells me, "No, you have to move your arms like this." She does a move, but so help me, I can't mimic it.

She's trying to teach me this dance, the name of which I can't remember, no matter how many times she tells me. To be fair, my age has nothing to do with it. I've never been much of a dancer, though I do love doing it. I learned long ago to not care about what others have to say about how I do it. That's why I find myself laughing along with my niece when she sees I have little coordination.

"I can't do it!"

"Yes, you can. Not with that attitude. For real. Watch me." She does the whole dance again for me. "Okay, now do the first part. Do this." She does it.

I successfully mimic it.

"See! Okay. Now do this." She does it.

"Okay." I pull that part off.

"Alright, now do them both back to back." She does it.

I fail and fall to the ground in defeat. She bursts out laughing.

"Aunt Greta!" she manages.

"No, I'm fine. Just going to lie here forever and ever."

She joins me. "Ah. This is actually comfortable."

We're in Sarah's backyard. The grass was recently cut, and it feels wonderful. It reminds me of my old backyard, which used to be my favorite place in the world.

"So, are you worried about getting old?" I ask her.

"I'm not old."

"I don't know. Leaving your teenage years is a big deal."

"I guess. I'm just more concerned with school and Dani and stuff."

"Your mom told me you got all A's and one B this semester."

"Yeah. Not sure how I pulled that off."

"I'm sure you're an excellent student."

"I'm okay."

I want to press her a little more but decide against it. The day is going so well that I don't want to rock the boat. Besides, it's Haley's life and her decisions – not mine. Of course, there's no harm in asking another kind of question.

"If you don't mind me asking, how *are* things going with Dani?"

"Pretty good. I do wish we saw each other more often, though. I mean, she drives me crazy sometimes. Like, she *never* locks her door. Who *does* that?!"

"That's pretty dangerous."

"Right?! Ugh. I swear. She also leaves hair, like, everywhere. It's disgusting."

I hold in laughter, hoping she doesn't see me. I can remember things Phillip used to do that drove me nuts. Everyone in relationships knows this. It's a part of it. I'm sure Haley will end up loving these things about Dani.

"She always thinks I'm cute when I get angry, and it just makes me more annoyed and angry."

"In fairness, you're always cute." I turn my head toward her and see her change from upset to relaxed, a smile forming on her face.

"Beside the point."

"Ha ha!"

"That's not the point. The point is, even through all of that, I still wanna be around her. I wanna talk to her. Listen to her. Hug her. Look at her. I love her so much." She turns her head to me and asks, "Do you think we'll last?"

"Oh, I can't answer that."

"Come on."

"What do *you* think? Right now?"

She takes a deep breath. "I kinda want to marry her."

"Then marry her."

"I'm not gonna *marry* her. We live apart from each other. I'm not even halfway through college. It's…."

"Well. Maybe after."

She adjusts her glasses and props herself up on her elbow, considering this. "What do you think mom would say?"

"Who cares? What do you think *Dani* would say?"

"I can't."

"Okay. Just know it's *your* decision. After all, I didn't get married until after college. Same with your mom and sisters. Plus, you don't *ever* have to get married."

"I do *want* to."

"Yeah?"

She nods. "Someday."

I wasn't trying to persuade her to propose or anything like that. I wanted her to understand her feelings and that whatever happens is up to her. It's not about anyone but her and Dani. Even then, she has to do what she believes is right. I'm not sure I made myself clear, but Haley is a sharp girl. I'm sure she picked it up, one way or another.

Later that day, she takes me to see Dani at her and Sasha's place. I watch as they set the table for lunch, perfectly in sync. Dani knows that Haley wants a paper plate, and Haley knows Dani doesn't want ice in her drink. Both make mistakes with Sasha, who tells me that no one ever remembers that she doesn't like ketchup.

"It's the same with me and mustard," I tell her.

"People, am I right?"

"Amen."

The four of us chow down on vegan hotdogs, courtesy of Sasha, and they're not half bad. Dani and Sasha premiere the trailer for their horror movie, and it looks impressive. I glance at Haley, who looks at Dani with loving pride, and I know right then they're going to be okay.

<u>Jess</u>

I go to see Mel the day after Christmas, and it turns out she and Stephen are hosting a post-Christmas kickback for Katie and her friends. Nothing elaborate, though they are barbequing.

"Smells amazing," I tell Stephen as I follow him into the kitchen.

"Right? I tell you, that sister of yours knows her way around a grill. I always seem to either burn or undercook anything out there. I've learned to get out of her way."

"Sounds wise."

"Why thank you, madam," he says, offering a bow.

"You may rise," I tell him. I like being able to joke with Stephen again. We've always gotten along well. So help me, I missed him when Mel and I were "separated."

"I'm gonna go say hi and then get out of you guys' hair."

"Oh, no – it's fine," he tells me as I head out.

"Don't worry about it. Just take those drinks to those girls. They're gonna eat you alive."

He smiles and waves, heading off to be a good dad.

Outside, I make sure Mel sees me before I get to her, so I don't startle her and she catches on fire or something insane.

"Hey," she says. "I didn't know you were coming by. I would've told you what was going on."

"Yeah. Pretty cool."

"Well, Katie's been getting along with more kids this year, so we thought this would help maintain any possible friendships. Plus, why not, right?"

"Yeah, totally." I suddenly feel bad. Not really jealous but more left out. I consider this as Mel starts to explain the proper way to check a meat's temperature. Why do I feel this way? After all this time, I got what I wanted. I'm close with my sister again. Still, I suppose time really has moved on. Mel was a mother long before we had our estrangement of sorts, but it feels like this is her life now. It's Stephen and Katie. And that's how it should be. Realizing this actually makes me feel better, and without knowing it, I'm smiling.

"What are you smiling about?" Mel asks.

"You have a good life," I tell her, which seems to catch her off guard.

"Thanks. It's a lot of work sometimes."

"Worth it, though."

"Yeah."

She seems to be feeling guilty, so I say this to make sure she knows how I feel: "Mel, I'm happy for you. It's as simple as that."

"I just wish you could've had this, too."

"Don't say that. This is how it turned out. And it's fine."

"Could've been great."

"Some days *are* great. Some days…maybe not. But regardless, good for you, little sis."

She smiles.

"Now, I'm gonna head out."

"No, stay."

"For real, it's fine. I'll swing by tomorrow. I just wanted to see you guys. Tell Katie I'll see her tomorrow."

"Okay. Are you sure?"

"Definitely. I got someone to see anyway."

Sam is eating the biggest damn sandwich I've ever seen her eat, and she looks like she's loving it. We're in the breakroom at her office, which is a lot cleaner than any breakroom I've ever been in. It also smells nice.

"Thanks for lunch," she tells me with her mouth full. I give her a thumbs up.

"I can't believe I've never been in here before."

"You've never come for lunch at my work before."

"Well, there's that."

"And, hey, as much as I love seeing you – and I do – why are you here? Are you okay? Or, are you just bored?"

"Neither. I wanted to come see you."

"You're bored."

"I'm not."

"Yes, you are. You don't have a job at the moment, so you need to kill time somewhere. How's that coming along actually? The job hunting."

"It's…fine. I haven't really been looking."

"Jess."

"I know. It's just…whoever I apply to, they're going to call my old place, and they're going to find out what happened, and I just don't – I'm not ready for that rejection."

"Maybe you won't get rejected."

"Maybe I will."

"If you're relying on a maybe then you need to realize it can go both ways. That's why I always look at the positive. Maybe you'll get a job. Maybe you won't. If it's maybe either way, go with the positive one."

"That makes sense, I guess."

She takes another big bite and with her mouth full again says, "I know. I'm a genius."

I smile. "Are we still on for New Year's Eve?"

"Oh, *hell* yes. Kris is going to deejay, by the way."

"Is that right? Coming out of retirement, huh?"

"Yes, ma'am. Get ready for a steady stream of Pet Shop Boys, Selena, and Daft Punk."

"Can't wait." Two people come in, talking amongst themselves. They acknowledge us and go on, as one of them heats up some soup in the microwave. "Do you like it here?" I ask her, lower than before but not quite at a whisper.

"Yeah. Why not?"

"I don't know. You wanted to be a dancer, right?"

"Yeah, when I was a kid."

"Up until college, if memory serves. One of the first conversations we ever had was about how you were taking a break from it so you could focus on getting a degree."

"I remember. I also remember you admitting that being a surgeon was not your *passion* but your *love*. *You* wanted to be a science teacher."

"That's right. Wow. I haven't thought about that in *years*."

"It's always an option."

"I'll teach high school biology if you join a community theatre company."

"Don't tempt me. I'll do it."

"Yeah, right."

Neither of us pursue the topic. In fact, Sam changes the subject and starts talking about how good her sandwich is.

The idea doesn't leave me, though. When I stop by Mel's the next day, I ask her about it while Stephen and Katie work on origami.

"I could *totally* see you doing that," she tells me.

"Really?"

"Sure. What's stopping you?"

"A few things. I like doing my own thing. I'd have to start following specific curriculum. Plus, I remember being in high school. Teenagers are dicks."

She laughs. "Yeah, that's never gonna change."

I look over at Katie who looks to be struggling with whatever it is she's folding. Stephen sees her and seems to calm her, eventually guiding her. It's a sweet moment that happens a lot probably.

"What about college?"

I turn back to Mel.

"Be a professor. You remember college, right? You can treat the students like adults because that's what they are. If they try to be asshats, you kick 'em out of class."

"Asshats?"

"What? What's wrong with that?"

"Nothing. I guess it's something to think about."

"The more I'm thinking about it, the more I'm certain you'd be a damn good professor."

"Well, even if that doesn't happen, I'm kind of a mentor now."

"What? Really? When did this happen? For whom?"

"Christmas Day. It's Riley Stafford."

"Oh, is *that* why she was at Christmas dinner? I thought you were just being nice."

"Yeah, well, I suppose I *was*."

"This is the one you helped get a job after you left the hospital?"

"That's her."

"And she wants you to mentor her? That's pretty cool."

"It definitely feels good. Sometimes I just think everything I do is meaningless."

"Tell me about it. There are times when I wonder whether I'm making any difference in Katie's life. I hope what I'm doing is positive. That I'm supportive. That I'm protective. That I'm loving. But I don't know. I feel like a failure sometimes."

"That's insane."

She shrugs.

"Mel, you're like Mom 2.0. Katie is *so* lucky to have you."

Speaking of Katie, she comes over and shows off the horse she's just made. "Oh, that's so cute," Mel tells her.

"And you made that yourself?" I ask. "What a showoff."

Katie hands it to me. "I made it for you."

"Thank you."

"You're welcome."

There was a time in my life when I wanted kids. That was never in the cards for me. I have the opportunity to be a great aunt to Katie, though. I can be the best mentor ever for Riley. I can make damn sure I'm the kind of older sister my family can depend on. That's a good life. It really is.

I need to talk to Penelope.

Later, once I'm home, I text her the following: "Hey. Sorry for just now getting back to you. I hope that's cool. Text me if you ever need anything, okay? That's what big sisters are for." The moment I hit SEND, I feel incredibly nervous. What if she doesn't respond? What if she takes months to reply, like I did?

In less than a minute, she replies, "Thank you so much!! I think you're awesome. Feel free to text me anytime to" This makes me feel really good, and I plan on texting her once a week from now on, whether she likes it or not.

That night, she texts around midnight, which I have to remember means it's only around 10:00 in California. It reads: "just so u know, I know what our dad did to u and I don't like it. Is it okay to say I love u? cause I do"

I reply, "of course. I love u too" – and then realize that I mean it.

Family is so goddamn important to me, and I've allowed stupid shit to cloud relationships with people I actually want to know and love. I'll never forgive my father, and I don't know just how much I can ever care about Clara. But Penelope? She's a part of me, and I vow to never forget that again.

New Year's Eve arrives, and Kris comes over early to set up her equipment.

"Jesus, how much did all of this cost?"

"A shitload. But it'll be worth it. Trust me."

"How exactly do you have so much money as a regional manager for a plastics company?"

"It's not just surgeons or lawyers that have the opportunity to make bank."

"Fair enough."

"When's the party starting?"

"I'm expecting people here by eight, so nine, I guess."

"Are your neighbors cool with this?"

"My neighbors go out for New Year's, so we're good."

"Sweet."

"Plus, we're not in our twenties anymore. Shit – our thirties."

"Fucking-A. Crazy how time passes."

"I'm thirsty," I say walking to the kitchen. "Want anything?" I call out.

"I'm good!"

I look in my fridge, curious about how I'm going to be tonight. I'm expecting just about everyone but me to be drinking. I know that people fighting an addiction can easily hang out with others who are doing the very thing they're addicted to, because I've lived that life for a long-ass time. Maddie seemingly always drinks when she's out or we're having dinner. "I don't drink when the sun's out" is her motto, and to be fair, she can also hold her liquor. I've seen her tipsy, but she's always in control. "Lucky," I say to myself, aloud.

"What?" Kris says, entering.

I jump. "Jesus."

Kris holds her arms up, unsure what to do.

"You scared the shit out of me."

"Sorry. I thought you heard me."

I take a deep breath.

"You okay?"

"Yeah. I just…." I close the refrigerator door. "I'm not thirsty actually."

"Okay…." I sit at the table, as Kris continues, "So, um, I was wondering if you could give me a thumbs up or thumbs down concerning the gift I got for Haley."

"Yeah, sure."

"Cool," she says, reaching into her back pocket and pulling out a lighter. "What do you think?"   She holds it out for me to take, which I do.

I inspect it. The thing looks crazy familiar. "Where do I know this from?"

"It's mine. We used to light our -."

"Oh, yeah. Damn. Haven't done *that* since college."

"Yeah, me neither. I found it when I went through stuff a few months ago. I was feeling nostalgic. Anyway, I cleaned it, filled it up, and I thought Haley could get some use out of it."

"You think my sister smokes weed?"

"No. Haley hates the smell of it."

"What?"

"We've talked."

"When?"

"I email her every now and then."

"Jesus, that girl emails and texts everyone, doesn't she?"

"She's a sweet girl. We all love her."

"She is, isn't she?"

"So, what do you think?"

"I like it. I think it's a good idea."

"Right? I'd get her a gift certificate to the Criterion Collection, but I swear – that girl has enough movies."

I smile. "She does."

Kris puts the lighter in her pocket and asks, "Should I wrap it?"

Things get loud around 10:30, and that's when Mel stops by, prompting an introduction by DJ Kris, who gets everyone to shout "whoo!" at her presence. She laughs, embarrassed, but clearly enjoying it. I go up to her, a bottled water in my hand.

"Hey," I yell over the music. "I was hoping you'd make it!"

"It's loud!"

"Yeah, it's great, right?!"

"Not really!"

I smile. "Follow me!" I take her down the hall to my bedroom. I close the door and we go into the bathroom. We can talk normally in here, even though it sounds like an IMAX movie through several layers of wall.

"Good to see you."

"Seriously, it's loud out there."

"Yeah, I know. We're probably gonna cut it short. We're all getting pretty tired at this point. Guess we really *are* old, huh?"

"I can't believe I used to love to sit next to the speakers."

"You were probably high."

"Probably," she says, embarrassed.

I laugh.

We end up just looking at each other, not really sure what to say. We end up talking about Haley's party and whether or not Kris knows what she's doing behind her table. After about ten minutes, Mel apologizes but she wants to get back home. "I need to wake up early to help Mom and Aunt Greta finish setting up. Plus, Dani wants to set up something in the backyard for the movie."

"That should be interesting."

She nods, awkward. "Well, Happy New Year."

"Happy New Year," I say, as we hug.

Within minutes, she's in her car, driving away. I go back inside and find Sam, who is dancing her ass off. I join her, and it feels like I'm twenty again, dancing at some party thrown by someone I never even met. I'm sober now, and it's so much better. Maybe it's because Sam and Kris are here. But that can't be it. They were there with me twenty years ago. I guess it's different now. We're that much older, and we've seen and done so much. Dancing like this isn't something we do often. It's a treat. It's special.

I wish I could've danced more with Thomas. Neither of us were particularly into dancing much, but when we did, it was nice. This is nice, too, but maybe it's because it's so rare. I'm not sure. Hell, there's so damn much I'm not sure about now, but I do know a few things. Sam and Kris are so much more than I thought they were, which is not a good thing to admit. What Kris said, about Mel being my best friend, I thought that was so true, and maybe it was at some point. But that time has passed. *Sam* is my best friend. Kris is my…*second* best friend? Best Friend the Second? I'll have to work on that, even though it's all just labels. I know what they mean to me. Perhaps I need to show it more and let them both know I'm happy that they're on this earth.

Tomorrow, my sister turns twenty, and for the first time in a long time, I feel like her oldest sister. I feel like I can protect her and be there for her.

All of this is a warm ball that fills my heart and my belly and my soul. I may not know what I'm doing, but at the same time, I got this.

<u>Maddie</u>

Marie visits, so Angie and I go have a few drinks with her. But, by the second round, the three of us agree that a quieter setting is more desirable, so we go back to my place. I open a bottle of vodka and put on some music, and we decide to play poker.

"So, what has the illustrious Marie Delgado been up to?" I ask, as I deal.

"Well, like I said, lots of picture taking."

"I'm sure she means personally," Angie says.

"That I do," I confirm.

"Oh. Well,…." Marie finds a picture on her phone and turns it to me and Angie. It's an insanely hot guy, obviously, but there's no harm in looking. *Damn*, I think to myself.

"Not bad," Angie tells her.

"The sex was okay, but I liked touching his body, so…."

"What happened?"

"You know. A little of this. A little of that. I wasn't planning on anything being all that serious, you know?"

376

"Sure."

"Okay, guys," I say. "Standard Texas Hold 'Em rules." I turn over three cards in the center. "Let's do this."

As we play, we drink, and talk, and laugh, and it's great. Eventually, once the pizza arrives, I switch the bottle with some wine, but the fun continues. Marie is kicking both of our asses, and I can't blame the alcohol.

"How in the *hell* did you learn to play so well?" Angie asks.

"Guys like to play. I like to hang out with guys."

"That's a little sexist, but I'll allow it."

Marie smiles and finishes her drink. I pour her some more, and we start the next hand.

"You know, I've been with you guys for a few hours now, and Maddie, you haven't said anything about your book. Are you almost done with it?"

"Just about."

"Really?" Angie asks.

I nod.

"Why didn't you tell me?"

I shrug. "I figured I would once I was done."

"That's so cool," Marie says. "How long is it?"

"A little over four hundred pages."

"Wow, that's a lot."

I nod. "I had a lot to say."

"How does that translate to when you actually publish? Will it be longer or shorter?"

"It depends on the page size and font and all of that. But we're getting a little ahead of it. I need an agent of my own and then editing with an actual editor starts."

"It shouldn't be too difficult, though. You used to *be* one. I'm sure there's little to be done. Plus, you can maybe go to your old job, right? I call, by the way."

Angie folds, but I'm in. I turn over the last card, and I have nothing. Marie lays down her cards to a full house.

"Shit," I say, a little frustrated.

"Ha-ha," Marie says, taking her chips.

"*Fuck*, you're good. And, *maybe* I'll take it to them. We'll see."

"Why are we even playing this?" Angie asks.

"Oh, come on, guys," Marie says. "We're not even playing for money. Should I *not* be trying to win?"

"No, you're right."

"We hate losing," I say. "Sue us."

"My bad," Marie says, stifling a laugh.

I shuffle the cards and say, "You know what? Let's change it up. Let's play 21."

We do, and Marie still kicks our asses. Eventually, it's late, so we call it a night. They ask to sleep over, and I tell them it's no problem, so long as they figure who's sleeping where. "I call couch!" Angie says.

"Really?" I ask.

"I like how couches feel."

"Okay. Marie, the guest bed is yours."

I leave them to take a shower and brush my teeth. When I head back, Marie is watching some movie on HBO. She tells me Angie's in the guest shower. I sit beside her and take her hand in mine.

"I'm glad you're here. I wish I saw you more."

"Hey, I come around a few times a year."

"Fair enough." I sit back to start watching the movie with her. I haven't seen this one.

"So, how's life in your thirties?"

"Ha!"

"That good, huh?"

"It's nothing special. I feel the exact same way I did this time last year."

"Yeah, but I'm sure that'll change in a few years."

"Maybe. I forget sometimes that Mel's just over seven years older than me."

"That's nuts."

"Right?"

"You in a good place?"

"As much as I can be, I suppose."

"It can totally be worse than it is."

"Oh, I know. Most days I don't acknowledge it – mostly because I don't see it or…I don't know – but I can be such a millennial."

"You and me both. I always think I'm above it, mostly because I'm not all that into social media or whatever."

"Says the girl with over a hundred thousand followers on Instagram."

"Fair enough," she says, and I smile to myself. "But I'm not attached to my phone. Neither of us are. Anyway, we did good after college. Maybe not great…. Angie's got a bookstore for crying out loud. Borders closed, but Angie grew from the ashes."

"I miss Borders like I miss Blockbuster. I just wish they were around."

"Me, too."

"You know, we were punk kids once."

"Oh, I know. I thought I knew it all. It's like the moment we can call bullshit on the adults in our lives we think we know the world. But we don't. Not really."

"I guess some of us...."

"Well, some of us is anything, right? Some people murder, but not everybody."

"Morbid, but I get it. I just think how I've technically been an adult for twelve years, but I'm just now beginning to feel like one. I went away to college. Still felt like a kid. I got an internship. Then a job. Then I quit to pursue a dream. Hell, I turned thirty! *Just* now, though."

"You think maybe it's because your little sister's turning twenty."

"Probably. It's just weird. I mean. When did you officially feel like an adult?"

"When I graduated high school."

"Really?"

"Yeah. I knew I was ready. Ready to leave home and do my own thing."

"That's impressive."

"I don't know about that."

"It is."

"Why?"

"Look at me. I moved right back home after college."

"Because that's where your job was."

"Because I didn't apply to places in New York or Chicago. Or somewhere out of this place. I stayed because I knew I could. Because it was safe."

"And, that's bad?"

"Yeah. I think. Isn't it? Shouldn't I be more confident? Shouldn't I be able to leave and start my own life away from my family?"

"If that's what you want. What do *you* want?"

"I don't know. And, I gotta say, as a thirty-year-old, that answer should not suffice."

"Maddie, I love you, so, with all due respect, you're whining."

"What? Is it my 'white privilege'?"

"No, but the fact you made that joke to me shows you have some. But that doesn't bother me – it never has. The point is that there's nothing wrong with your life. What are you complaining about?"

"I know. Angie pretty much got on me over this."

"When?"

"I don't know. A while ago."

"And no change?"

"Nope."

"Mads. Come on. What's the problem?"

"I don't know."

"Think about it. Even if it's one thing. What's the *one* thing that makes you happy?"

"A lot of things make me happy. But I'm happiest when I write."

"Then do that."

"It's stupid, though."

"Why?"

"Jess is a doctor. Mel works in an office, but what she does affects people."

"Mad -."

"My mom's a psychiatrist. My aunt's a professor. Freakin' Haley's going to be someone awesome. Everybody knows it."

Marie shakes her head and looks down.

"Katie wants to be a research scientist. She wants to cure a disease. And – what? – I want to write some stories? What the hell kind of life is that?"

She looks back up. "I take pictures." She turns to me. "What does that say about me?"

"Marie -."

"No. What about me? You say writing a novel is meaningless. What about photography?"

"That's different."

"How?"

"Because what you do affects people."

"And what you want to do doesn't?"

"It's different."

"How?"

"Because who the hell wants to read a book, let alone mine?"

She lets it sit there for a moment before saying, "Do you know how stupid that sounds knowing your best friend literally owns a place that sells these worthless things no one apparently wants to read?"

I start to calm down.

"Maddie, fuck everybody and what they *might* think. Because I'm assuming this isn't you. I'm assuming this is what you think others say or believe – that writing accomplishes nothing. But it does. And if you don't think so tell that to the literal millions of people who are and have been affected by stories since Guttenberg. Fuck. I *wish* I could do what you do."

Angie slowly enters. We look up at her.

"Hey," she says, awkwardly.

Marie turns to me. "So?" she asks.

I'm a writer, I think. I turn to her. "I'm a writer."

"Good. Angie? What do you think? Is Maddie a writer?"

"Hell, yeah, she is."

I want to hug them both, and soon enough I do. Angie joins us, and we watch some TV. She's the first to fall asleep. Marie and I leave her alone. Before I leave her to the guest room, I tell her thank you. She slightly smiles and tells me it's nothing. "Love you," she says, closing the door.

"Love you," I tell her. I go to sleep feeling pretty good.

Here's the thing: my kid sister's growing up, but that doesn't mean she won't be getting her birthday spanks. I volunteer to be the one who picks her up from Dani's and drives her to Mom's for the big event. Angie and Marie leave me to it, saying they'll meet me that night at the party. A few days ago, I called Dani to let her in on my plans. She thought it sounded hilarious.

"You do this every year?"

"Oh, yeah. Ever since she was ten."

"Ten?"

"Yep. A full decade and counting. It's definitely a tradition."

"Does anyone else do this?"

"No – just me."

It's true. I tried to get Jess and Mel in on it, but they scoffed and said the spanks were all me. Mom doesn't think there's much harm in it. I mean, it's not like I make them hurt. Twenty spanks *are* a lot, though.

I arrive about a half hour early to do this. After Dani lets me in and I lock the apartment door, she goes to tell Haley I'm here. "She's in the shower."

"I can wait," I say, taking off my jacket.

Sasha's in the kitchen typing something on her laptop.

"What's up, Sasha?"

"You know, applications for film festivals suck. I feel like I'm applying for college again."

"I didn't know you applied."

"I got into UT and A&M."

"No shit. Why didn't you go?"

"Eh," she says with a shrug. I sit at the kitchen table, sort of across from her, and say, "I like the red streak." I point to my own head.

"Oh. Yeah. I figured since Dani went back to her natural hair, someone had to bring a little color into the picture."

"Well, red's a good color on you."

"Thanks."

Dani comes in and leans on the counter. "She'll be done in a bit."

"Do you know what's about to happen?" I ask Sasha.

"You mean the 'birthday tradition'? I do."

"Well, okay then."

"I think it's hilarious."

Haley comes out in a robe, her hair completely dry – probably didn't wash it. She freezes when she sees me. "No."

I stand. "Yes."

"No!" she yells and runs back into the bedroom, closing the door on me. I try to turn the knob, but she's holding it from the other side. "Open, you dork!"

"You're not getting me this year!"

Dani and Sasha are loving this. I smile and glance their way. Both give me a thumbs up. "I'm going to break down the door."

"Then you'll have to pay for it."

"Dani? Do you mind? A new door on me?"

"Don't you dare!" Haley yells from the other side.

Dani sighs and comes over. "Haley, just let Maddie in."

"What?! Do you know what she's going to do?"

"Spank you? It doesn't seem like the end of the world."

"You know?!"

"Family talks to one another," I say. Dani smirks, looking moved by what I've said.

I hear a very audible sigh and the knob loosens. I let go. The door opens, and Haley looks defeated. "Fine." She goes to her bed, and I enter. She throws herself on the bed, face first. I make a big deal, rubbing my hands together Mr. Miyaki style. Dani and Sasha stand at the door, waiting. I lift my hand and bring it down, lightly tapping Haley's big butt.

She turns her head to face me, confused. "What was that?"

"The end of an era." I get off the bed and reach my hand out. She takes it, apprehensively, and I help her up. "Happy Birthday, baby sis."

She turns to the girls and asks, "You knew about this?"

"Of course," Sasha says.

Dani adds, giving me a quick glance, "Family talks to one another."

I help Haley get dressed, and soon, the four of us are on the road.

"Who's texting you?"

Haley looks at her phone. "It's Penelope." She looks at something and starts giggling. She shows the other two in the backseat. They giggle as well.

"What? What is it?"

We come to a stop, and Haley shows me. It's a .gif of Will Ferrell from *Elf* screaming, "SANTA!" but because it's a meme, it reads, "HAPPY BIRTHDAY!" So help me, I giggle, too.

Hitting the gas, I tell her, "Oh, by the way, Nicole and Sophia are here."

I glance over and see Haley about to explode. "Are you serious?"

"It's a big day. We flew them here."

"Eek!" She hugs me, and I nearly swerve.

"I can't wait to meet this mysterious Nicole," Dani says from the backseat.

"You guys will love her."

"I haven't seen Sophia since high school," Sasha mentions. "Wonder what she's been up to."

"I email her from time to time, but I'm curious, too."

By the time we get there, the sun begins its descent.

I wake up around nine. In over twelve hours, I'll officially no longer be a teenager, and even though turning 21 does *seem* like a bigger deal, I'm excited.

Dad's sent me an email. I give it a cursory glance and then go about my morning routine. It's nothing special. He wishes he could be here, he loves me, blah, blah, blah. As I brush my teeth, I get a text from Dani. She's sent a photo of herself in a pair of glasses just like mine, and I realize I've left them at her place, and they *are* mine. I put on my damn contacts, practically counting the seconds before I can get to Dani and Sasha's so I can swap them with my specs. I finish up and text her back: "look whos sexy…"

She sends back a winking face. As much as I hate my contacts, I'm trying to use them up. Seems like a waste if I don't.

I get dressed and have a late lunch with Mom and Aunt Greta. They ask me if I'm excited for the party tonight, and I let them know that of course I am, because of course I am. Throughout the meal, I constantly have the feeling like they want to tell me something, and since I figure it has to do with my birthday, I don't say anything about it. Once it comes time for me to leave to see Dani, Aunt Greta excuses herself. Mom tells me Aunt Greta has something for me. She returns with a small-ish box, moving my plate

aside and laying it on the table in front of me. I'm definitely curious.

"It's something I've been planning for a few months, *but* I want it clear

that you – by no means – have to do this."

"O-*kay*...."

She opens it and lets me look. It's a lot of travel stuff, all having to do

with a Viking Cruise. *Holy crap!* I want to yell. I pull out a brochure and

then a travel guide to Paris. Eventually, I find my ticket. I look up at her,

and she seems excited herself. I look back at the ticket. "Aunt Greta...."

"What do you think?"

"This is on *your* bucket list."

"And *yours*, if I remember correctly."

I find a smile slowly making its way across my face. "Seriously?" I ask,

making sure I haven't gotten the wrong idea.

"Seriously, birthday girl."

I get up and give her the biggest hug.

"Thank you so much."

"Absolutely."

We break apart and I ask," Mom?"

"You'll be back before school starts. It's up to you."

"Oh, I *want* to go."

"Then it's settled," Aunt Greta says.

I turn to her. "You and me for about a week?"

"You got it."

"Sweet."

It's a hell of a way to start my birthday, that's for sure.

"I'm jealous," Dani admits when I tell her. "I wish *I* had a cool aunt like that. Does this mean you've been rich this whole time?"

I scoff, and she smiles. I shake my head and smirk.

"When do you leave?" Sasha asks.

"Next week."

"Awesome."

"Right?"

"Where're you going exactly?" Dani asks me.

"Paris. Well, France, mostly. Paris for about two days."

"Please tell me you're going to the Louvre."

"Duh."

"Oh – don't forget about Notre Dame," Sasha adds. "Hopefully it won't burn down before you get to see it."

"That's horrible. And kinda true, I guess."

"Honestly," Dani says, moving closer. "Pretty badass gift."

We kiss, and I can see Sasha get up to give us some alone time. We're in her and Dani's living room, on the couch, and sure enough, we keep making out.

"So, I have a little bit of a surprise for tonight. But I figured I'd tell you now, because it's also a little bit selfish."

"What is it?"

"We're premiering our movie after the party ends. Your mom and sisters are cool with it, as long as Katie's asleep by then."

"Oh."

"Now, I know it's going to be weird seeing yourself and having the people you love seeing you act and all of that, but baby, you're so good in it."

"You have to say that."

"I really don't. It's the truth. Frankly, if you weren't good, Sasha would've recast you and reshot all of your scenes."

"Really?"

"Yep. She told me. When I wanted you in it more, she told me if you weren't good, you'd be -," she finishes with a "cut" sound.

"Huh," I say. I'm equally hurt and impressed with Sasha. For the first time, the film seems real, and not something they just wanted to really do. They *are* filmmakers. Shame on me for thinking otherwise.

"You good?"

"Yeah, I think I am. Just hold my hand during all my scenes."

"I'll hold your hand throughout." She kisses me and then adds, "Even when your hands get clammy."

"They don't get…." I sigh. "Fair enough."

Maddie comes to pick us up and to give me my birthday spanks. Dani's in on it, and I do actually feel betrayed, but then it ends up being a tap – and the tradition seems to come to an end. I doubt I'll miss it.

On the way to Mom's, Penelope sends me a few texts, including one I show everyone, which is a pretty hilarious meme. The other two I keep to myself. The first one says: "love u sis. You're my role model. Thanks for everything"

The second one, after the meme, says, "I hope we can all be together one day."

"I hope so too," I write back. I do.

I'm told that my roommate and old best friend will be in attendance, and when I show up, everybody's there already. It feels like the end of a movie, when all the cast of characters are gathered. Of course, Dad's not here, but it's not like he's really missed. I acknowledge this feeling and move on. Dani, maybe sensing this, gives me a peck on the cheek. "Dry the Rain" by The Beta Band plays, and I know it's Jess who's selected the playlist, especially when the song fades into New Order's "Temptation" immediately after.

After the usual entering-a-party pleasantries, my family leaves me alone so I can go hang out with my friends. Before that, though, I take my mom's hand. "Mom?" I ask.

"Yes, hon'?"

"Can I ask you a question?"

"Absolutely."

"Are you okay?"

"What?" she asks, almost laughing.

"Is everything good?"

"Why wouldn't it be?"

I shrug. "It's been a crazy year."

"I know. But I have my sister. I have all of you."

"Mom, I'm so much younger than everyone."

"I'm sure Katie would take offense to that."

I look down and away. She's not getting it.

"Haley, things are great right now. And, yes, I'm okay."

"I just worry about you sometimes."

"Why?"

"I don't know."

"Yes, you do."

I try to find the right words but just end up saying, "You're getting old."

She stares at me for a moment and then bursts out laughing so loudly that I actually get a little embarrassed. "Oh, honey," she says, touching my cheek. "I'm fine. I'm not *that* old yet." "Yeah, but you *will* be."

"I know. And so will your aunt Greta. And Jess. And Mel. And Maddie. And even Katie. She's getting tall, you know."

"Yeah."

"We all get old. And it's okay. We're here. Together. Let's not think about stuff like that right now."

I nod.

She knows that my feelings aren't going anywhere, so she hugs me, and it *does* make me feel better. I return it. "Happy Birthday, Sweetie." She kisses my other cheek and tells me to hang out with my friends. I watch her walk away and then do just that.

"This is actually a pretty cool party, even with all the old people here," Nicole says, which makes Sasha laugh.

I find out that Nicole and Sophia have been hanging out for the past few hours, and I'm thankful for that. While Sophia is a bit unsure how to act now that I'm back together with Dani, Nicole says she's happy to finally meet her.

"Haley told me how great you've been with her," Dani tells her.

"I do my best. I think we've got each other's backs."

"How *are* things?" Sophia asks both of us.

Dani says, "Great."

"I love her," I say.

All three are slightly stunned and then react in slightly different ways. Sasha says, "Awesome," and toasts us. Nicole smiles. Sophia nods. "Good for you guys," she says. We'll definitely talk later.

The sun is already gone, but it's that time of day when it's still not quite night yet. I find myself near the back windows with Jess, the backyard I used to spend an inordinate amount of time in taking up my peripheral. It feels comforting. I mention to Jess how much I love the music, and she puts her hands below her chin, smiling and posing. It's a dorky thing to do, and I'm reminded how she can consistently pull off being mature, cool, endearing, confident, intimidating, and caring all at the same time – or be able to swap at the drop of a hat. I hug her.

"Oh," she says, sounding surprised. "Okay. Always welcome a hug." She hugs me back, and it feels really good. I realize we don't hug all that often. That needs to change, especially since I don't see her much anymore.

I want to suddenly burst into tears. As we pull apart, she sees this and gets really worried.

"Whoa – what's wrong?"

Tears fall on their own, even as I try to hold them back. I don't care if anyone ever sees me crying, but I don't want to make a scene and throw off the night. It's going well enough so far. I swallow hard and find myself asking, "Why did you try to kill yourself?" It's a question I've wanted a real answer to for nearly a year but could never actually bring myself to ask it clearly and directly to her. The plan, obviously, wasn't to do it now, but I want an answer.

Jess, meanwhile, is completely taken aback – truly shocked. She takes a moment and then says, "I don't know."

"What do you mean you don't know?"

"I mean…I was sad. I was…I was really sad. But I don't know *why* I did it."

"I know how much Thomas meant. I really do. But, Jess, come on. You called Mel, and she didn't want to talk to you."

"Okay, no one should've told you that," she says, but I continue over her.

"But, what about me? What about Maddie? What about *Mom*?"

She tries to find an answer, eventually settling on, "I called Sam. I'm sorry, but…I don't know. You know, I think maybe I just wanted to…. I think I knew she would come over. I didn't…. You have to know that I wasn't in my right mind."

I shake my head, anger starting to form.

"Hales, I would *never* actually do something like that without saying goodbye."

"Except you did. That's what you did. You went home and tried to kill yourself."

She's speechless. Twice she tries to say something, but nothing comes out. My anger doesn't reach the surface and fades away. The tears are beginning to dry up. I sniffle. "I'm sorry," she says quietly. "I'm not…. I'm *not* a very good older sister."

I feel like shit, because I know that's not true. "Jess, that's not what I meant." I take a few steps away. "Fuck," I say quietly. I turn back around. She looks to me, hoping I can tell her what she can do for me. There's pleading in her eyes. I've never seen that before. New Kids on the Block begins to play. I start to listen to it. So does she. We make eye contact again, and for some reason, smiles form on both of our faces. I rub my eyes and walk back up to her.

I take a deep breath. "I guess I have some feelings about what you did."

"Yeah – I should've, uh…should've known that. I'm truly sorry."

"Ehh."

"No, for real. You know – I just want you to know a few things. One. I love you. Two. I'm *always* here for you. Three. Don't ever worry about me. And, four." She gives me a hug. "Even if we're not together, we're together. Got me?"

"I got you."

We pull back, but Jess holds onto me. She pushes my bushy hair back and gives me a look. "You are so beautiful."

I feel like I'm turning red.

"Dani's a lucky girl."

"Even with the glasses?" I ask.

"*Especially* with the glasses, kid," she answers with a smile. With that, she puts her right arm around me, and we go to find Maddie, who is listening intently to Nicole tell a story to her, Dani, and Sasha.

"I have no idea what was happening, but it sounded fun," she says. Maddie smiles.

"You talking about me?" I ask.

"I was, actually. I was letting them know about your midterm and final exam meltdowns."

"Sounds intense," Maddie tells me.

"Yeah, I get a little crazy when I'm studying."

"You need to relax. Trust me. Most jobs'll never even look at your GPA when you apply for them."

"For real?" Nicole says like she can't believe it.

"Yeah."

"Well, that blows my mind."

"I'm getting a snack," Jess tells me, her indication being that she's walking away for the time being. She touches my shoulder and leaves. The conversation continues on as I watch her go. I'm so glad I finally asked her about what happened and let her know how I feel. It's insane that it took so long, though. I see her walk up to Mel and Katie. She picks up our little niece, surprising her. They laugh, and she puts her back down. I go to find Sophia.

She's alone in the kitchen, a drink in her hand, seemingly deep in thought. I snap her out of it when I walk in. "Hey," she says.

"Hey yourself," I say, leaning on the counter beside her. "So, what's up?"

Looking at the ground, she shrugs and says, "Nothing."

"Nothing, huh? Okay. Just thought maybe you had some thoughts about me and Dani getting back together."

"You love her?" she asks, looking at me.

"Yeah, I do."

"I remember how hard it was for you. When she broke up with you."

"We've talked about that."

"Yeah?"

"Yeah. And, what can I say? We're in love."

"I just want you to be happy."

"I'm happiest when I'm with her."

"Well, okay then. You know…I wish we talked more."

I nod. "Yeah – you know, I have a step-sister."

"Penelope," she says, nodding back.

"Yeah. Well, she lives out in California. I've known about her for as long as I can remember. Met only once a few years ago. But I only really started talking to her when I moved away to college. It's weird how we can just go on with our lives without people who are supposed to be important to us." I turn to her. "I'm sorry."

"Hey, I could've texted the last year or so, too."

"You did when Thomas died. That was pretty cool of you."

"Well, I wanted to do more when Dani told me. I just thought it'd be weird or something – me showing up after not seeing you for so long."

"You're always welcome in my life."

"You, too."

I smirk. "So, how's Notre Dame?"

"Pretty great. Weather's a lot nicer there. Except when it snows."

"I bet."

"It's funny, though. It gets to, like, 70, and everybody's all hot. I'm still wearing pants, laughing to myself at everyone wearing shorts."

"Get to see the leaves change?"

"I have. It's gorgeous."

"I'm happy you're here." I put my arm around her. She reciprocates.

"Ditto."

Soon enough, it's time for cake. Thankfully, I won't have to open gifts in front of everyone, which is always such an awkward experience. I count that as a birthday gift from my family. They get me.

The cake is awesome. It's yellow cake with chocolate frosting, but a screenshot of Joel and Clementine on the frozen lake from *Eternal Sunshine of the Spotless Mind* sits on top. "Oh, mom," I say. She's beaming.

"That is so cool," Sasha adds.

There's only one candle, and I blow it out once everyone sings "Happy Birthday." There's applause, followed by the cutting, which I offer to do and then decide against it, because I cannot ruin this work of art. Maddie has no problem doing so. She takes the knife and cuts right into it with delight.

It's delicious. I don't have cake all that often, so when I do, I savor every bite. Given the amount of people here, it goes fast, but I manage a second slice. Maddie stays by my side, eventually eating one of her own once everyone's gotten theirs.

"Quite the shindig," she tells me.

"I know. You guys went all out."

"We did our best. Make sure to thank Mom, though. She thought of most of this."

"I will."

"By the way, I'm so looking forward to your Oscar performance later on."

"Oh God."

She stifles a laugh and says, "I'm sure you'll be at least fine."

"How's your new book coming along?"

"Not bad, actually. I wrote nearly twenty pages yesterday, which was just the best. I'm looking forward to spending time with this one. I love my characters already."

"Will I be the first to read it?"

"We'll see."

"Can I ask you something?"

"Always."

"Is it weird that I want to marry Dani?"

"Why would that be weird?"

"Because we just got back together, and who even marries anymore?"

"Who gives a shit what anyone else does? You love each other, why not marry?"

"Well, I don't plan on asking – or saying yes, if she asks. Just wanted to know your stance on it."

She mumbles a little and then clearly says, "In that case, I'll say this: it's not for me. Unless I find the right person, I'm good being by myself. I mean, come on. I have Angie. I have Marie. I have you and Mom and everyone. Let's just say I like going home to an empty house and waking up alone. It's freeing."

"Sounds good."

"It is."

"But waking up next to Dani's better. For me, anyway."

"Fair enough."

"I guess writing is the great love of your life."

"Seems like it so far." She smiles at me. Maddie's happy, and that makes *me* happy.

Mel and Stephen have to leave to take Katie home. They tell me to come by sometime tomorrow night. Katie will be at a sleepover, and they really want to see my movie. I give them both a hug, and whisper, "Thanks for everything," to Mel when we embrace. "Anything for you," she answers.

I get to Katie's level and ask her what she got me for my birthday.

"I can't tell you that."

"Why not?"

"Because it's a surprise."

"Aw, c'mon. Not even a hint?"

"Nope."

"Sticking to your principles. Good girl." We high-five.

Mom and I see them out, and then it's time for the movie.

In lieu of having Dani and Sasha introduce the thing, they tell me to get in front of everyone and say a few things. It's my birthday, after all. I soon find myself in front of about two dozen people, sort of hating that they're all taller than I am – except, perhaps, Dani and Jess. I feel really small, though, but I clear my throat and say, "Hi."

Most everyone says it back, with a few giggles throughout. I see Dani in the front row next to Sasha, and I'm reminded of Open-Mic Night. I feel slightly better. "Um. So, my friends Dani and Sasha over there." I point them out, even though at this point everyone knows who they are. "They made a horror movie this past year. Which is pretty cool. And, I'm in it. For some reason." Over that last bit, someone – probably Maddie – yells, "Woo!" Again, some giggles. "Thank you, mystery woo-er."

"It was me!" Maddie yells. She's in the back. There's laughter now. Ice officially broken; at least, from my point of view.

"Thanks, Mad. Um. I guess I should say something about today. I'm…twenty years old." Some applause. "Thank you. I've lived two whole decades. Knowing that a lot of people don't get that opportunity because…. Anyway, I guess that's quite an achievement, isn't it? We're beginning a new year. 2020. I have hope that it'll be better than 2019, but I've been wrong before." Everyone's listening intently now. I somehow find the words and continue. "I'm really lucky, though. I'm lucky because I have everyone in this room. I know all of you. And, there's a few *not* in this room whom I love, too. I have a biological family who I not only love, but that I'm *friends* with as well. I'm not sure they could honestly say the same, but I would be friends with each of my sisters if they weren't my sisters." Maddie looks touched, and Jess sports glassy eyes. "And, then there's extended family. Aunt Greta, I love you." She mouths the same to me. "And, of course, my friends, whom I consider family. Nicole. Sophia. Sasha. Angie. Sam. Kris." I take a deep breath. "Yeah. I'm lucky. And, then I think about how much living I still have to do. How I get to go to college. How I have my own car. Enough money to afford food other than ramen. Which I love." I look at mom. "Mom, you did a hell of a job. Thank you." She smiles. "And, you," I finally say, turning to Dani. "You're the love of my life. I don't know what's going to happen. We'll probably have good times, and other times, we'll fight and not want to be around one another. But, right now – at this moment – I know I don't want to not be with you. Even knowing we can't physically be with one another when I'm off at school, I don't know – I take comfort in knowing that I care for you and that you care for me." I turn back toward everyone else, and say, "And, with that, let's watch a zombie movie, huh?"

Lots of "yeah's" and applause. I'm met with hugs and "I love you's." It's wonderful. Dani touches my shoulder lightly, and then she and Sasha set up the movie. Soon, the backyard lights are off, and it begins.

<u>Katie</u>

Aunt Haley comes over the day after her birthday party, and she shows me an old movie called *Carnival of Souls*, which she says is kinda like the movie her friends made, which I can't see until I'm in middle school.

Mom is the one who says this. Haley said high school first. Mom's cooler than I thought, because I start middle school later this year. Guess I'll be watching it for Halloween. I'm already looking forward to it.

Once it's over, mom tells me I have to clean my room. "Oh, I'll help," Aunt Haley offers, but mom shoots her down, and I'm off on my own. I leave my door open and start by fixing my bed. I realize I haven't looked beneath my mattress in ages. My lip gloss is still there.

I hear laughter coming from down the hall – probably the kitchen. Mom laughs a lot more now. Dad said it's because this weight has been lifted from her. I asked if that has to do with Aunt Jess. He nodded, but then added, "And your grandpa, too."

"I wish your parents were still around so at least I could have *one* grandpa who wants to see me."

"Sweetie, don't say that. I'm sure your mom's father wants to see you."

"But he hasn't."

"Life's more complicated than you think."

"Doesn't seem that complicated. If I had a child, I'd want to see her *all* the time."

He smiled and kissed my forehead. "Good to know," he said.

I take the empty container from my closet and proceed to put all the stuff that doesn't really belong anywhere into it. I shut the lid and put it back. Aunt Maddie taught me that trick. She doesn't like to get rid of stuff, but whenever she has something that doesn't have a place on a shelf or something, into a container it goes. *I wonder if we're hoarders*, I think to myself. I go to my desk and end up bumping the mouse to my computer, which was a hand-me-down from Aunt Haley, and lo and behold: my wallpaper brings a smile to my face, like it always does. It's a picture of me and Mom from about a month ago. Aunt Jess took it. We're in the backyard, and Mom's hugging me from behind. I'm in the middle of bursting with giggles.

Knock-knock. I turn to see Aunt Haley in my doorway.

"Hey. Need help?" she asks.

"I thought Mom said you couldn't."

"Eh, I talked her down."

Haley's been more confident lately. I like it. She comes in and sits at the edge of the bed.

"No!" I say.

"What?"

"I just made it."

"Oh. My bad." She gets up, straightens the comforter and points to the chair by the window. I nod. "Sorry," she says, sitting.

"No, it's nothing. I just like to keep things looking good for as a long as I can after I've cleaned 'em."

"I feel you. After I vacuum, *no one* is allowed to walk on the carpet for at least an hour."

"You get it," I say, sitting down at the desk. "So, how's it feel no longer being a teenager?"

"Not that special."

"Yeah. I didn't feel all that different when I turned ten last year."

"Geez. You're already coming up on eleven."

"Yup."

"Wow. We're getting old, aren't we?"

"We're not *that* old."

"How old is old?"

"I don't know. How old is Grandma?"

"My mom?" Haley asks, wanting to laugh. She gives it a thought and says, "Sixty-one."

"That's old."

"Not young, that's for sure." She adds, sort of like she's half-playing and half-serious, "My mom's an old lady. I need to keep a closer eye on her."

"My mom's got it covered."

Aunt Haley looks at me and slightly smirks. "Yeah. I think you're right about that."

I scratch my head and decide to ask her something I wanted to ask the night before. "So, are you and Dani officially back together?"

"Yeah."

"What does Mom think?"

"Honestly, she's happy for me."

"That's great," I say, smiling.

"We've been smiling a lot lately, haven't we?"

"Yeah."

"Probably a good thing. There's nothing wrong with expressing yourself, as long as it's honest. We should all smile more. And cry. And get angry. And ignore people. And say thank you. And say no more often."

"You should give a TED Talk."

"No way. All those people in the crowd staring at me. Sounds horrible."

"I think you can do it."

"Thanks, cuz."

One day, Jess comes over. It's an average visit. We eat and hang out. Eventually, we end up outside, and Jess leaves to get something from her car. When she returns, she holds a camera. Mom says, "Ahh!" and laughs. Dad stands up and accepts the camera from her. She walks up to Mom and says, "Let's go."

We go to a quiet, sunny area of the yard.

"What's going on?" I ask.

"We're fulfilling a plan," Mom says.

I watch as they sit on the grass and rest their heads on one another. Dad takes a few shots, and then we all look at them under the tree. My mom and Aunt Jess look so pretty in them. "How about one with the three of you?" Jess asks.

Several days later, Aunt Jess arrives with about two dozen photos she had "developed," whatever that means, and we all look at them. I love the one with all four of us. Mom and Aunt Jess seem to really like the first one that was taken, the one with just the two of them. I look at the duplicate and think how beautiful they both are, outside and inside. At this moment, I realize I'm not worried about Aunt Jess anymore.

Mom comes to see me before I go to bed that night. She seems like she wants to tell me something serious, but she's not acting the way she was the night Uncle Thomas died. This is different. She sits beside me on the bed, takes a deep breath, and says, "I know about the lip gloss."

I want to say, "What lip gloss?" Instead, I mumble, "Okay."

"Where did you get it?"

I opt to tell the truth, rather than lie. "I stole it."

She closes her eyes for a moment. "When was this?"

"The day before Uncle Thomas died."

She nods. "Okay. Where did you steal it from?"

"Target."

"Why?"

I shrug.

"That's not good enough, Katie."

I struggle to find the words. The truth is that I wanted it, but I didn't want Mom seeing me buy it. Is this a good answer? Will she understand?

"I'm not angry at you. What's done is done. Just tell me why you'd steal."

It takes a few tries, but eventually, I do get it out. "Because you wouldn't have bought it for me. Right?"

She thinks about it and then says, "Yeah. Probably. That doesn't excuse it, though."

"I know."

"So, what do we do about it?"

Well, mom. For one thing, how about you stop going through my stuff? Aw, crap. Does that mean you saw the book Maddie sent to me? The letters from Aunt Jess? I feel guilty, and I *hate* feeling guilty. I think she senses this and puts her arm around me, pulling me closer to her. I slide over. She ends up hugging me. I'm confused. Is she about to kill me?

"I guess this is your one chance. Next time, just be honest with me."

"Mom, you would have said no and then lectured me about being too young -."

"Yeah, I absolutely would've done that. And, it's true." She lets me go and sort of slumps ever-so-slightly. "But I still want you to tell me things. I still want you to ask me questions. I'm here. Don't forget that."

She *is* here. Always. She didn't abandon me and my dad. She didn't give up when things got difficult. She used to be an irresponsible, immature young woman. And then she wasn't. She helped raise Aunt Maddie. She